The Third Way

The Third Way

Colin D. Peel

ROBERT HALE · LONDON

ISBN 978-0-7090-8287-3

Robert Hale Limited
Clerkenwell House
Clerkenwell Green
London EC1R 0HT

2 4 6 8 10 9 7 5 3 1

Typeset in 11/13pt Baskerville
by Derek Doyle & Associates, Shaw Heath
Printed and bound in Great Britain
by Biddles Limited, King's Lynn

Since no nation threatens China, why these continuing large and expanding arms purchases?

US Secretary of Defence
Donald Rumsfeld

We have the best relations with China that we've had in some time – perhaps ever.

US Secretary of State
Dr Condoleezza Rice

CHAPTER 1

Long before the end of his first assignment in the Tarim Basin, Driscoll had sworn never to return to this godforsaken place. Yet, three years later, here he was, back piloting the same kind of aircraft, flying over the same part of the country for the same damn reason.

Viewed from the Cessna's cockpit on this bleak February afternoon, the wasteland below him looked as foreign and desolate as it had looked when he'd been here last. Despite having flown over it more times than he cared to remember, nothing about it was even faintly familiar.

Instead, stretching ahead of him through the windshield for as far as he could see was the usual featureless expanse of shifting sand and giant dunes; another vast and forbidding chunk of the Chinese north-west desert – a part of the world that should have been left to itself, but which was slowly being inhabited by men working at well heads in one of the remotest and loneliest places on Earth.

In ways he'd rather not consider, he was no better than the roughnecks on the rigs, Driscoll decided, as hungry for the easy money as they were, and for a while at least, prepared to put his life on hold while he joined the scramble to open up the oil fields that lay hidden under the sand 5000 feet beneath the Cessna's wings.

If the scientist seated beside him was here for the money, so far the young man had been careful not to mention it. In the four days since they'd started the survey, Charles Collier had been largely uncommunicative, either intimidated by the environment, or still coming to grips with the primitive conditions under which he was being forced to work.

Collier was a pale-faced 23-year-old Cambridge graduate who'd confessed to having been outside of Europe only once before, an admission that had made Driscoll wonder why he'd wanted the job, and how the hell he'd got it to begin with, although he seemed to know more or less what he was doing, even if it was often hard to tell whether he did or not.

Driscoll checked his altitude before turning his attention to the flight display screen, waiting impatiently for the red light that would signal the beginning of the new survey leg.

'You ready?' He glanced at Collier. 'Are you getting a proper readout from the gradiometer?'

'Yep.' Collier kept his eyes on his laptop.

'How about the laser and the magnetometer?'

'You don't have to keep asking. I'll tell you if we get an interruption in any of the feeds.'

'You didn't tell me last time.' Driscoll punched a button on the Sat Nav. 'That's why we're still out here instead of sitting in the warm having a beer back at our hotel.'

Collier said nothing, using his laptop to make sure that the stream of incoming data was being stored correctly, and only occasionally looking up to cross-reference their position with the aircraft's GPS.

Now the light had flickered on, for the next thirty minutes Driscoll was able to relax, knowing that the low level run they'd make later in the week would correct any errors caused by turbulence or the odd air pocket, and content to let the Energex system do his job for him while he tried to figure out what he was doing in this part of the desert at all.

The Chinese had offered no reason for insisting that, before he started out on the fly-over of the new B7 Block, he was first to repeat a sweep of the old B5 Block – a part of the desert that had not only been surveyed by Driscoll himself three years ago, but which was dotted with wells that were producing oil already.

Far away to the west he could see one of them now. Like others in the area, it was in the middle of nowhere, surrounded by the usual collection of corrugated iron shacks, the remains of a derrick and piles of discarded pipes and casings; a dirty smudge on the desert floor where, twenty-four hours a day, men were labouring to satisfy the never-ending energy needs of China's burgeoning economy.

So, if the wells in B5 had already been brought in, why the hell would the Chinese want the same block to be resurveyed, Driscoll wondered?

Whatever the reason happened to be, because Energex were paying him only for his expenses, the fuel and his flying time, and since the company were almost certainly charging the Chinese an exorbitant consulting fee, he was disinclined to seek an explanation. If the China National Petroleum Corporation were happy to pay for a survey of the whole half million square kilometres of the Tarim Basin, that was fine and, as long as Collier was smart enough not to rock the boat, the pair of them would make a good deal more money than they would otherwise have done.

'How's it going?' Driscoll had been watching the thickening cloud cover.

'All right. Better than this morning.' Collier continued studying the coloured traces that were creeping across the screen of his laptop. 'Except I hadn't bargained on such big fluctuations in the sandstone topography. If the software can't handle it, someone back home is going to have a problem when they come to do the analysis.'

'It wasn't a problem three years ago.' Driscoll pointed out the window. 'That well down there only exists because Energex was able to tell the CNPC where to drill their hole.'

'So why are we surveying this block again?'

'Beats me. Does it matter?'

'No. I just thought you'd know.'

'First rule for working in China – always do what the Chinese want you to do. The second rule is never ask them why.' Driscoll checked the horizon for more clouds. 'Soon as we're finished here we'll head on back. We don't want to be hitting the airstrip in the dark.'

His weather predictions proved to be wrong. In a dull but steadily clearing sky, shortly before four o'clock, with their repeat sweep of the B5 Block more than half completed, he'd stopped following the river and was banking the Cessna high above the thin black ribbon of the road between Kargilik and the old silk city of Hotan, preparing for his approach to the tiny desert landing strip where he'd chosen to base the aircraft.

The strip itself was nothing more than a bumpy piece of tarmac, a part of the old road that had been bypassed by the much-improved highway that had been pushed through the region some years ago. Flanked by low dunes and a number of ramshackle sheds and run-down workshops, as well as being bumpy, more often than not the strip was covered in windblown sand making the surface difficult to pick out when the sun was overhead, and even harder to see later in the day because of shadows.

For a change, this afternoon Driscoll's landing was all but perfect. By

9

touching down more than halfway along he managed to avoid the worst of the washboard, and there was none of the slewing at the far end as there had been yesterday when he'd underestimated the drag from the surface sand.

He turned off the strip in front of the building where their CNPC loan car was parked, and where four men were standing beside a black Mercedes – an uncommon sight anywhere in the Tarim Basin, let alone at a place like this.

Driscoll kept the Cessna rolling, taxiing past the fuel bowser until he reached the tie-down eye that he'd been using to secure the aircraft against the desert wind, making sure they wouldn't have to do any pushing before he cut the engine and climbed out in to the cold to stretch his legs.

More weary than he cared to admit, he was getting hungry, and for the first time in three days he was ready to let Collier take over the driving duties for the trip back to their hotel in Hotan.

Collier had not yet left the cockpit. Still wearing his head-set, he was fussing around inside to satisfy himself that all of the instrumentation had been switched off and properly put to bed, and that his precious laptop contained the data he'd need to determine how well or how badly they'd performed today.

One of the men from the Mercedes came over to speak to Driscoll. For a Chinese he was quite tall, with none of the features of the local Uighurs or Kazakhs, and while his three companions were less well-insulated against the cold, he was wearing gloves, an expensive fur hat and an overcoat that reached almost to the ground.

'You are Peter Driscoll?' he asked.

'That's me.'

'And this is your aircraft?'

'You've just seen me land it.'

'But it is owned by the Energex Corporation, is it not?'

Driscoll started paying more attention. Instead of what he'd guessed was going to be a routine examination of their flight plans or an inspection of their survey permit, this was something different. The visitor's English was too good, and his manner was as out of place as the Mercedes was.

'You will give me your passport.' The man held out his hand.

'It's back at my hotel,' Driscoll said. 'I don't carry it with me, and even if I did, why should I show it to you?'

'May I assume the colleague who accompanies you is Mr Charles

Collier, and that you are both employed by Energex in London?'

'Assume what you like,' Driscoll said. 'Look, unless you tell me who you work for and what you want, I don't have to answer your questions. I've been flying all day, I need a leak, I'm cold, I'm tired and I'm dirty, so if there's some kind of problem, come and see me in the morning. I'll be back here at nine o'clock.'

Collier had finally disembarked and was wandering over to discover what was going on.

'Have we done something we shouldn't have done?' he asked.

'Who knows?' Before Driscoll could decide whether or not it would be prudent to walk away, the man reached out for Collier's laptop.

'I will take that,' he said.

'Like hell you will.' Stepping forward, Driscoll intervened.

'It is better you do what I say.' The man beckoned to his companions.

Not yet certain if he was dealing with an oil industry executive or a senior government official, and preferring to avoid a confrontation, Driscoll followed his own rules.

Taking the laptop from Collier, he handed it over. 'There you go,' he said. 'But if you're hoping to download any useful information, you're going to be shit out of luck. The only software that can analyse the data in there is sitting in an office five thousand miles away in London.'

There was no change in the man's expression. 'You do not understand,' he said. 'You will remain here while your friend returns to the aircraft.'

'I don't think so.' Driscoll's wariness was being replaced by concern. Sacrificing the computer had done nothing to defuse the situation and he was beginning to think they'd become inadvertently caught up in some kind of turf war between rival prospecting companies.

Collier seemed to have reached the same conclusion. He was being escorted back to the Cessna by two of the men, but managed to stop and turn round for a moment.

'What shall I do if they ask me to give them the gradiometer?' he called.

Driscoll wished he knew. Compared with the loss of the computer, any pirating of the aircraft's recording equipment would be a more serious matter altogether, and if these people were to get their hands on the gradiometer, there'd be hell to pay in London and New York, and even the Russians were going to be pissed off.

But Collier wasn't being asked to do anything. Instead, he'd been forcibly bundled into the cockpit by a man who was now lashing a rope around the fuselage, while his companion was busy taping something to the strut of the Cessna's nose wheel.

The rope was to keep the doors shut, Driscoll realized, to keep Collier inside.

'OK.' He endeavoured to stay calm. 'What is it you want?'

The man in the fur hat made no attempt to reply, standing impassively with his arms by his side as though nothing was happening.

'You listen to me,' Driscoll said. 'My company's under contract to the CNPC. That means you're going to be in deep shit with Beijing unless I get some answers out of you real quick.'

The man took a camera from his pocket. 'You should wait in my car,' he said.

'Why would I want to do that?'

'It is better you do not look.'

'Jesus Christ.' Driscoll's mouth had gone dry, and his stomach had started to lurch.

The man who had been kneeling beside the undercarriage had gone over to the bowser and was using the hose nozzle to direct a stream of aviation fuel on to the apron beneath the Cessna.

Disbelievingly, Driscoll watched the pool of fuel spread out, refusing to accept the unthinkable until he caught sight of Collier at the window.

The young man's face was a mask. Trapped inside and terrified by the smell of fuel, he was using all his strength in a bid to escape, kicking at the door and hammering helplessly against the perspex with his fists.

Slow though Driscoll had been to understand, now that he did, he was quick to act.

But he wasn't quick enough. And he'd failed to detect the presence of the fourth man who had come to stand behind him.

Before he could make his move, the strut of the Cessna's nose wheel was shattered by the blast from an explosive charge, and he was driven to his knees by a blow to the back of his head.

Too dizzy to get to his feet, he began crawling towards the aircraft, insensitive to the wall of heat from flames that were engulfing the fuselage from one end to the other – doing everything he could to hurry, because if he didn't, he knew he'd never be able to forgive himself.

He was making good progress, still crawling and still fighting to remain conscious when his face was slammed against the tarmac by the detonation of the Cessna's fuel tank, and the sky above the dunes became suddenly filled with fire.

CHAPTER 2

The officer was embarrassed. He wasn't much older than Collier had been, and his previous duties as a member of the People's Liberation Army had clearly not included the delivery of a foreigner to an address in downtown Shanghai.

He'd instructed his driver to turn right on to Zhongshan Dong Lu and had just realized that, instead of heading north towards the Waibaidu bridge, they were travelling south along the waterfront.

Driscoll was past caring. No closer to understanding what was going on than he had been after the horror at the airstrip three days ago, and too weary and too strung out to worry about what direction the car was travelling in, he kept his mouth shut and continued looking out the window.

To correct the officer's mistake, the driver used his initiative. Without waiting to be told, he swung left into a street that would take him across to the People's Park, and was soon able to enter the stream of north-bound traffic on the Henan Zhong.

Five minutes later, the car was double-parked outside the front entrance of the Huangpu building.

The officer handed Driscoll a ballpoint pen and a sheet of paper. 'You will put your name,' he said.

'Why?' The piece of paper appeared to be some kind of form, but because it was printed in Chinese, Driscoll had no idea what it was for.

'It is to say I have completed my task.' The officer pointed to the glass doors of the building. 'Is this not the address where your company has their office?'

'Yeah, yeah.' Driscoll scribbled down his signature. 'Are we all done?'

'You may go.' The officer leaned across to open Driscoll's door for him. 'Your passport will be returned to you tomorrow.'

Although the day had dawned cool, and it was still fairly early in the morning, because the sun had come out, the Shanghai waterfront was already heaving with people and alive with noise and colour.

All along the Bund, businessmen with cell phones in hand were rubbing shoulders with shoppers and tourists of almost every nationality, generating the same atmosphere of bustling optimism that Driscoll had encountered during his previous visits here.

Today, though, he barely noticed, uncomfortably conscious of being a foreigner as he pushed through the crowds on the sidewalk and made his way into the foyer where he took the elevator to the fourth floor.

By the standards of modern Shanghai, the Huangpu building was architecturally unremarkable; a seven storey glass-fronted office block that three years ago had been occupied solely by Energex.

Since then, like everything else in Shanghai, much had changed. Instead of Energex having the place to themselves, nowadays they were sharing it with nearly twenty other offshore companies and corporations, including one from Sweden that – according to Ji Siu-kai – had just pulled off a $14 million deal to supply sandalwood-scented condoms to a local pharmaceutical distributor.

Ji was Energex's only permanent employee in China, a solidly-built, middle-aged Shanghainese who acted as office manager, translator, secretary, travel agent and housemother.

When Driscoll entered the office she was sitting at her computer, balancing a cup on her knee and pushing buttons on a calculator.

'Oh, Mr Driscoll.' She stood up so quickly she spilled her tea. 'I have been most worried.'

He could tell. So relieved did she seem to be that for a moment he thought she might forget herself and hug him.

'When did you hear?' he said.

'The day before yesterday.' She found a chair for him. 'I first receive a phone call from the CNPC to say there has been an accident, and then one hour later a man calls from the office of the Liberation Army and Air Force Department in Beijing. It is from him I learn that Mr Collier has died in the crash, but no one could tell me how badly you yourself had been hurt.'

Driscoll sat down. 'Accident,' he said. 'And a crash?'

'I have not the words to say how sorry I am.' She came over to inspect the bruise on his forehead.

'There's a better one on the back of my head somewhere.' Although he had only a hazy recollection of being knocked unconscious by the blast from the Cessna, he could remember being hit from behind as clearly as he could remember waking up in the back of the Mercedes.

'Goodness me.' Using her fingers, Ji gently parted his hair. 'You should have had that stitched. It has not even been cleaned up properly.'

'I know. Stop fussing. I'm OK.'

'You do not look OK. And if you will permit me to say so, you are in need of a shower.'

'I haven't had much of a chance.' Driscoll was too confused to be worrying about how badly he needed a shower. 'What have you heard about the accident?' he asked.

'Only that your plane has crashed while landing and that you were saved from the fire, but that Mr Collier was not so lucky.'

'Was there someone at the strip who saw what happened?'

'Do you not know?'

'Know what?'

'I think you should have coffee.' She spoke firmly. 'If you bring your chair, you can talk to me while I make some for you.'

Driscoll didn't bother with the chair. Wondering what else it was he was supposed to know that he didn't know, he followed her into the kitchenette and waited while she busied herself at the little office espresso machine.

'You and I have worked together before,' she said.

'Yeah, we have.' He tried to guess what was coming.

'So you understand that like many people in Shanghai I do not always believe what I am supposed to believe, and I know that things I read in Chinese newspapers are not always true.'

She was feeling awkward, he decided, which meant he was probably pushing too hard for information. 'Have you been expecting me?' he asked.

'This morning there is an email from Mr Gorman in London. But it says only that you are arriving in Shanghai today, and that according to the Chinese authorities, you are required to leave the country before the weekend.' She handed him a cup. 'If you must soon return to England, why first do you travel all the way back from the Tarim Basin to Shanghai?'

It was a question that had been exercising Driscoll too, but like all the other questions he had, one for which he had no answer. 'It wasn't my idea,' he said. 'I didn't exactly ask to be stuck on a flight to Kashgar and locked up in a stinking police cell for two days, and I sure as hell didn't ask to be handcuffed on board an Air Force Antanov for eleven hours and flown back to the airbase at Changshu. The Antanov smelt like a urinal, and every two hours the damn thing had to stop somewhere to refuel.'

'Perhaps you are brought back here because this is where Energex have their office, or because your journey to the oil fields started from Shanghai and not from London. We Chinese are very logical. But I think you already know that.'

In his present circumstances, Driscoll would have welcomed any kind of logic. 'You haven't told me who was supposed to have seen my plane crash,' he said.

'In the *China Daily* yesterday there was a small report about it.'

'Do you still have the paper?' He finished his coffee and carefully put down his cup.

'You wish me to read it to you?'

'If whoever wrote the article knows more about what happened than I do, I need to talk to them.'

'Because you cannot remember the crash, or because you believe it was not an accident? You think perhaps someone sabotaged your plane?'

Not knowing what to think, he accompanied her back to the office, wondering what version of the story London had been told and trying to decide whether or not to risk implicating Ji by confiding in her.

Opening a drawer in her filing cabinet she took out a folded newspaper and spread it out on her desk. 'You will forgive me if my translation is not good,' she said. 'For me, reading is more difficult than talking face to face.'

He pointed to a small article at the bottom of the page. 'Is that it there?'

She nodded. 'The title says *Xinjiang oil survey plane crashes near Hotan.*'

'Is that what it says exactly?' Driscoll knew he was interrupting. 'You're certain there isn't another way you could translate it?'

'I am certain.' She looked up and smiled. 'Am I permitted to continue?'

'Sorry. I just wanted to be sure.'

'Perhaps the report will make things clearer for you.' She cleared her throat and began again. '*The fatal crash of a light aircraft at a makeshift runway near the main highway west of Hotan has claimed the life of Charles Collier, a 23-year-old scientist and son of a member of the British Parliament. His companion, British pilot Peter Driscoll, is reported to have been dragged uninjured from the burning aircraft by agents of the National Narcotics Control Commission who were waiting to question him in connection with the trafficking of illegal drugs. Both men were employees of the Energex Corporation, an international oil exploration company owned jointly by American, Russian and British interests which is presently conducting aerial surveys of the Tarim Basin on behalf of the CNPC.'*

Driscoll was bewildered. He hadn't been expecting the truth, but he certainly hadn't expected this. Why the Chinese had concocted a story about him crashing the Cessna and trafficking drugs was as incomprehensible as the brutality they'd shown in killing Collier by burning him alive.

Ji could see he was struggling. 'If the report is inaccurate, would it not be best for you to tell me?' she said. 'Then perhaps I can telephone the newspaper so they will be able to correct their story.'

'There wasn't any crash,' Driscoll said slowly.

'And there were no drugs on the plane?'

'What do you think? The whole north-west is already awash with heroin and opium. And you know as well as I do what the penalty is for drug trafficking in China.'

'Then how is it poor Mr Collier has come to lose his life?'

'I don't know.' Endeavouring to think with a head full of cotton wool, Driscoll was still reluctant to disclose what had really taken place. 'I didn't realize Collier's father was an MP,' he said. 'Did you know?'

Ji shook her head. 'Not until his secretary phoned me at my home last night from London. She wished to ask if I would speak to Mr Collier directly. I think it was not an easy call for him to make, and it was also hard for me because there was nothing I could tell him that he had not already learned from Mr Gorman.'

Driscoll could understand why Collier's father had made the call. Mick Gorman was the operations manager of Energex in London, a hard-nosed Texan who was under the impression that straight talking was a substitute for competence, and whose sympathy would have sounded as contrived as it would have been insincere.

'Have you spoken to Gorman yourself?' Driscoll guessed she would have done.

'For long enough to know he is angry about many things. You will have much talking to do on your return to London, I think.'

Driscoll thought so too. In the absence of any explanation that made the slightest sense, Collier's death and the loss of the Cessna were big enough problems without him being accused of running drugs as well.

'Have you heard from anyone else?' he asked.

'People from other offices have come to say they are sorry, and there have been three phone calls from an American journalist who says she works in Shanghai. She wishes to know more about you and about the crash.'

'What did you tell her?'

'Nothing, but twice she asks what time you will be back in Shanghai, so she may have information sources of her own.'

'If she calls again, tell her to get lost, or say I've gone straight back to London.' Driscoll went over to stand by the window. 'I suppose you'd better book me a flight,' he said. 'And I'll need somewhere to get my head down for a couple of nights.'

'Already I have reserved a room for you at the Shangwai.' Ji joined him at the window. 'It is not as nice as the Four Seasons or the Hyatt, but there will be fewer westerners, so you are not so likely to be bothered by people who wish to ask you silly questions.'

Aware that she was being careful to avoid asking questions of her own, he thanked her for her thoughtfulness and went back to the kitchenette to make himself more coffee while she ordered him a taxi and started checking out the availability of flights from Pudong to Heathrow.

He woke up slowly, unsure of his surroundings until he glanced around the hotel bedroom. Lined up on the top of the mini-bar, a row of empty bottles explained why his brain was still refusing to work, and sunlight filtering through the curtains told him that he either hadn't been asleep for very long, or that it was morning, in which case he'd been asleep for the best part of fifteen hours.

To discover which, he went to the bathroom and searched for his watch. It was on the vanity where he'd left it, lying between yet another bottle and the new razor he'd bought.

He could remember feeling better after his shower, but his headache was back again – not necessarily because of the Scotch and the vodka, he decided, but mostly because he hadn't eaten anything since yesterday.

Having determined that it was still only late afternoon, he returned to the bedroom and was consulting the room service menu when his phone rang.

Without thinking, he picked up the receiver, realizing his mistake when the operator told him that a young lady was waiting to see him in reception.

Driscoll had a fair idea who his visitor might be, but he was surprised she'd been able to track him down so quickly. 'Does she have a name?' he asked.

'One moment please.' The operator sounded apologetic. 'Her name is Natalie Washburn, and she says that if it is not inconvenient she would very much like to talk with you.'

Against his better judgement, and unable to imagine why anyone would be taking the trouble to follow up a story that was hardly big news in Hotan, let alone in Shanghai, he asked the operator to put her on the line.

'Is that Mr Peter Driscoll?' Natalie Washburn spoke before he could say hello.

'Yep. What can I do for you?'

'I'm not really sure, but you are the pilot of that plane that crashed over in Xinjiang, aren't you?'

Hardly the most promising of openings, Driscoll thought, but at least she hadn't tried to be cute, and she didn't sound like a smart-arsed reporter who was after an angle on the drugs. Instead, she had the pleasant voice of a well-educated American who was slightly less than confident about herself.

'Look,' he said, 'I'm not much interested in talking to anyone about what happened. You'd be better off chasing another story.'

'Oh.' She hesitated. 'Won't you give me the chance to explain? There's a really nice bar down here in the hotel where we could have a drink.'

The last thing Driscoll wanted was another drink. 'Try talking to the CNPC,' he said. 'Or get hold of someone at the Energex Corporation and see what they have to say. It was their plane.'

'I've already done both those things. And I've made some other calls as well. That's why I'm here.'

'Who did you speak to at Energex?'

'I called their office in New York, but they said I should contact a Mr Gorman in London, so I did.'

'What did he tell you?'

'Nothing.' She paused for a moment. 'Well, more or less nothing. He wasn't very helpful, except for saying you're a dick-head cowboy who thinks that crashing planes is almost as much fun as flying them.'

Amused by her frankness and inclined to believe she might have more information than she was admitting, Driscoll reconsidered his strategy.

'OK,' he said. 'No promises, no tape recorders and you don't take notes. There's a restaurant next door to one of the banquet rooms that has a Chinese name I can't pronounce. I'll see you there in five minutes.'

He hung up before he could change his mind, more curious about the reason for her visit than he had been before, and equally curious to discover what kind of person she would turn out to be.

To find out, after a quick check in the mirror, he put on the fresh shirt and the jeans he'd bought this morning and made his way down-stairs.

Most of the tables in the restaurant were already occupied by well-heeled and elegantly-dressed Shanghainese who were preparing them-selves for an evening out, but alone at a table at the far end, a young woman had seen him coming and was beginning to stand up.

But she wasn't the white American Driscoll had been expecting to meet. Natalie Washburn was a rather pretty Eurasian. In her mid or late twenties and wearing sensible shoes, tailored slacks and a bright-red, high-collared jacket, she was small with dark hair and large eyes, and with features that were slightly more European than they were Chinese.

Perhaps because she was uncertain of her ground, there was some-thing not quite right about the smile she gave him when Driscoll intro-duced himself.

'Who told you I was staying here?' He waited for her to sit down before joining her at the table.

'Nobody. I just made a list of hotels and started ringing them. I worked out how long each call would take before I began.'

'So you could decide whether it was worth wasting all that time.'

'Mm.' She gave him the same peculiar smile. 'Five seconds to ring each number, a four second wait for someone to answer, six for me to give them your name, and fifteen for them to check their guest lists.'

'How many calls?'

'Not many. I'm good at guessing.'

'Am I expected to guess who you're working for?'

'Oh. I'm sorry.' She handed him a business card. 'I work for myself. Up until last Christmas I had a job with Associated Press in New York, but I thought I'd made enough contacts to see if I could freelance – well, for a while anyway.'

'That doesn't explain why you're interested in talking to me.'

'No.' She hesitated for a moment. 'It's partly because you're a foreigner, and partly because air accidents are always news – not necessarily in China, but overseas they are – even if yours was only a light aircraft, and the crash happened as far away as yours did.'

'Do you write mostly for overseas markets?'

She nodded. 'I sell nearly all my stuff to British and US magazines and newspapers. A piece I wrote last year was published in four US trade periodicals, but because it was about the Chinese oil industry, it was picked up by the *China Economic Quarterly* as well.'

'If that's the best reason you can come up with for being here, you and I won't be getting very far,' Driscoll said. 'Do you want to try again?'

The arrival of a waiter provided her with some breathing space. She ordered a white wine, speaking in fluent Chinese until she quickly changed to English.

Driscoll didn't bother with the menu, ordering himself a club sandwich and a glass of water before he asked her where she learned her Mandarin.

'I was born in China. My mother's Chinese. My father went back to the States when I was seventeen, and my mother lives in Paris now, but I grew up speaking Mandarin.'

'Is that why you're working in Shanghai?'

'I like it.'

Driscoll looked at her. 'Are you going to tell me what it is you're after?'

'There's nothing complicated about it. I just thought there would be a market in the UK for a story about the death of Charles Collier.'

'Because he was the son of a British politician?'

'Yes.' She compressed her lips. 'I know how that sounds, but I make my living following up those kind of stories.'

'And this one's almost as good as Margaret Thatcher's son trying to overthrow the government in Equatorial Guinea. Is that the sort of thing you had in mind?'

'It depends.'

'On what?'

'On whether there's something else behind what happened. I thought there might be – you know, because of the reports of you. . . .' Her voice tailed off.

'Trafficking drugs.' Driscoll finished the sentence for her. 'And you figured I'd tell you what's really been going on.'

'Yes.'

In spite of her believing the newspaper article, she was at least being more honest now, he decided, even if she was still keeping something to herself.

'What makes you think there could be a story in it?' he asked.

'Well, I didn't just read about the crash in the paper. I got a fax about it too. I don't know who sent the fax, but the wording was the same as the wording in the *China Daily*, so I assumed it was a government press release from *The Xinhua News Agency*.'

'Why would Beijing be sending a copy of a press release to you?'

'Maybe because of the piece I wrote about the Chinese oil industry. That's what I first thought.' She paused. 'But then, yesterday afternoon there was a message on my answering machine saying you'd be in Shanghai today. I don't know who that was from either.'

The arrival of their order interrupted her, but it wasn't hard for Driscoll to imagine what conclusion she'd come to.

'So you figured someone was trying to tell you something,' he said.

'Yes.'

Although the waiter had left the table, she seemed reluctant to continue.

'Keep going,' Driscoll said.

She sipped at her wine. 'I'm not sure how right this is, but it sounds as though someone might want me to expose a drug ring that's operating out in the Tarim Basin oil fields – so whoever it is, or whoever they are, can take over the business for themselves.'

It wasn't a bad guess, Driscoll thought, but it wasn't a good one either. In such a poor and sparsely populated part of the country, even if there had been a shortage of heroin or opium – which there wasn't – a war between drug rings was about as unlikely as the idea of oil companies fighting over the survey data.

'And you've been following up the tip-off.' He started on his sandwich.

'There wasn't much to go on. That's why I telephoned Energex, and why I phoned the Smuggling Prevention Department and the NNCC – that's the Chinese National Narcotics Control Commission.'

'The NNCC are the guys who were supposed to have rescued me from my burning plane, are they?'

She nodded. 'Except they've never heard of anyone called Peter Driscoll. According to them, the NNCC only have a handful of people working in the whole of the Xinjiang region, and they're all up in Ürümqi trying to stop methamphetamines from being exported into Russia through Kazakhstan. They hadn't heard about a plane crashing either. They didn't even know there was an airstrip near Hotan, and they said that even if they had known, they wouldn't have cared.'

'There you go then.' Driscoll spoke with his mouth full.

'What do you mean?'

'If there were any Narcotics Commission agents at the strip, they sure as hell didn't introduce themselves to me.' He took a gamble. 'Look, there wasn't any accident, and there weren't any drugs.'

'I don't believe you.' She frowned. 'If your plane didn't crash, why is Charles Collier dead, and how did you get that nasty bruise on your forehead?'

'Long story.'

'I won't write it up unless you want me to.'

'You're not going to write up anything. You've already said you don't believe me, so you haven't got much of a story to write, have you?'

'I will if I can get some more information. If I can, will it be all right if I come to see you again?'

'I don't think so.' By being cautious he knew he was sounding cynical. 'If I change my mind, I'll give you a call.'

'No you won't. That's not a very original line. Anyway, I'm out of town for the next two weeks.' She finished her drink and stood up. 'I'm sorry for wasting your time, and I'm sorry you won't trust me enough to tell me the truth. Goodbye, Mr Driscoll.'

So quickly had she cut her losses that, before he could think of anything appropriate to say, he was left alone at the table with his glass of water and a half-eaten sandwich, wondering who the hell had put her on to him and aware that, unless he'd badly misjudged her motives, he'd just lost the opportunity to enlist the help of someone who could have found out more than he was ever going to find out by himself.

*

The flight attendant had assumed he was asleep and was shaking him by the shoulder.

Driscoll opened his eyes. 'Hi there,' he said.

'You are the passenger who asks to know when we are four and one half hours into the flight?'

'That's me.'

She leaned across to collect his empty glass and fold up his tray. 'If you wish to know where we are, I can ask the captain.'

'It's OK. I've got a fair idea, thanks.'

She had a nice figure and she was close enough for him to smell her perfume – the same perfume Natalie Washburn had been wearing at their aborted meeting in the hotel restaurant.

Not that telling the truth to a journalist would have made the meeting any more useful, Driscoll decided, nor would it have changed much. Even if she'd believed him and leaked the information to the British press, Energex were always going to swallow the official Chinese story, because the official Chinese story was perfectly plausible, whereas the truth most certainly was not.

'May I bring you another drink?' The flight attendant interrupted his thoughts.

'I'll only go to sleep.' He smiled at her. 'Later maybe.'

For a few minutes after she'd gone, he did nothing, wondering if he'd be better off not looking out of the window as he'd planned to do.

In the end he did so anyway, doubting he'd be able to see much, but unable to prevent himself from trying in case he could.

A week ago he'd been flying over a not dissimilar part of the country in the Cessna. But viewed from an altitude of 35,000 feet, apart from the washed-out colour and the twin forks of the Hotan river that he fancied he could just pick out in the distance, the desert bore no resemblance to the wilderness it was – proof of how easily you could get the wrong impression about a place, Driscoll realized, and a reminder of why nothing about the Tarim Basin was ever quite what it seemed to be.

CHAPTER 3

The buckle on Gorman's belt was as tasteless as the paintings of rodeo scenes adorning the walls of his office. Driscoll had seen the paintings before, but the belt buckle was new – an ostentatious brass oval on which was stamped the stylized outline of a longhorn bull.

Having given Driscoll the opportunity to admire it, Gorman stopped pacing round the room and returned to his desk. 'Right,' he said. 'Let's get to it, shall we?'

'Look,' Driscoll tried to sound indifferent, 'do you want to hear what happened, or don't you?'

'Your version, you mean – the one where you don't set fire to Collier to stop him from spoiling the nice little business you were running on the side. Or would that be the version where you don't come in to the strip so goddamn hard there'll be no evidence left of anything after the fire?'

'You don't believe that,' Driscoll said.

'Who gives a fuck? You still wrote off three-quarters of a million pounds' worth of equipment, you still lost us the Chinese contract, and as far as I know, Collier is still dead.'

'It wasn't like that,' Driscoll said. 'You don't have any proof, you won't find any, and you're wrong.'

Gorman raised his eyebrows. 'What are these then?' He tossed an envelope across the desk. 'Take a look.'

The envelope contained three A4 colour prints, the first of which showed the Cessna tipped up on its nose with flames starting to lick around the wing roots. Another photo showed the whole aircraft enveloped in fire, and the third was a close-up of the burnt-out remains sitting on the blackened apron in front of the building where Driscoll had parked it.

At first sight, the photographs were an irrefutable record of an accident, but the longer he studied them, the easier it was to see that they revealed more of the truth than he'd first thought.

'Where did you get these?' he asked.

'They came by courier from Beijing. The Chinese figured they'd help us with our insurance claim.'

'It was a lucky coincidence, wasn't it?'

'What?'

'Someone with a camera being at the strip at exactly the right time.'

'You're the lucky prick.' Gorman put his hands behind his head. 'If those Narcotics Control guys hadn't been there to take pictures of the drugs you had on board, you wouldn't just have that nice bruise on your head, you'd be toast. The way I see it, they made a big mistake. If it'd been me, I'd have pulled out Collier and left you to take your chances.'

Driscoll slid the first of the photos across the desk. 'See the nose wheel strut and the propeller?'

'What about them?'

'If I'd gone in too hard, the strut would have snapped off backwards. So why is it sticking out forwards?'

Gorman shrugged.

'And the propeller's fine.' Driscoll showed him. 'You know damn well I wouldn't have tried landing without power on. So, if the nose wheel strut had collapsed while the propeller had still been rotating, why aren't the tips of the prop all bent?'

'What's your point?'

'What the hell do you think? If you don't believe me, what about the buildings and the sand dunes in the background? Does it look as though the Cessna's sitting on a runway or at the end of a landing strip?'

'How would I know?' Gorman was uninterested. 'You were the guy doing the work there, not me.'

Now Driscoll had come to inspect the second photo more closely, he'd noticed something else he'd missed. Encircling the Cessna's fuselage close to the leading edge of the wings, a telltale ring of brighter fire showed where the nylon or polypropylene rope had been burning.

Not that it was the kind of evidence that would cut any ice with Gorman, he thought, especially when it was part of such an improbable explanation that no one would be willing to accept it.

'You're being sold a fairy story,' Driscoll said. 'You need to find out what game the Chinese are trying to make you play.'

'I don't need to.' Gorman slipped the photos back into the envelope. 'I've got all I want right here.'

'No you haven't. I had no reason to kill Collier. I didn't crash the plane and I wouldn't have been crazy enough to risk being shot for selling drugs in China. You're going off half-cocked.'

Because this was the third occasion in as many days that Driscoll had said much the same thing to three different people, he was under no illusions about how his statements were being received. In Shanghai, Ji at least had given him the benefit of the doubt, but Natalie Washburn hadn't and Gorman had hardly bothered to listen.

The American took a file from a drawer in his desk. 'You're full of shit, Driscoll,' he said. 'You've always been full of it. You were on the bones of your arse in Angola before we gave you a job – and what did you do? You gave us a whole lot of trouble, and you've been trouble ever since. If you're dumb enough to think we're going off half-cocked, you'd better see how deep a hole you've dug for yourself this time.'

Driscoll remained silent.

'How about we start here?' Gorman opened his file and took out a fuzzy black and white photograph. 'Recognize this place?' He held up the photo. 'It's your hotel in Hotan.'

'So?'

'What about this guy?' Gorman pointed to a man who had been snapped on his way out of the hotel entrance.

Driscoll had never seen him before. 'Who is he?'

'According to the Chinese, a small time drug dealer called Wen Jintao who operates across the north-west. They think he was delivering a five-kilogram package of opium to you.'

Unable to think of anything sensible to say, Driscoll waited to hear the rest of it.

'Then there's this.' Gorman waved another photograph. 'A picture of you handing over a packet to some whacked-out junkie at the airstrip.'

Driscoll had heard enough. 'It was cigarettes,' he said. 'The carton was to pay him for keeping an eye on the plane at night.'

'He lived there, did he?'

'He had a bunk in a shed at the back of one of the workshops.'

'So he'll be able to confirm your story about the Cessna – because he was there, right?'

'Get someone to ask him. See what he says.'

27

'I don't need to.' Gorman handed over a sheet of paper. 'That's a statement from the bank account we set up for you in Shanghai. The Chinese thought they ought to send us a copy. It's a bummer for you that they can access the accounts of anyone in China whenever they want. Pity we can't do that here. It'd save a lot of trouble sometimes. How do you explain that 17 February deposit for a hundred thousand yuan?'

If he hadn't suspected it before, by now Driscoll was beginning to appreciate how thoroughly he'd been framed. Without realizing, he'd been trying to solve a puzzle in which he, himself, had always been a part – not as an observer, but as a participant in some kind of subterfuge that had cost Charles Collier his life.

Knowing that Gorman was expecting him to deny all knowledge of the 100,000 yuan, Driscoll decided not to waste his breath, preferring to try and collect his thoughts in case there were more surprises to come.

There were.

'Whichever way you look at it, I'd say you're pretty much fucked, wouldn't you?' Gorman said. 'Sir Oliver wants your head on a spike and I want you off the payroll by midday.'

Sir Oliver Fox was one of the three directors of Energex, a self-important, florid-faced industrialist whom Driscoll had once met at a company dinner in Cape Town, someone who would normally never be involved in the dismissal of an employee unless they'd been groping his secretary or vandalizing his Rolls.

'What's any of this got to do with Sir Oliver?' Driscoll said.

'Use your imagination. Collier's father is holding you responsible for the death of his son. That's why he had a private meeting with Sir Oliver yesterday afternoon. You see, Driscoll, you weren't even close to being smart enough. You were so busy looking after yourself that you didn't know Collier had sent an email to his father, did you?'

'Saying what?'

'See for yourself.' Gorman removed another sheet of paper from his file. 'Then tell me all this is a big mistake.'

Prepared for the worst, Driscoll picked up the email and began to read:

Dear Dad
Sorry I've been too busy to get in touch until tonight. The days

are very long, and although I spend them sitting in a plane, by the time I've had dinner and finished checking our survey results, I'm usually more than ready for bed.

The job is all right, but the place is much worse than I expected it to be – mostly because of the cold, and because there's absolutely nothing here except oil wells and sand dunes.

The Chinese call the Tarim Basin 'The Sea of Death', which is exactly how it looks from the air – and sometimes from the ground as well.

Peter Driscoll is a good pilot, but I'm sure he's operating a business of his own to supplement his income. It's probably drugs. Everyone knows there's a market for them out in the oil fields, and a couple of times I've seen him handing stuff to rig workers who call by on their days off or when they have shift change.

I'm not sure whether I should tell anyone. What do you think?

Give Shirley my love and tell her that I bet it's twice as cold here than it'll be when she arrives in Reykjavik.

All the best for now,

Charles

To disguise his discomfort, Driscoll switched to the attack. 'Collier didn't write that,' he said. 'He couldn't have done. Why don't you fax the National Narcotics Control Commission in Beijing? Ask them how many men they sent out to the airstrip, and see if they can tell you what kind of car they were driving. They won't know because no one from the NNCC was there.'

Gorman ignored the suggestion. 'Are you going to be at your flat for the next few days?'

'You just fired me, didn't you? Why would you care?'

'I don't. Collier's father wanted me to ask where he could get in touch with you.'

'What for?'

'He didn't say. Maybe so he can explain why you'll be losing your flying licence, and why you won't be getting any more work in the UK, or Africa, or China, or any place else where he can put in a good word.'

'I don't know where I'll be.' The lie came easily – the result of Driscoll's conviction that, before very long, he needed to be as far away as he could get from Gorman and from Energex, and probably from London too.

He left the email lying on the desk and stood up. 'Tell Collier's father I'm sorry,' he said.

'Tell him yourself.' Gorman sounded more conciliatory. 'Seeing as how you were the last person to see his son alive, say what he wants to hear. So long as you don't screw up our insurance claim, no one at Energex is going to give two fucks what story you spin him, and Collier won't know whether it's true one way or another, will he?'

Driscoll thought for a moment. 'I'll be at my brother's place in Wiltshire,' he said. 'Give me a pen and I'll write down the phone number for you.'

'It's not me who wants it. I've got better things to do than pass on messages for you. Leave it with my secretary. If you feel like calling Collier before he calls you, she can give you his private number.' Gorman went to open the door. 'Good luck finding another job.'

Driscoll didn't bother to answer. Nor did he say goodbye, as glad to be leaving the office with its tacky paintings as he was to be leaving Gorman, who, by hooking his thumbs into his belt to display his buckle once again, was managing to look even more ridiculous than he had done before.

The drive down to Mere had taken longer than he'd expected. It had also been a mistake.

All the windows of the house were closed, one of the gutters had been overflowing, and the place looked as though it had been unoccupied for some time, Driscoll thought, which meant that, if he didn't want to face the trip all the way back to his flat in Kensington, and if the key wasn't hidden where it usually was, he'd have to find somewhere else in the village to stay – an unwelcome alternative in his present frame of mind.

After locking up his rental car, he opened the gate at the side of the house and went to see whether the plank across the stream was still in place.

It was, but there was no key under the triangular-shaped rock on the other side, and none of the other rocks had keys beneath them either.

He was halfway back across the plank when a young woman appeared at the gate.

She had long dark hair that was beginning to escape from the ribbon she'd used to tie it back and she was wearing gumboots and a pair of muddy overalls.

'Hi there.' He waved at her. 'I'm not trying to break in.'

'I didn't think you were.' She smiled as she came to meet him. 'I saw your car.'

Driscoll thought he recognized her. 'I'm Jeremy's brother, Peter. You live next door, don't you?'

'Rebecca.' She wiped her hands on her overalls before she shook hands with him. 'Rebecca Wilson. You were here for a weekend last summer. I remember. You're the pilot.'

'Yep. Do you know where Jeremy is?'

'Scotland – something to do with measuring oxygen levels in one of the lochs. He won't be back until next week. Were you looking for the key?'

'It's not there,' Driscoll said. 'But that's OK. It's my fault for not phoning first. I'll find a motel or get a room in the village somewhere.'

'That's silly. Jeremy left the key with me. He won't mind me letting you have it. Here.' She produced it from the pocket of her overalls and gave it to him. 'I'm afraid you won't find much food in the cupboards or the fridge, though. You know what Jeremy's like. But you're welcome to borrow stuff from me if you'd rather not go shopping right away.'

'I don't want to put you to any trouble.' Driscoll returned her smile. 'Did I interrupt your gardening?'

'I was just trying to drain water off the lawn. We had loads of rain last night. Would you like me to go in with you to show you where things are?'

'I'll be fine. If I'm not, I'll come and bang on your door for help.' Anxious to end the conversation before she asked him about his bruise, he went to open the gate for her.

'It's all right.' She headed off across the back garden towards a gap in the hedge. 'I can go this way. Don't forget to turn on the hot water. The switch is in the airing cupboard.'

'Thanks.' He waited until she'd disappeared from sight, then let himself in and went straight to the phone in the hall, ready to do what he'd known he was going to do for the last two hours, and unwilling to put it off any longer.

After he'd punched in the international prefix for China and the 21 for Shanghai he hesitated for a second, wondering what he should say before he carried on and pressed the buttons for the number on Natalie Washburn's business card.

The click of her answering machine was an anti-climax – not

because he'd been in too much of a hurry to take account of the time difference, he realized, but because she was out of town just as she'd told him she would be.

Annoyed with himself for forgetting, he let her outgoing recording play right through, listening to the Mandarin version as well as the English one, but too frustrated to pay much attention to the alternative number she gave in her message.

It was only after he'd replaced the receiver that he began to wonder if he'd been too hasty. The other number had started with a double zero, which meant she was overseas somewhere, but if the double three that had followed was the code for the country he thought it was, then maybe the setback wasn't a setback after all.

Pushing the recall button, he listened to the recording again, this time scribbling down the number and checking the prefix in the phone book.

He'd been right. Natalie Washburn was in France, almost certainly visiting her mother in Paris, and thousands of miles closer to him than she would have otherwise been.

Believing his luck might be taking a turn for the better, he placed the call and waited.

A woman with a pleasant voice answered in French.

'I'm sorry to bother you,' Driscoll said. 'Is Natalie Washburn there?'

'I shall fetch her for you.'

Some muffled conversation was followed by another voice saying hello.

'Is that Natalie?' he asked.

'Yes it is.'

'Hi. This is Peter Driscoll.'

'Oh.' She didn't sound surprised. 'I was wrong then.'

'About what?'

'About you getting in touch with me if you changed your mind.'

'I've sort of had my mind changed for me.'

'Are you calling from England?' she asked.

'Is that a guess?'

'Not really. I found out you weren't being allowed to stay in China, but no one at the CNPC could tell me when you were leaving Shanghai or where you were supposed to be going, so I tried your boss again. When I finally got through, in between him being ruder to me than he was before, he sort of said you were in Europe.'

Driscoll could imagine how her call had been received. What he couldn't imagine was why she'd been prepared to risk getting another mouthful from Gorman. 'Remember me saying that what happened at the airstrip was kind of complicated?' he said.

'You said it was a long story. Has it got longer?'

He could tell she already knew it had. 'Not just longer. I think that whatever's going on could be fairly serious.'

'I think so too. That's why I've been trying to contact you. I'm really pleased you've called.'

'Because you believe what I told you in Shanghai is true now?'

'Partly. Mostly it's because I think I know the reason for what happened to Charles Collier, and I'm fairly sure you don't. If you did, you wouldn't be talking to me again, would you?'

Whether that meant she'd found the right explanation, Driscoll wasn't certain, but it sounded as though she'd come up with something.

Her next remark confirmed his suspicions. It also caught him off-guard.

'If I catch an early flight I can meet you in London tomorrow morning,' she said, 'unless you don't want me to, or you'd rather come to France.'

He'd been planning to provide her with a suitably graphic account of the way Collier had died, but instead, without any help from him, she'd evidently decided that there was a good deal more to the story than she'd first believed.

'I'm not in London,' Driscoll said.

'That's all right. As long as you're not miles and miles away, I can get a hire car. I like driving.'

'Just hold on a second there.' He attempted to slow her down. 'Before you start booking flights and renting cars, how about telling me why all this is so important to you?'

'It's only important if you can back up what I think I've uncovered.'

'Which is?'

'More than I bargained for. I started off by finding out everything I could about the oil industry in the Tarim Basin, which turned out to be a weird kind of exercise. It was too easy, almost as though I was being deliberately fed the information I wanted, so I acted on a hunch and changed tack.'

Driscoll interrupted her. 'Is something going on in the oil fields?'

'As far as I can make out, it looks as though the Chinese might not be getting hold of the right survey data, but that hasn't got anything to do with you or Charles Collier. It's something completely different: it's Collier's father.'

'What do you mean? What about him?'

'I spent a whole morning checking out his background and his career. It's his political views you've got yourself involved with.'

'How?' Driscoll wasn't keeping up.

'It has to do with the tension between Mainland China and the Taiwanese movement for independence. You see, what you probably don't know is that Johnathon Collier's second wife is Taiwanese, and that he's made five official visits to Taiwan in the last two years. He's a personal friend of Chen Shui-bian, the Taiwanese president, and he's on record everywhere as being an advocate of Taiwanese independence. That means he'll have been tagged as a priority two enemy of the Chinese government. The Communists hate people like him.'

'Enough to shut him up by killing his son and blaming me for it? Is that what you're saying?'

'It all fits. The Chinese have used you as a scapegoat to solve one of their problems. Johnathon Collier still has a wife and a grown up daughter to worry about, so it was an easy way to keep him quiet from now on.'

'And a scoop with a nice pay cheque for you,' Driscoll said. 'If you're right.'

'If I am, it'll clear your name, won't it? Isn't that a good reason for us to see whether I am or not?'

It was good enough, he thought. And even if she was wrong, after his experiences of the last few days, the prospect of meeting her again was, at least, something positive he could look forward to.

Feeling more optimistic than he had done for a while, he gave her Jeremy's street address and phone number, then, after retrieving his map from the car, spent the next five minutes providing her with directions on the simplest route out of Heathrow and explaining how she should find her way on to the A303.

CHAPTER 4

Rebecca Wilson was the kind of neighbour Driscoll could have done without. She was well-meaning and pleasant enough, but after yesterday evening when she'd called round unannounced and stayed for nearly an hour, he was being careful not to encourage her this morning.

She'd come over to help him unload the last of his shopping bags from the car and was hovering while he closed the boot lid.

'I could've got this for you,' she said. 'I'm going in to Gillingham later on, and things are cheaper at the supermarket there.'

'I have someone coming to see me.' Driscoll took the bag from her. 'I thought I'd better stock up on some bits and pieces before she arrives.'

'She?'

'Just a friend from France.' He wished he hadn't opened his mouth. 'You don't have a phone number for Jeremy, do you?'

She shook her head. 'You don't look as though you slept very well.'

He hadn't, but he had no intention of telling her so. 'I'll let you know if I run out of anything,' he said.

Before she could speak again, he left her standing in the drive and went to unpack his shopping, making a quick detour on his way in to the kitchen so he could glance at himself in the hall mirror.

Except for his bruise being a different colour, it seemed to be no better and it wasn't hard to see what had prompted Rebecca Wilson's comment.

He'd slept only fitfully, willing himself to forget the recurring image of Charles Collier's face at the window of the Cessna in case it triggered the dreams that had kept him awake for the last four nights, and twice getting out of bed to wander round the house in the hope of being able to think about something else.

This morning, he was glad to have Natalie Washburn's theory to occupy his mind, an explanation that in the light of Johnathon Collier's political stand on Taiwanese independence was fairly believable, even if it seemed a little thin now he'd had longer to think about it.

To see if he could fault the logic, after making himself toast and coffee, he sat down at the kitchen table with a pen and a pad of paper and endeavoured to link what he knew for certain with what Natalie Washburn had discovered – an exercise that ended up proving not very much at all, but one that kept him busy until shortly before 12.30 when a red Ford Fiesta pulled in to the driveway.

Pleased that his visitor had arrived early, and hoping his neighbour was still away on her shopping trip, Driscoll went to say hello.

Today, Natalie Washburn had her hair in a ponytail, and in place of the semi-formal, high-collared jacket she'd been wearing in Shanghai, she was dressed more casually in designer jeans and a cream-coloured sweater that revealed more of her figure than the jacket had done. She was also wearing heels and carrying a slim, state-of-the-art laptop computer beneath her arm.

'You didn't get lost then?' Driscoll said.

'No. I very nearly didn't get here at all, though.' She accompanied him to the front door, but stopped to look back at her car. 'Someone tried to run me off the road.'

'Where?' He could see she was still shaken.

'After I'd gone past Stonehenge. A man driving a white van came up really close behind and pushed me sideways towards the oncoming traffic. I don't know how much damage he's done to the bumper.'

'Probably some idiot having fun.'

'I don't think so. He did it twice – both times when there were trucks coming the other way.' She made an effort to pull herself together. 'I'm sorry. I didn't mean to arrive here sounding like a helpless female. I'm not usually like that.'

'I should've driven up to London and met you there,' Driscoll said. 'It's my fault for not offering when you called me back to say you'd booked your flight. Come on in, and I'll fix you a brandy.'

'I don't want a brandy. It'll make me sleepy.' She followed him inside. 'Is this your place?'

'It's my brother's. I'm sort of squatting in it while he's away in Scotland. If you don't want to fall asleep, how about some coffee?'

'That would be nice. Thank you. Did you find somewhere for me to stay tonight?'

'Yep. There's a motel on the other side of the village. It's nothing special, but it's clean and tidy. I've reserved you a double room at the back where there won't be so much traffic noise. Will that be OK?' He escorted her in to the kitchen.

'Of course it will.' She looked at him. 'You know, I never really expected to see you again.'

'Because I was a bit offhand.' Driscoll concentrated on making the coffee.

'No. I just didn't think things would turn out the way they have.' She placed her laptop on the table and sat down. 'Has your boss seen the report about you in the *China Daily*?'

'Among other things. That's why I lost my job yesterday. The Chinese sent Energex a photo of a local drug dealer visiting my hotel in Hotan, and there's another photo of me handing over a package to someone at the airstrip. It was a carton of cigarettes, but you can't tell what the hell it is from the print.'

'And that was all the proof your company needed to fire you?'

'There were a few other things,' Driscoll said. 'A statement from my Shanghai bank showing a big chunk of money in my account that I know nothing about, and a copy of an email Collier is supposed to have sent to his father saying he was sure I was running drugs on the side. Whoever's stitched me up hasn't messed about.'

'You know who's done it. I told you.' She took the cup of coffee he gave her. 'And you know why they have.'

Driscoll joined her at the table. 'Tell me something,' he said. 'What makes you think the Chinese government will let you get away with selling a story like this? You'll either get yourself locked up, or they'll throw you out of China more quickly than they threw me out.'

'Not if they don't know who wrote it.'

'Suppose you're wrong. What if there's another explanation? For all you know, Collier's father could've been targeted by a terrorist group that has nothing to do with Taiwan or Beijing.'

'And they threatened to kill his son unless he paid them a couple of million dollars or something? Is that what you mean?'

'It's how the Chinese Triads work, isn't it?'

She shook her head. 'The Triads wouldn't take the trouble to blame someone else. If Collier's father didn't pay up, they'd have just stuck a knife in Charles and walked away. I like my idea better.' She drank some of her coffee. 'When are you going to tell me what really happened?'

'Anytime you like. What about having some lunch first?'

She shook her head. 'I'm not hungry. I had a big breakfast at the airport, and I still don't feel very good – you know, because of that driver. Don't let me stop you, though.'

Driscoll wasn't hungry either, preferring to get down to business if that was what she wanted. 'There's not that much to tell,' he said.

'Do you mind if I take notes this time?' She opened up the screen of her computer. 'Then I won't have to keep asking questions as we go.'

'No, I don't mind.' He forced himself to remember his last day at the airstrip, wondering whether he should edit out some of the details, but deciding not to in case they were to prove important later.

He began by describing his uneventful landing, then went on to provide her with an account of everything that had occurred up to the moment when he'd heard the bang from the explosive charge and seen the wheel strut collapse beneath the Cessna's nose.

'Is that when you knew things were going wrong?' she said.

'I knew before then. There's only one reason why anyone would rope the doors shut and spray aviation fuel around. I can understand the Chinese wanting to make it look as though Collier had lost his life in a crash, but they didn't have to burn him alive and blame me for it.'

'It's more awful than I thought it would be.' She shivered. 'I don't see how anybody could do something like that. Have you any idea why they took away his computer?'

'God knows. They'd have been better off with the gradiometer, but they didn't even look at it. Do you want to hear the rest?'

She nodded.

To get it over with, he gave her a brief summary of his attempt to reach the burning plane, taking care to avoid over-dramatizing it and making light of the blow to his head before he explained how he'd lost consciousness after the Cessna's fuel tank had exploded.

Once he'd finished, she said nothing for nearly thirty seconds, either too taken aback or too busy assembling the questions he knew she was going to ask him.

'The Chinese have screwed themselves,' Driscoll said. 'To make sure people think it was my fault, they've told the CNPC to cancel their survey contract with Energex.'

'Oh.' She looked at him. 'The CNPC didn't tell me. Perhaps that's why someone wanted Collier's computer – so the data wouldn't be lost in the fire.'

'Wrong.' Driscoll said. 'All we'd done was a sweep of the block that I'd already surveyed before. Anyway, the computer data won't be any use to them – not without the right software to interpret it properly.'

'Don't the Chinese have that?'

'No. It belongs to Energex. No one else anywhere in the world has anything like it. The gravity gradiometer and the terrain mapping laser are real clever pieces of equipment, but you need software to correct all the errors caused by the aircraft moving around during its flight. Unless you've pre-calibrated the characteristics of the plane you're using, geological mapping from the air is a waste of time. You're better off just doing a seismic survey.'

'Is that where geologists set off explosives in the ground and record the shockwaves as they bounce back off different layers of rock?'

'That's it.' He wasn't surprised she knew. 'Until Energex spent millions developing the gradiometer technology, the oil companies had to rely on the results from seismic exploration and a whole lot of luck.'

'Maybe that man in the fur hat took the laptop so he could use it to send the fake email to Collier's father.'

'The timing's wrong,' Driscoll said. 'It was sent the day before Collier was killed. You can't fake an email date because it's recorded by the internet service provider as soon as they receive it.'

'So it was sent the day before by someone else from somewhere else?'

'It must have been. That's what I meant about the Chinese trying so damn hard to make things look right.'

'It's not that.' For the first time that day she smiled at him. 'It's because you don't understand Chinese culture.'

Ever since Driscoll had met her in Shanghai, for reasons that were still unclear to him, he'd been able to recall nearly everything about her. He hadn't forgotten her eyes, or the colour of her skin, or the shape of her mouth, nor had he forgotten how pretty she was.

But it was her smile he remembered most – not because it made her more attractive, but because it didn't.

Today's smile, fleeting though it had been, had lasted just long enough for him to notice the asymmetry of it – as though she was wary of giving the wrong impression and allowing only part of her face to smile while she kept the rest of it unchanged.

'Did I say something?' she asked.

'No. I was thinking about the email.'

'No you weren't.' She left the table and went over to stand with her back to the wall. 'It's all right. I'm used to it.'

'What?'

'How people look at me when I smile at them.'

'I'm sorry.' He realized he'd been staring. 'I didn't mean to be rude.'

'It's my mother's fault – well, she thinks it is. She says it's genetic. She calls it my broken smile.'

Although it was hard to think of a better description, there was more behind Natalie Washburn's broken smile than genetics, Driscoll thought, not the least of which was the easy way she combined her frankness with a reserve that surfaced whenever she thought her self-assuredness was slipping.

'OK.' He chose another subject. 'Let's have a look at the information you've got on Johnathon Collier. Maybe there's something that'll tell us whether he's ever been threatened by the Chinese government.'

'I don't think there is.' Returning to the table, she sat down next to him and adjusted the position of the laptop so they could view the screen together. 'There's a simpler way.'

'Ask him.'

'Can we do that?'

'It's worth a try. According to Gorman, he wants to talk to me anyway, and we can get his private number from Gorman's secretary. I should've asked her for it yesterday, but I can give her a call.'

'Well, that makes it even simpler, doesn't it?' She tried not to look too pleased. 'It'll be the best lead we could have, as long as he isn't paranoid about protecting the rest of his family.'

'You can promise not to use anything he tells us in your story, unless he's bitter enough to want the truth out in the open. It depends what kind of person he is.'

'No it doesn't. It depends on whether the British government are prepared to accuse Beijing of murdering a British national for political purposes.' She pressed a key on her computer. 'If you read these press clippings, you'll understand how incredibly sensitive the issue of Taiwan is – not just to China and Taiwan, but to the Japanese, the US and half of Europe too. It's a potential flash-point like Israel and Iran or North Korea.'

The clippings she'd found were as numerous as they were varied. Unsurprisingly, the reports from the West or Taiwan tended to limit themselves to recycling the pro-independence speeches that Johnathon Collier had made, although a few international journals contained statements pointing out that his views were controversial and unlikely to meet with much favour in Beijing.

By way of contrast, Natalie's translations of articles from Chinese newspapers presented a different picture. As well as being universally hostile, condemning Collier for meddling in affairs that he knew little about, in several instances he was being blamed for rekindling the political tension that had existed between Britain and China before the handover of Hong Kong.

Driscoll didn't read them all, relying on Natalie to highlight any she considered particularly relevant, but knowing that irrespective of what the Chinese thought or said, press clippings were just press clippings, and constituted proof of exactly nothing.

She pushed another key to scroll back through the text. 'Now do you believe I'm right?' she asked.

Driscoll was still trying to make up his mind when a coloured map of the Tarim Basin oil fields flashed up on the screen.

'Hold on there.' He made her stop. 'What's that?'

'You can see what it is. I've already told you about it. The CNPC gave me dozens of maps like this one.'

'Part of the information you thought was too easy to get – before you changed horses and started researching Johnathon Collier?'

'Yes. I'll show it to you later if you want. Some of it's quite interesting.' She switched off the computer. 'Now you've read all about Johnathon Collier, and now I know what happened to you in China, we should be able to connect everything together, don't you think?'

To guard against the possibility of her preferred connection being the wrong one, Driscoll spent the rest of the afternoon persuading her to consider other possibilities, enjoying her single-mindedness as much as he enjoyed her company, and only remembering he hadn't offered her a late lunch when she went over to look inside the freezer and started opening cupboards.

'Are you ready to eat?' he asked.

'I thought I could fix us something for dinner.'

'You don't have to do that. We'll go out, then I can drop you off afterwards at your motel so you won't have to find it in the dark.'

'We don't need to eat out.' She turned around. 'There's a packet of spaghetti and a can of tomato puree in the top cupboard. And there's some olive oil and you have beef mince in the freezer. That's enough for spaghetti Bolognese – well, almost enough.'

'You've come all the way from Paris,' Driscoll said. 'You don't have to start cooking.'

41

'I like it. And I'm good at it.' She gave him one of her smiles. 'Don't you want to see?'

'What else do you need?'

'Is there a local shop where you could buy onions? Some oregano would be nice as well, but I'm not sure where you'd get that.'

'We might be out of luck.' He checked his watch. 'This isn't exactly the big city, and it's getting pretty late.'

'Oh.' She looked disappointed.

Reluctant to embark on another shopping expedition, he took the easy way out. Picking up the phone, he dialled the number for next door, speaking as briefly as he could to Rebecca Wilson, and after twice assuring her that onions and oregano were all he needed, cut the conversation short by thanking her for her offer to bring them over.

Natalie was amused. 'Your brother's friendly neighbour,' she said.

'Bit too friendly. Don't give her a chance to start talking.'

He should have saved his breath. Within a minute of Rebecca Wilson appearing at the back door, she'd manoeuvred her way into the kitchen and was standing by the cooker telling Natalie how her husband, who was a gunnery instructor in the army, had only last night phoned to say that, because the course he was taking had been extended for a further day, he wouldn't be home until tomorrow.

Having heard all about it before, Driscoll was inclined to believe that her husband might be glad of the respite, while Natalie, having made the mistake of sounding sympathetic, was looking as though she needed rescuing.

He went to interrupt, hoping to persuade his neighbour to go home and stay home by thanking her again for her trouble and promising to replace the items she'd brought over.

'Don't be silly. I'm happy to help.' She picked up the bottle of olive oil. 'Do you know how much they charge for this in the village?'

It was a typically inconsequential question, and the last one Rebecca Wilson would ever ask.

At the same time as the window behind Driscoll shattered in to a thousand pieces, the bottle slipped from her grasp, and a tiny red-rimmed hole appeared in the centre of her forehead.

She was dead before her knees began to buckle, killed in an instant by a hollow-point bullet that had torn away half the back of her head and sprayed a soup of her blood and brains across the range-hood and the wall beneath it.

CHAPTER 5

Once, at a fog-bound airstrip near the edge of Namibia's western desert, Driscoll had witnessed a small-scale massacre when rebel soldiers high on crystal meth had executed the entire family of a deserter who had returned to his village to help an ailing father.

The soldiers had been armed with high-powered hunting rifles, the effects of which Driscoll had hoped to never see again.

Yet here he was, not back in Africa and no longer in China, but in England of all places, where the chances of something like this occurring were so unlikely that he'd never believed they could.

The shock had slowed him down. More than a second had passed before he started to react, and it took him another second to hit the light switch and yell at Natalie.

She too was slow to move, without thinking stepping into the line of fire.

Driscoll did his best to save her, tackling her round the waist and pulling her down onto the floor beside him.

'Listen to me,' he said. 'If you want to stay alive, you have to crawl to the bathroom. Knock on the bath with your knuckles. If it's made of cast iron, get in it and stay in it. If it's plastic just keep lying on the floor.'

'I can't.' She could barely speak and started to shake.

'You have to. Whoever fired that shot wasn't trying to kill Rebecca Wilson. If they realize they've made a mistake, they're going to try again.'

'You don't know that.' She gripped his arm. 'I can't go by myself. And you can't make me.'

He didn't answer her, struggling to recall whether he'd heard the crack of a rifle above the sound of breaking glass, and unwilling to gamble on neighbours having heard something in case the gunman had used a moderator or a silencer.

'We have to call the police.' She spoke so quietly, he could hardly hear her.

'And tell them what? I'm a drug trafficker who's already supposed to have killed the son of a British politician – remember? Explaining this would be about as easy as explaining why there wasn't a plane crash in China. The police aren't going to listen to anything I have to say.'

She fell silent, maintaining her hold on his arm as though to help stop herself from trembling.

Driscoll prised her fingers away. 'Stay here then,' he said. 'Don't go near the phone and don't stick your head up either.'

'If someone's still out there, they can't see us – not now you've turned off the lights.'

'If they have night vision equipment they can.' Hoping she'd do what he'd told her to do, he used his shoe to clear away some of the glass and began to inch his way over to the window through the spreading pool of blood and olive oil.

There was nothing unusual to see outside. The street was in darkness and undisturbed. His car was still parked in front of Natalie's car in the driveway, there was no sound of shouting, and no lights were being switched on in any of the surrounding houses.

So where the hell had the shot come from, Driscoll wondered? And had the gunman gone, secure in the knowledge that his job had been carried out successfully?

'What are we going to do?' Natalie whispered.

'I don't know. Shut up a minute. I'm trying to listen.' It was a lie. He wasn't listening. He was endeavouring to think, as numbed as she was, bewildered by the second cold-blooded murder he'd been forced to confront in the space of eight short days.

Natalie came to join him at the window. 'Don't you think one of us should check her pulse?' she said.

It was a pointless question, but he was careful with his reply, knowing he couldn't afford to have her any closer to the edge than she was already.

'That won't help her,' he said. 'And it isn't going to help us. Right now, all we have to worry about is you.'

'Because I'm the one the bullet was meant for?'

'Someone wants you dead,' Driscoll said, 'someone who used that message on your Shanghai answering machine to track you down in France. They could even have been on the plane with you this morning. When they couldn't run you off the road on your way here, this was their next best option.'

'Why would anyone want to kill me? What have I done?'

He had no idea. Nor did he have his nerves properly under control, conscious of the need to do something, even if it was only making the decision to wait.

She started to speak again, but had to turn away to vomit, a clear indication to Driscoll of how little use she was going to be unless she was able to pull herself together.

'I'm sorry.' She coughed. 'I've seen traffic accidents, but I've never seen anybody shot before.'

'Give me your car keys.' He held out his hand.

'They're on the table. You won't leave me alone here, will you?'

'No. We'll stay where we are for a while. Then, I'm going to reverse your car out of the drive and back it up to mine so it's facing the right way. When you see me kick open the passenger door, you run like hell and jump in. If something happens to me before that, get out of the house by the back door and head for the stream that runs along the bottom of the garden. There's a plank you can use to get across. Once you're on the other side, all you'll have to do is keep going until you come to a boundary fence and some houses. Bang on the first door you come to and tell them you need help.'

'The best place for us to get help is from the police. I still think we ought to phone them.'

'I don't care what you think.' Driscoll looked at her. 'Do you want to make a run for it out the back while I wait here?'

'No I don't.' She made an attempt to collect herself. 'Why are you so sure I was the target?'

'You're about the same height as Rebecca Wilson. You both have the same colour hair, and you've got yours tied back like hers was.'

'Mine's in a ponytail; hers wasn't.'

'Not much difference if the light's not good and you're behind a telescopic sight sighting through a gap in the curtains,' Driscoll said. 'Whoever pulled the trigger either knew this is where you'd be, or he saw you arrive. He wouldn't have known Rebecca had come across through her back garden.'

'I didn't tell anyone where I was going except my mother, and all I gave her was your phone number.' She raised her head to peer out of the broken window. 'You didn't see a white van, did you?'

'No. Are you going to do what I said?'

'You're not giving me a choice.' She glanced back at the body. 'How can you be so matter of fact after someone's been murdered right in front of you?'

'What do you want me to say? I'm just trying to make sure you don't get a bullet through your head as well. You can agonize over it all you want later. Right now we have to get away from here and lose ourselves so we can figure out what in the hell is going on and see what we can do about it.'

By engaging her in conversation, Driscoll had allowed his concentration to slip. Among the bushes and trees on the other side of the street, where more and more shadows seemed to be forming and dissolving, the half-imagined outline of a man was there one minute and gone the next, a figure that appeared only after he blinked or in his peripheral vision when he was looking somewhere else – a situation that was being aggravated by the knowledge that the longer he waited, the more his courage was draining away.

He reconsidered his plan, wondering if they'd be better off not risking a run for the car, but rejecting the idea once he saw rain glistening on the street and realized how vulnerable they'd be on foot when neither of them was familiar with the area.

For the next quarter of an hour he kept watch, trying to believe that by outwaiting the gunman he was minimizing his chances of taking a bullet before he could reach the car, but failing to convince himself and growing more apprehensive as time wore on.

Eventually, the wait became unbearable. As ready as he was ever going to be, he repeated his instructions to Natalie, then, after retrieving her keys from the table, went to the door, hesitating just for a second before he embarked on a nerve-racking sprint for the Fiesta.

Getting into it was easy. Starting it was not.

The engine caught on his third attempt, but stuttered and almost died on him while he was engaging gear.

To prevent it from happening again, he floored the accelerator, reversing with his tyres spraying gravel until he hit the tarmac out in the street and was able to complete his manoeuvre.

Natalie had been over-eager. Holding her laptop in both hands, she'd left the house too early, and he only saw her at the last minute in his mirror and nearly knocked her over.

The car was still moving when she wrenched open the door without his help, and threw herself inside.

Beginning to believe they might just get away with it, he rammed the Fiesta in to first gear and dropped the clutch, spinning his wheels again, but this time facing forwards and ready for the jolt when the tyres started to bite harder.

He headed for the village centre, driving as fast as he dared, watching for lights behind him and for any sign of a parked white van until they reached the comparative safety of the A303, by which time Natalie seemed to have partially recovered, although she still had no colour to her face.

'Did you see or hear anything before we left?' Driscoll asked.

She shook her head. 'Where are we going?'

'I haven't decided. Are you all right?'

'No. Of course I'm not all right. How can you ask me that?'

'Do you want me to drop you off somewhere?'

'I don't know. I can't stop thinking about that poor woman.'

'Think about this instead,' Driscoll said. 'Your theory about the Chinese wanting to hammer Johnathon Collier for his stand on Taiwanese independence has just blown up in your face. This can't have anything to do with China and Taiwan. Whatever crazy ideas the Chinese think you might have come up with, you're no threat to them.'

'You don't have to keep explaining. I'm not stupid.'

'I didn't say you were. I just want you to understand that whatever mess it is you and I are in, it's a whole lot bigger mess than you thought it was.'

'Why wouldn't I understand? Twenty minutes ago someone was shot to death while I was standing beside them in your brother's kitchen – someone who was supposed to be me. Don't you think that might have given me a clue?'

It wasn't a clue, he thought. It was a full-blown fucking disaster. Worse still, with his rental car parked back in Jeremy's drive, and with Rebecca Wilson's husband due home tomorrow, they were running out of time as quickly as they were running out of ideas.

'If we don't crack this soon, we're going to have the police to worry about as well,' he said.

'As well as us having to worry about the man who shot Rebecca?'

'It won't take him long to figure out he's screwed up.' Driscoll was wondering whether to head for the coast on minor roads where it would be easier to detect the presence of a following car. 'We need some help – serious help.'

She brushed raindrops off her computer and reached over to place it on the back seat. 'There isn't anyone we can ask,' she said, 'not if you won't go to the police.'

'Yes there is. Johnathon Collier.'

'I thought my theory about him had blown up in my face.'

'If I can convince him that his son didn't die in a plane crash, he's the best chance we have. You said that yourself.'

'I said he'd be able to give us the best lead. It's not the same.'

'Do you have a better idea?'

'Tell him everything, you mean?' She sounded doubtful. 'About tonight too?'

'We can't make any sense out of it. Let's see if he can.'

Faced with the unwanted complication of her safety to consider, Driscoll knew the suggestion was not without risk, but on a long drive to nowhere on a winter's night that was growing steadily colder and darker as the rain started coming down in sheets, and now he'd begun to realize how truly limited his options were, the further he drove, the more attractive the idea of approaching Collier became.

At Wincanton, for no good reason he could think of, he turned to the south, his concern about being tailed replaced by the need to find somewhere safe for them to spend the night now that the young woman beside him had grown so withdrawn, he feared she could be suffering the after effects of shock.

What should have been easy ended up occupying them for the next two hours. After a succession of frustrating phone calls made from petrol stations carrying bed and breakfast listings in directories that were either out of date or which applied only to the summer months, Driscoll was able to locate only three places which would accept late guests on a cold February night.

In the circumstances, he would have been willing to stay almost anywhere. But even he was appalled by the standard of accommodation offered at the first of the houses they visited.

As a consequence, it was nearly 10.30 before they were being shown to a small self-contained bed-sitting room at the rear of a Charminster farmhouse off the A3143.

If the farmer's wife had noticed Natalie's distress, she'd been too polite to mention it, bringing them sandwiches and a hot drink before bidding them goodnight and leaving them to an unsettling and anxious wait until morning when Driscoll could attempt to contact Collier – a call that he guessed would be at best a long shot and, at worst, a mistake that could see Natalie placed in even greater danger.

Fifty miles away, enjoying a cognac in the second most expensive suite in Bath's Regency Hotel, Victor Melinkov was contemplating the repercussions from a mistake he had already made – or one that he rather thought he had.

As he'd expected, his evening's work had been both unsatisfying and distasteful – a legacy from a *Red-Ops* mission in the Sudan where, four years ago at a remote Chinese-owned oil installation, he'd been forced to shoot two Darfurian women.

They had been sheltering there, their children already dead from starvation and the heat – victims of ethnic cleansing by the Arab *Janjaweed* militia that had driven countless thousands of other women and children from their homes to perish in the wilderness of the desert.

Melinkov had been wiring explosives to the wellhead when they had appeared like ghosts, unwitting spectators to an act of sabotage he could never have allowed them to witness.

But tonight had been different, he thought. If indeed he'd made an unfortunate mistake, the reason for it was understandable.

In the pictures he'd been sent, the girl had been photographed exclusively in profile, and the presence of a second female in the house had only become apparent after he'd squeezed off the shot.

So, should he have waited? While he'd still been in position, and before the lights had been extinguished, should he have used his initiative and shot the other girl as well? Or was it his aversion to killing women that had prevented him from making certain of things?

The situation would clarify itself, he decided. If he'd been unlucky in his choice of target, Washington, Moscow and London would be expressing their displeasure soon enough, and even if they were slow to comment, the English newspapers could be relied on to confirm whether or not he had fulfilled his contractual obligations.

CHAPTER 6

The overnight rain had left the countryside looking grey and dreary. During their drive, surface water had been lying in the fields alongside the main road, and even here on the outskirts of Dorchester, where there was more tarmac than grass, everything had the appearance of being colourless and washed-out.

In the car-park of The Black Swan, where they'd been sitting in the Fiesta for the last two hours, the majority of the puddles had been dispersed by the passage of patrons' cars, but with the sky looking more threatening, and with more rain in the air, Driscoll thought it wouldn't be long before the place became as waterlogged as it had been when they'd arrived.

He'd selected The Black Swan principally because its car-park had four exits, two of which led out on to the main road from Charminster, and another two that offered an alternative escape route via a lane that ran along the back of the pub – a precaution he was beginning to think had been unnecessary.

Earlier today, after obtaining Collier's number from Gorman's secretary, it had been Natalie's idea to make two separate phone calls – the first giving Driscoll the chance to introduce himself and to discover whether the MP would be agreeable to a meeting, the second to confirm when and where, but only after Driscoll had conducted a quick reconnaissance of the area.

Finding Collier at home had been a lucky break. That he'd been willing to cancel his appointments and drive down to Dorchester had persuaded Driscoll that the risks of trusting him were low. But over the last thirty minutes or so, with no sign of him arriving, the wait was starting to tell on Natalie.

Largely as a result of their overnight stay in the comparative safety of the Charminster farmhouse, she'd recovered well, talking quietly to him for several hours about what had happened before finally falling asleep in a chair shortly before dawn.

Breakfast had helped to wake her up, surprising Driscoll who'd suspected she would still have been too shocked to want anything to eat.

She'd continued to surprise him during their drive this morning. Like him, she was wary of each new vehicle that pulled into the car-park, but there was no doubt her spirits were improving, and she seemed to have regained at least some of her confidence.

'You should've asked Collier what kind of car he'd be driving,' she said.

'I should've asked him to come alone too.'

'Why would he want company?'

'Depends if there's anything in the London papers about Rebecca Wilson. That might have made him decide to bring some help, or warn the police.' By purposely not mentioning Rebecca Wilson during his phone calls, Driscoll had taken a gamble he was beginning to regret. 'Maybe he's heard or read something that's put him off.'

'He hasn't been. Look.' She pointed to a black Rover that had stopped in one of the car-park entrances.

The driver was being cautious, either uncertain of where he was, or searching for the least muddy route between the potholes.

'Are you sure that's him?' Driscoll slid back in his seat.

'As sure as I can be. Don't you recognize him? There were photos of him in two of those press clippings I showed you.'

'OK. You keep your eyes on him while I watch for other cars that might have come along for the ride.'

'There aren't any other cars. He's by himself.'

'We don't know that yet. You were the one who decided we ought to be careful – remember?'

She ignored the remark. 'He's parked and he's getting out. And the only thing he has with him is a briefcase. Is anyone else showing up?'

'Not so far.' Having switched his attention to the grey-haired stranger who was strolling over to the front door of the pub, Driscoll was trying to match his features with those of the man in her photographs.

For such a bleak day, The Black Swan was doing good business. Nearly two-thirds of the parking slots were occupied and there were even some hardy souls arriving on foot with their collars turned up against the cold.

'Right.' Driscoll checked his watch against hers. 'If I'm not back in five minutes, take off by yourself.'

'To where?'

'Wherever you think is best.' He was reluctant to leave her alone. 'If something goes wrong, push the horn button and hold it down.'

'No.' She opened the door. 'Nothing's going to happen. We'll go in together.'

In no mood to argue, Driscoll climbed out and started walking across the car-park to the building, waiting for her to catch him up before he used the remote to lock the doors of the Fiesta behind him.

'Are we going to talk to him here?' she asked. 'Or do you think we should ask him to go somewhere else with us – you know, to be safer?'

'We'll wait and see.' Driscoll let her enter the pub ahead of him. 'He's over there – standing by himself at the bar.'

Johnathon Collier had the bearing of a man who was as at ease buying a beer in the pub as he would have been addressing an electorate or debating affairs of state in the House of Commons. In his fifties, with a distinguished if rather lined and careworn face, he was wearing a coloured tie to offset the otherwise traditional drabness of his business suit and overcoat.

Driscoll approached him directly, introducing Natalie before he shook hands.

'I'm most pleased to meet you both.' Collier beckoned to the barmaid. 'May I get you something to drink? I'm afraid I've ordered already. I wasn't sure you'd wait for me. The traffic out of London was atrocious, and there are major roadworks this side of Salisbury.'

For a father mourning the loss of his son, the MP was too friendly and too controlled, Driscoll thought, the characteristics of a politician so accustomed to concealing his emotions that his manner could easily be a front.

It was hard to tell whether Natalie had similar misgivings. Like Driscoll, she'd declined the offer of a drink and had waited until Collier had been paying for his beer before raising her eyebrows as if to question how they should proceed.

Collier provided the answer himself. 'I realize how difficult this must be for you,' he said. 'If you prefer we speak elsewhere, I'd be glad to accompany you to a place of your choosing. However, before you decide, please let me say I've never been entirely happy with the reports I've received about the death of my son. I'm not by nature a suspicious person, but in this instance I must confess to being somewhat mistrustful of the official explanation – which, of course, is why I've been anxious to talk to you.'

Driscoll made up his mind. 'Do you think we can find somewhere better to talk,' he said, 'somewhere a bit quieter?'

'I shall enquire.' Collier left them for a moment, returning in the company of the barmaid who was folding notes and slipping them into her pocket. 'This young lady has kindly agreed to let us use a small room at the back,' he said, 'one that I understand is normally reserved by the Rotary Club. She'll show us to it now.'

As well as being small and smelling faintly of smoke, the room was windowless, but it was as warm as the bar had been and furnished with several well-used settees, a number of easy chairs and an imposing sideboard on which stood a silver tray and a matching pair of cups.

'Please.' Collier waved at one of the settees. 'If we have as much to go over as I believe we do, we should at least make ourselves comfortable, don't you think?'

Driscoll sat down next to Natalie. 'I'm sorry about Charles,' he said.

'Your condolences have already been passed on to me through Mr Gorman. But thank you for the thought.'

'Did he tell you I've been fired?'

'He told me a great many things about you.' Collier removed his overcoat and opened his briefcase before sitting down with the glass of beer he'd brought with him. 'I must say you've led a considerably more varied and interesting life than I have. Your exploits in Africa make me feel a rather ordinary person.'

'If Gorman got round to telling you about Africa, he wouldn't have stopped there,' Driscoll said. 'He'd have given you his version of what happened in China too – which means you know all about the hundred thousand yuan that's turned up in my Shanghai bank account, you'll have been shown proof that I was selling drugs to rig workers out in the desert, and you'll have seen photos of the Cessna on fire after I'd crashed it to stop Charles from turning me in to the Chinese Narcotics Control people who were waiting to arrest me at the airstrip. How does that sound?'

'A fair summary, shall we say.'

'How much of it do you believe?'

'That's what I'm here to find out.' Collier drank some of his beer. 'Before we go any further though, there are two things you should know. Both have to do with the email Charles was supposed to have sent me the day before your accident. I believe Gorman showed you a copy.'

'What about it?'

'Well, first of all I'm as certain as I can be that it wasn't from my son.' Opening his case, Collier took out a folded magazine. 'This is the March edition of an Oxford University newsletter. As you can see, it's dated nearly a month before you and Charles left for China. It has nothing to do with either of you, but it does contain an article about my daughter. She's studying at Oxford – or until last week she was.' He gave the magazine to Natalie. 'You and Mr Driscoll may like to skip through the write up on page five.'

Driscoll didn't skip through it. Instead, after a quick glance at the accompanying photo of a smiling young woman, he read every word:

Shirley Collier, 28, daughter of well-known MP Johnathon Collier, is one of three international graduates selected to join a prestigious research project at Vanderbilt University in Nashville Tennessee.

Known to family, friends and everyone else as Furl, Shirley will utilize her experiences of modelling the electrical activity of the heart to help develop a three-dimensional computerized model of the human digestive system.

Although this appointment will prevent her from presenting her paper on medical modelling at the 9 Feb Icelandic conference in Reykjavik, she thinks the weather will be warmer in Tennessee.

'And I might enjoy the music more in Nashville,' she laughs.

Driscoll was the first to comment. 'So Charles knew all along that his sister wasn't going to Reykjavik,' he said.

Collier nodded. 'Everyone knew. He had no cause to joke about how cold she'd be in Iceland because he knew very well she wasn't going there. Nor would he have ever called her Shirley. When he was young, Charles couldn't pronounce the word properly, so it became Furley. Then later as he began to grow up, the name was adopted by the family and abbreviated to Furl. My daughter hasn't been called anything but Furl for twenty years. She likes it.'

Which certainly seemed to confirm that someone other than Charles had sent the email, Driscoll thought, even if it didn't confirm much else.

Natalie had a different opinion. Up to now, she'd been content to listen, but she was suddenly eager to interrupt. 'Have you thought that the mistakes could've been deliberate?' she said. 'Suppose whoever wrote the email wanted you to recognize it as a fake?'

'Indeed.' Collier returned the magazine to his briefcase. 'A not so subtle means of persuading me to investigate the reason for my son's death more thoroughly than I would otherwise have done.' He held up his hand. 'Before you ask if I've tried to trace the sender of the email – yes, of course I have. My secretary has spent some hours endeavouring to do so, but she tells me the chances of success are not good.'

'*Anonymousemail dot com*,' Natalie said. 'That's just one of a dozen websites you can use to send anonymous emails. For twenty dollars a year they'll guarantee a service that blocks anyone from ever tracing an email back to you.'

Collier nodded. 'So I understand.'

'Did you tell Gorman?' Driscoll asked.

'I fear Mr Gorman has something of a closed mind. I wasn't inclined to discuss the matter with him.'

'How about Oliver Fox?'

'Sir Oliver is a busy man. I'd prefer not to bother him again until I have more information.' Collier closed the lid of his case. 'Now then, I seem to be doing all the talking. Perhaps this would be a good time for you to tell me your side of the story.'

'It's not something you're going to want to hear. It's pretty tough.'

'Mr Driscoll, my son is already dead. I'm not expecting your account to sit well with me. I do, however, expect it to be the truth.'

'OK.' Having described the events at the airstrip to Natalie only twenty-four hours ago, this time Driscoll was able to make a better job of it. As he had done yesterday, he left out nothing, pretending not to notice Collier's discomfort and attempting to finish on a positive note by suggesting the MP should examine the photos that the Chinese had sent to Gorman.

'For what purpose?'

'So you can check out the Cessna's nose wheel strut and have a look at the propeller. You'll be able to see how the strut's collapsed forward instead of backward, and you won't find anything wrong with the propeller. Not even the tips are bent.'

Earlier in his summary, Driscoll had been unable to avoid mentioning the rope, but he'd chosen not to describe how the photo showed it burning more fiercely than the surrounding airframe. Nor had he said anything about the young scientist's desperate attempts to escape.

But he might as well have done.

To conceal his disquiet, Collier had walked over to the sideboard where he was inspecting an engraved motif on the silver tray. 'I'm told there was little left of my son to identify,' he said, 'but the Chinese authorities have been characteristically stubborn. They insisted on conducting a full autopsy before they would agree to release his remains. According to their findings, the cause of death is unequivocal, but like them I had supposed the broken bones they discovered in my son's feet and hands were the result of the crash.' He turned round. 'Which is not the case, is it?'

Driscoll shook his head. 'He fought real hard to get out. If I'd been more awake to what was happening, maybe I could've done something.'

'I'm sure you did your best.' Collier returned to his chair. 'I'm grateful for your frankness. I realize it can't have been easy for you.'

'You haven't heard it all,' Driscoll said. 'I know you won't want to hear this either, but a woman was murdered in my brother's house last night. She took a bullet in the head – a bullet that was meant for Natalie.'

'God in Heaven.' Collier made no effort to disguise his disbelief. 'Here? In this country?'

'Twenty-five miles away. In Mere.' Driscoll wasn't surprised by the MP's reaction. Until now, Collier had seemed willing to accept what he'd been told, but his expression showed that this was more than he could handle.

'Who?' he asked quietly. 'Who was she?'

'Rebecca Wilson, my brother's next door neighbour. That's the main reason we phoned you. If Natalie and I get any further out of our depth, we're going to drown without ever knowing why. Do you want me to go on? Or will that put you in too difficult a position?'

Either Natalie didn't care about placing Collier in a difficult position, or she'd already made up her mind to tell him everything. Giving him no opportunity to reply, she launched in to her own hesitant account of the circumstances that had led up to the kitchen window exploding, going on to describe their departure from the house before she explained their reasons for concluding that Rebecca Wilson had never been the intended target.

'And there's no possible reason you know of why anyone would have done this?' Collier said.

She shook her head. 'Not that I can think of, but that doesn't mean a lot. I've been getting everything wrong. Until last night I thought your son might have been killed by the Chinese to stop you supporting the movement for Taiwan's independence – you know, because you're a politician. But I don't believe that's right any more.'

'No. I don't believe it is. Beijing may not like me expressing my views on the subject, but I'm sure I'm no more than a minor irritant to them. They have far more dangerous and influential people than me to worry about. Was that the only idea you had?'

Driscoll was half-expecting her to carry on now she'd begun talking more freely. But he was mistaken.

She'd placed each of her hands palm down on her lap, and instead of answering Collier's question she was sitting absolutely still with patches of colour on her cheeks.

'I know.' She glanced at him. 'I know.'

'What?'

'Look at us – the three of us. A week ago we'd never heard of each other. I'm a journalist, you're a pilot and Mr Collier's a politician. There's not a single thing we have in common. But here we are today, all sitting in the same room trying to solve the same problem. Don't you see? We're doing what we've been forced into doing – which is exactly what the Chinese wanted. It's a set-up.'

'What do you mean?' Driscoll wasn't following her reasoning.

'Think. The Chinese could've arrested you for selling drugs, or they could've deported you straight back to England. But they didn't do either of those things. They flew you to Shanghai where they'd already made sure I'd interview you by sending me that newsflash and leaving me a message on my answering machine. They picked me because of my article on the Chinese oil industry. They picked you because they knew you'd be so horrified by what you'd seen that you'd have to find out the reason for it. And to make Mr Collier start an investigation in to his son's death, they sent him an email he'd know could never have been sent by Charles.' She paused to catch her breath. 'It's been a set-up all along – right from the very beginning.'

'To bring us together?' Driscoll said.

'Yes.'

'So we'd do what?' He had the answer before he'd finished speaking. 'Jesus,' he said slowly. 'Oil. Chinese oil. That's why they made us carry out a repeat sweep of a block that's already producing, and why the bastards took away our computer. They want us to think they can check the results of the survey Energex did for them three years ago. They're pointing us smack bang at their oil fields in the Tarim Basin.'

Collier was looking doubtful. 'Are you sure the pair of you aren't adding two and two to make five,' he said. 'No matter how aggressive the Chinese are being in their efforts to find more oil, I can't believe my son's death was simply a way for them to attract our attention.'

Natalie shook her head. 'You don't understand how they think,' she said. 'In Chinese culture, the lives of individuals aren't important. I know that must sound awful to you, but you can't apply Western values when you're trying to work out why they do something or say something.'

'So you're suggesting this set-up, as you call it, is a means of compelling us to uncover some kind of anomaly in their Tarim Basin oil business – one so serious and so critical that they're not prepared to deal with it themselves.'

She nodded. 'Because they can't prove there is an anomaly – not without help from the West. We've been programmed into getting the proof for them.'

'Do you realize the implications of what you've just said?' Collier's voice had assumed a harder edge. 'If you're right, it means the Chinese wish to make it clear they're questioning the authenticity of the information Energex supplied to them. How can you possibly be sure of that?'

Natalie was more than sure. Collecting the car keys from the arm of the settee, she headed for the door. 'Don't go any further until I fetch my computer,' she said. 'I'll be back right away.'

Collier waited until she'd gone before he spoke again. 'What now, I wonder?' he said. 'I must say your friend is almost as surprising as she is attractive.'

'She's not my friend. I only met her five days ago. She's a freelance journalist.'

'Then you won't mind me remarking on the effect she had in the bar.'

Driscoll didn't mind. Twenty minutes ago, when she'd first entered The Black Swan, the drop in noise level had been as obvious as the looks she'd received. In the Shanghai restaurant it had been the same – except then she'd been aware of it, whereas this morning she'd either still been too shaken to notice, or she hadn't cared.

Judging by how damp and out of breath she was when she re-entered the room, the rain had started again.

'Do you want me to find you some paper towels?' Driscoll asked.

'This is more important.' She placed her computer on the sideboard, then hurriedly dried her hands on the inside of her sweater and flipped up the screen. 'Before I show you what I want you to see, have a quick look at my other files first,' she said. 'They're a bit boring, but it'll be good background, and they'll give you an idea of how dependent the Chinese economy is on oil and why the Chinese need so much of it. I'll start at the beginning.'

It was hard not to be impressed by the quantity of data she'd been able to accumulate. There were graphs and pie charts mixed up with bar-charts, and statistical projections along with quote after quote from documents and publications she'd obtained from sources all over the world.

So comprehensive was the information that Driscoll had given up trying to read it all when she pressed a key to display a summary file:

NW FILE 02
PEOPLE'S REPUBLIC OF CHINA (GENERAL)

- Area: 9.6 million sq. kms.
- Will be world's largest economy by 2050.
- Population: 1.3 billion.
- Growth in GDP: 9.5%.
- Growth of exports to USA: 1600% in last five years.
- World's fastest growing economy.
- World's largest army (2.5 million men).
- Foreign investment: $60 billion.
- Exports: $600 billion.
- World's largest producer of: coal, steel, cement.
- World's fourth largest defence budget – increasing at 10% per annum.
- Producers of: Two-thirds of the world's photocopiers, microwave ovens, DVD players and shoes. Half the world's cameras. One third of the world's televisions.

OIL

- Projected demand by 2010: 8 million barrels/day.
- Projected production by 2010: 3.3 million barrels/day.
- World's second largest importer of crude (doubling every 3 years).
- Country's reserves expected to be depleted in less than 12

years unless Tarim Basin fields prove more productive.
- Consumption projected to grow at 7% per annum.
- Consumption this year: record 110 million tons (21% more than last year).
- Current investment in Sudanese wells: $15 billion, much of it being wasted because of terrorist attacks.
- Half of all oil imports come from unstable Middle East countries.
- Leading contributor to the world reaching the *Hubbert Peak* for oil production whereby half of all the oil on the entire planet will have been exhausted.
- Negotiations currently underway to purchase two major Canadian oil fields and two more in Peru. Bidding for oil development rights in Venezuela, Indonesia, India and Russia.
- Considering construction of pipeline through Uzbekistan and Kazakhstan – a project unlikely to proceed because China is as starved for capital as it is for oil.

Collier was a quicker reader than Driscoll who was still absorbing the information when Natalie pressed another key – this time to bring up a coloured map of the Tarim Basin. It was the map he'd seen on her screen yesterday, a chart of the Xinjiang desert region that was dotted with dozens of tiny flags.

'This is the interesting bit,' she said. 'Each flag represents a well or a group of wells that have been sunk on the advice of Energex.'

Driscoll inspected one which he guessed was somewhere near the centre of Block 5. 'Sunk after the Chinese had conducted their own seismic survey, you mean?' he said.

'Yes. And after they'd done trial drillings to make sure the oil was there.'

'Is this the data the CNPC gave you? The stuff you said was too easy to get?'

'Some of it. I understand why they were so happy to hand it over now.'

Collier pointed at the screen. 'What do the three numbers on the flags signify?' he asked.

'The first one just identifies the location of the well.' To show him, she selected a flag near the desert border with Kirghistan. 'The second number is the barrels per day the well is producing, and the one underneath is the total amount of oil that's been pumped out in the last twelve months. It's an easy way to compare the output from different wells in different places.'

'Easy for who?' Driscoll asked.

'People like us. Look.' She pressed another key to display a smaller scale map – this one incorporating wells that had been drilled in the neighbouring countries to the west.

'Were the positions of all these recommended by Energex too?' Collier asked.

'That's what the CNPC said. Can you spot the difference? Compare the output of the Tarim Basin wells with the output of the ones in Kazakhstan. Do that first.'

Driscoll was already trying, but it wasn't until she began highlighting flags in adjoining countries that he properly understood.

'The Chinese wells are running out,' he said. 'The number of barrels a day isn't too bad, but the total output from them is right down.' He looked at her. 'Which means a whole lot of them are drying up.'

'If they haven't dried up already.' She highlighted more flags. 'The wells that Energex pin-pointed for the Chinese all produce oil, or used to produce oil, but they haven't produced much of it.'

'While the wells surveyed by Energex in other countries have continued to be profitable.' Collier peered at the screen. 'But how can that be when the results of seismic testing and experimental drilling would surely have alerted the Chinese to the small size of these fields?'

Driscoll answered for her. 'They didn't have a choice,' he said. 'According to Natalie's data, by 2010 they're facing a shortfall of more than four million barrels a day. That won't just cripple the Chinese economy, it'll stop it dead in its tracks – particularly if the foreign wells they own are being blown up every day by terrorists. What would you do if you were in their position? They need every damn barrel they can get out of the ground, and they know it.'

Collier turned to Natalie. 'So you believe that the Chinese are aware of this deception and have decided to do something about it.'

'What the hell can they do?' Driscoll said. 'On the face of it, there's nothing wrong with the survey data Energex gave them. None of the Tarim Basin wells were actually dry. They were just drilled into small or unproductive pockets. Beijing can't accuse Energex of supplying skewed results because they haven't any proof they were skewed.'

'Not to mention how politically unwise it would be for them to do so,' Collier said. 'The way things are with China's trade imbalance, Beijing can hardly afford to start accusing a major multi-national corporation of tampering with the results of an aerial survey when there's no rational reason for Energex to be doing such a thing.'

'Which is why they've involved us,' Natalie said. 'When we've discovered what the reason is, they're expecting us to expose Energex to the American and British and Russian governments. That's the only way they'll be able to get compensation and force Energex to hand over the right survey information they should've been given to begin with.'

It was easy to believe she'd cracked it, Driscoll thought. But she hadn't. In her enthusiasm to put the jigsaw together, she'd failed to realize that one of the pieces didn't fit.

'What about last night?' he said. 'If the Chinese have taken all this trouble to set us up, they wouldn't be trying to get rid of you, would they?'

'Suppose it's not them.'

'Who the hell else would it be?'

'Well, because I started off thinking I'd be writing a story about you crashing your plane, I collected as much information about Energex as I could. I didn't make a secret of what I was doing. I contacted all sorts of people in all sorts of places – not just in China, but in America and Russia too. I told you I phoned the Energex office in New York before I called Mr Gorman in London.' She put her hands behind her back. 'Then I went and called Gorman again two days ago.'

As though Collier was reluctant to listen any longer, over the last few minutes he'd been checking his watch and had already gone to collect his coat and briefcase from his chair. 'I think it best if we don't get too far ahead of ourselves,' he said. 'I regret having to leave when our discussion has reached such an interesting point, but my son's remains are being flown back from Kashgar today and I have funeral arrangements to attend to.' He handed Driscoll a business card. 'If Miss Washburn will send me copies of her maps, I shall take the responsibility of investigating what exactly Energex have been up to. In the meantime, I think we should keep these suspicions to ourselves. It may also be prudent for me to maintain the pretence of believing Charles was a victim of an accident.'

Natalie closed the lid of her laptop. 'Do you want me to send you maps of Russian oil fields as well?' she asked. 'The CNPC gave me some of those too. Goodness knows how the Chinese got hold of them.'

'Same way they got hold of us,' Driscoll said. 'Part of their long-term plan. This isn't something they thought up over a weekend.'

Collier went to the door. 'If the Russian maps illustrate the same pattern of oil production, I'd certainly like to have them.' He gave Natalie a brief smile. 'Do please telephone if you need to contact me before I see you again. I'm sorry we haven't met under more pleasant circumstances. Goodbye to you both.'

In spite of the progress they'd made, the MP's departure was an anti-climax – one that had left Driscoll feeling dissatisfied and short-changed. Not that it was hard to believe a rival international oil company could be giving Energex kick-backs for falsifying the Tarim Basin survey data, he thought. And it was even possible to believe Natalie was right about the reason for Charles Collier's death. In the worldwide rush for oil, and in the aftermath of the fiasco in Iraq, so cut-throat was the competition that the Chinese would be as desperate to expose what Energex were doing to their economy as Energex would be to stop Natalie from delving any further into their affairs.

Now they were once again by themselves, she was back at work on the puzzle. Avoiding any mention of the danger she was in, and not commenting on how conveniently Collier had side-stepped the problem of what they should do once Rebecca Wilson's body had been discovered, she fetched them sandwiches and coffee from the bar before engaging Driscoll in two and a half hours of fruitless discussion that ended only when she took exception to him telling her to stop going over ground they'd already covered.

She was still resentful when they left The Black Swan in the dark to commence their drive back to Charminster, sitting tight-lipped beside him without speaking until he pulled off the A3143 on to the narrow service road leading to the farmhouse, where he made the mistake of asking her to get ready to open the gate.

If she'd been in a better mood, she wouldn't have made a point of looking away. And if she hadn't looked away, she would never have seen a white van concealed in shadows at the entrance to the barn.

CHAPTER 7

Melinkov was cold. He'd been cold when he'd first arrived at the farm, and after sitting in an unheated van for the last two hours, and as a result of his cautious exploration of the area surrounding the farmhouse and the barn, he'd gradually grown colder still and had started to wonder if the details of the address he'd been sent were no better than the original information he'd received about the girl.

He was also inclined to believe that *Red-Ops* were taking advantage of him. By neglecting to mention anything in the way of an additional payment for the inclusion of the girl's companion in his contract, they were exploiting his mistake of yesterday, he'd decided – almost certainly a deliberate oversight that had still been irritating him when the red Fiesta had appeared.

Had he been less cold and less preoccupied he would have been able to react more swiftly. As it was, by the time he'd got the Transit's engine started, the driver of the Fiesta had executed a u-turn by putting his car into a slide at the gateway to the house and was already accelerating back the way he'd come.

Too late to block its path, Melinkov watched the car slither by in front of him on the gravel, its driver electing not to change gear until he turned north on to the main road.

Melinkov's own departure was less hurried. He set off at a more leisurely pace, making no immediate attempt to give chase or to match the speed of the car he was following, confident of his ability to choose the right place and the right time to make his move.

His confidence came from his experience of yesterday morning, when twice he had only narrowly failed to nudge the same car into the path of an oncoming truck. On each of those occasions, the commendable performance of the Transit had been hard to fault – a sign, perhaps, that *Red-Ops* were at last beginning to supply him with modi-fied vehicles.

Apart from its lowered suspension and twin exhausts, the otherwise ordinary-looking van had been ready for him to collect at Heathrow, along with the disassembled rifle and his encoded instructions confirm-ing that the girl who he'd been following from Paris had now become the subject of something other than a watching brief.

But that had been yesterday, Melinkov reminded himself – before his mission had started going wrong, and before the pilot Driscoll had turned up to complicate matters.

It would be the pilot at the wheel this evening, he decided, someone more skilled than the Washburn girl had been, but still unable to extend his lead with so little power at his disposal, unless he began taking risks that sooner or later would end with him losing the car on a high speed bend, or smacking it into a roadside tree – all but inevitable scenarios given the kind of pressure the van was capable of exerting.

To test the pilot's response, Melinkov dropped a gear and let the Transit have its head, closing the gap until he was travelling only a few feet behind the car, flashing his headlights on and off at random inter-vals to see how successful the strategy would be.

The effect was precisely the one he'd hoped for. The driver of the Fiesta increased his speed, reaching a peak of nearly 80 miles an hour and was starting to rely on the flicker of oncoming lights to warn him of approaching traffic before swinging out over the centre line to use all the road on bends made slippery by rain and patches of sodden leaves.

Yet what at first had seemed easy was to prove not so easy after all. Over the next four or five miles, during which Melinkov was to use the tactic no less than seven times, not once did the Fiesta lose its footing, and because under certain conditions the little car was more nimble than the van, not once had he been able to get sufficiently close to unsettle it with his bumper as he had done yesterday.

More annoyingly, a minute ago he'd been unprepared when the driver had suddenly abandoned the main A352 in favour of a side road where tighter bends were putting the Transit at a disadvantage.

Unable to consider using the rifle and wondering whether the occu-pants of the car might be in possession of a cell phone, Melinkov recon-sidered his position before switching on his interior light in order to consult his map.

It was only then he noticed a set of lights in his mirror that he recalled having seen before – recognizable in part by their intensity, and partly by the low-level yellow fog lamps the driver was choosing to employ.

A coincidence, he wondered? Or an indication perhaps that just as he was following the Fiesta, so someone was following him – an unlikely possibility in this part of the world, unless his mistake of last night had given *Red-Ops* an excuse to double up on the job because of its importance?

Whoever it was, they were being careful to keep their distance, and for the moment they were too far away to interfere – which meant there was nothing to prevent him making a final and more aggressive run at the Fiesta while the opportunity still existed for him to do so – this time exploiting the Transit's superior straight line speed and relying on its reinforced front bumper and its greater mass.

To prepare for the ram, he first made certain his rifle was stowed away safely beneath the passenger seat then, after checking the inertia reel of his seat belt he settled back to wait for a suitably deserted piece of road.

For Driscoll, drenched in sweat from pushing the Fiesta well beyond its limits on an unfamiliar road in the dark, the appearance of another set of headlights should have been a welcome sight.

Instead, he was suspicious, aware that the driver of the second vehicle seemed to be acting in consort with the driver of the van, in recent minutes neither of them drawing any closer nor falling any further behind as though they shared a common purpose.

Natalie had seen the lights too. She'd been doing her best to navigate under impossible conditions, hanging on whenever Driscoll stood on the brakes and closing her eyes when, once or twice he'd gone in to heart-stopping slides after committing himself to bends that had tightened up on him halfway round.

It had been her idea to leave the A352, a suggestion that had allowed them to extend their lead, but one that had seen them driving deep in to the countryside where the chances of them seeking help from a local garage or a passing motorist were becoming as slim as Driscoll's chances of continuing to keep the Fiesta on the tarmac.

'What are we going to do?' she shouted.

'I don't know. The bastards are waiting for something.'

'What?'

He didn't know that either, too busy concentrating on his driving to guess what might happen next, and too concerned to answer her now there was another equally fast vehicle on their tail.

Last night, during their high-speed drive from Mere to Charminster, Driscoll had discovered how suddenly the Fiesta's tendency to under-steer could switch to oversteer if he made the mistake of lifting off in the middle of a bend. But he'd also learned how quickly the car could be made to corner on a wet road as long as he was careful with the throttle – the principal reason he'd been able to keep in front of what he'd known from the beginning was no ordinary Transit van.

On the straights, though, everything was different, the Fiesta being hopelessly outclassed and no more able to match the van's top speed than Driscoll was able to consistently out brake it.

Which meant their advantage was about to disappear, he realized. Over the last mile and a half, the countryside had begun to flatten out and, as a consequence, the bends were becoming fewer – a recipe for disaster unless Natalie could identify an alternative route for them to take.

At their present speed, her efforts to read her map were being hampered by the jolting and jarring from the Fiesta's overworked suspension. But that hadn't stopped her from trying.

As she had done earlier, she'd unbuckled her seat belt and was hold-ing the map closer to the interior light, bracing herself against the dash-board and refusing to acknowledge Driscoll's warnings about upcom-ing bends.

'I still can't see properly.' She threw down the map in frustration and refastened her belt. 'I think we need to head for a place called Alton Pancras at the next intersection.'

'Why?'

'Because the road to it looks twisty. What else can we do?'

There was nothing else they could do, but it was a lousy option, and she knew it, Driscoll thought. A twisty road wasn't going to get them out of this, especially if he was right about the straighter stretches that lay ahead.

For as far as he could see beyond a cluster of signposts and markers announcing the presence of a roundabout, there wasn't a bend in sight.

With the double set of lights growing rapidly in his mirror and with the Fiesta's speedometer needle stuck stubbornly on ninety miles an hour, Driscoll willed the damn thing to go faster, easing his wheels out to straddle the white line while he strained his eyes in a vain attempt to pick out the furthermost point at which he would dare to leave his braking.

His plan was as short-lived as it had been optimistic.

So great was the closing speed of the vehicles behind him that, before he knew it, they were on him, the van to his left, and to his right what looked like a Series 7 BMW, both drivers matching their speed to his speed until at the last possible minute Driscoll hit his brakes.

Pedal shuddering against his foot as the Fiesta's ABS cut in, but still travelling too fast towards what by now he could see was a large, shrub-covered traffic island, he did the only thing he could do.

Wrenching on the wheel, first in one direction and then the other, he tried to scrub off speed against the flanks of the van and the car that had come to box him in.

It was a contest he was never going to win. No sooner was the sound of tearing metal accompanied by a shower of sparks, than a violent sideways lurch ripped off one of the Fiesta's door handles and destroyed the only remaining outside mirror.

A second later, Driscoll saw the nose of the BMW begin to dip and skitter as the driver applied his own brakes. Then all three vehicles entered the roundabout together.

Still boxed in and fighting to regain control, for the briefest of moments Driscoll sensed an opportunity.

By holding its position, the van was blocking all routes to his left, but the BMW had failed to keep up, and the exit directly ahead of him lay open and unprotected.

It wasn't until he heard Natalie shouting that he realized his mistake.

Instead of dropping back, the driver of the BMW had accelerated around the traffic island the wrong way, not only gaining enough ground to close the trap, but already lining up his car with the Fiesta's bonnet.

To avoid a head-on collision, and with nowhere else to go, Driscoll wrenched despairingly on the wheel for one last time, sliding the Fiesta wildly inwards towards the centre of the island.

Because he'd known the kerb was always going to be too high, the severity of the impact was not much worse than he'd expected. And because he'd known the car was always going to roll, long before the suspension tore itself to pieces and one of the tyres blew out, he'd stopped thinking about how bad it was going to be, and had begun worrying about who was going to look after Natalie if she were to escape uninjured and he did not.

CHAPTER 8

By absorbing the shock, the shrubbery slowed the Fiesta's progress across the traffic island. Flattening a swathe of plants, the car rolled twice before cannoning off a large bush to become temporarily airborne.

For Driscoll, confronted with a revolving horizon while he fought to deflate an air bag that had exploded in his face, the rolling seemed to last forever, ending in another shower of sparks when what was left of the car crashed back on its wheels somewhere out on the tarmac.

The smell of leaking petrol was still only faint, but it was bringing back memories of the airstrip, making him search frantically for the ignition switch before he checked to find out if Natalie was all right.

Like him, she was smothered in white powder from the air bags, but she didn't appear to be seriously hurt.

'Are you OK?' He tried to see her face.

'I'm not sure. I think I am.' She fumbled to unfasten her seat belt and attempted unsuccessfully to force open her door. 'I'll have to get out your side.'

'Hold on.' Driscoll's door was already hanging off one of its hinges, and so badly buckled that it almost fell off when he leaned against it. 'I'll yank yours open from the outside.'

She shielded her eyes from the headlights of the now stationary BMW. 'There isn't time. Someone's coming.'

'Leave this to me.' Gritting his teeth, and conscious of how hollow his statement had sounded, he went to meet two men who were hurrying towards the car.

The tallest of them was approaching Driscoll, leaving his companion to go round and check on Natalie.

'Leave her alone,' Driscoll said. 'If you've got something to say, you say it to me.'

'Well,' the tall man said, 'how very surprising.'

He might have been surprised, but he was nothing like as surprised as Driscoll was.

The man was not a stranger. He was the Chinese from the Hotan airstrip; the man in the fur hat who had stood by calmly taking photos of the Cessna after he'd issued instructions for it to be set alight.

Driscoll was too disoriented to think straight. 'Where's the van?' he said.

'You believe the Russian will return?'

'The white van,' Driscoll said. 'Where is it?'

'The driver has gone. We frighten him away, I think.' The man stooped to peer inside the Fiesta. 'I see your passenger is Miss Washburn. How badly is she hurt?'

'I don't know.' Driscoll shoved him out of the way and helped Natalie to scramble out through the driver's door.

She was unsteady on her feet and biting her lip, endeavouring to wipe the white powder out of her eyes and mouth and holding on to him at the same time.

'It's OK.' He put his arm round her. 'We may have got things wrong.'

'What do you mean? Where did the van go?' She was trying to see across to the other side of the roundabout. 'Who are these people?'

'Guess.' Driscoll looked at the tall man. 'Do you have a name?'

'You may call me Feng Shan.' Turning to his companion who had returned from his examination of the wrecked Fiesta, he exchanged a few words in Mandarin before stepping closer to Natalie.

'After such an accident, it is good you have suffered no injuries,' he said. 'It is lucky for you we follow the Russian tonight. But we should not stay here in the cold where we will be interrupted by the first driver who comes along. Since your own car is badly damaged, I shall be pleased to give you a lift to a place of your choosing where you and Mr Driscoll may recover.'

'Screw you,' Driscoll said. 'Stick your lift. If you think either of us are going anywhere with you, you're out of your fucking mind.'

Feng's expression remained unchanged. 'Have you learned nothing?' he said. 'Do you not understand the danger you are in?'

'From this Russian character?'

'More from the people he works for. We did not imagine they would be so quick to hunt for you, but it seems you have already made many waves in many places. So, it is best you come with me. Miss Washburn is already shivering and I can assure you I mean you no harm.'

'The same way you meant no harm to Charles Collier.' Driscoll had only the vaguest idea of what he was up against, and even less idea of how to deal with a situation that apparently Feng himself had not foreseen.

'You weren't following us, were you?' Natalie said quietly. 'You were chasing that van.'

'Of course. Earlier this evening when I am informed that the Russian leaves the hotel where he has been staying, we decide to see where it is he goes. For the past eleven months in more than four countries we have been tracing his movements in this way.'

Towards the end of the crashing and banging before the Fiesta had come to rest, Driscoll had been expecting the worst. Now, stranded at night without transport somewhere in the Dorset countryside, he felt as helpless as he had done then. The only thing that was going to make a difference was the answer to one crucial question.

'The Russian,' he said, 'who does he work for?'

'In most countries he masquerades as a businessman who operates under the name of Victor Melinkov.' Feng pointed at some skid marks. 'Not often have we come this close to him.'

'Answer my question,' Driscoll said.

'We believe that, like you, he works for the Energex Corporation. Had you not guessed?'

The last piece of Natalie's jigsaw had slipped in to place so neatly that for a second Driscoll made the mistake of believing the picture was complete. It wasn't, he realized. It wasn't even close to being complete, but in their present predicament, close enough maybe for them to risk accepting what looked like the only chance they were going to have.

'You are ready to go?' Feng enquired.

Driscoll was. Natalie was not. She too seemed to understand that one part of the puzzle had been solved, but instead of going to the BMW she'd returned to the Fiesta.

'What are you doing?' He went to see.

'Getting this.' She held up her laptop.

Taking her arm, he escorted her over to the BMW where the other man was already seated behind the wheel. He was Chinese as well, but Driscoll didn't recognize him, and it seemed unlikely that he'd been one of the others at the airstrip.

'Please.' Feng opened a rear door for Natalie. 'Once you and Mr Driscoll have chosen where it is you wish to go, I shall instruct my driver.'

Driscoll got in beside her, wary of making any decisions until he'd come to terms with the behaviour of someone who had thought nothing of incinerating another human being, yet who would open a car door for a young woman he'd never met before.

Once the BMW was underway again and completing its circle of the roundabout, Natalie's expression showed that she shared his misgivings. 'We can't go back to Charminster,' she whispered. 'Someone found out where we were staying.'

Driscoll knew who it had been. 'It's my fault,' he said. 'If I'd had any damn sense, I'd never have used the phone from there.'

'Why would Collier have traced our address from the number we called him from?'

'It wasn't him. I had to get his number from Gorman's secretary first – remember? Five minutes after I'd spoken to her, Energex would've been in touch with their Russian friend. We might as well have told him where to wait for us tonight.'

Feng turned round from the front seat. 'You have talked with Collier?' he asked.

'Yep.' Driscoll nodded.

'Then it is a pity things have not gone so well for us. But perhaps you will still be able to do what we had hoped you would do for us.'

'Shaft Energex for you,' Driscoll said. 'If you think we haven't got that figured out, you're dead wrong. We know your Tarim Basin oil wells are drying up, and we know you don't stand a snowball's chance in hell of proving that Energex has been feeding you with doctored data.'

Feng smiled slightly. 'Then you understand why it is we enlist your help. The world must be shown how the future of the Chinese People's Republic is being undermined. In the search for oil, China has come to expect such things, but at the same time we are learning how to combat them.'

'By killing innocent people like Charles Collier?'

'Mr Driscoll, spare me your sensibilities. Every day in my country, countless thousands of people die from diseases that are easily preventable in the more prosperous nations of the world. By providing us with false information, and by sabotaging our foreign-owned wells, the Energex Corporation is responsible not just for the death of one person, but also for the deaths of hundreds of thousands of innocent Chinese. Your enmity would be better directed at the company you work for.'

'I don't work for Energex any more. You made sure of that – the same way you made sure Collier and Natalie got themselves mixed up in this stupid fucking plan of yours.'

Feng showed no emotion. 'You have never been part of what you term our plan,' he said. 'For longer than one year now, we have been developing a sophisticated and wide-ranging programme that will see China compensated in full for all of its lost production. You and the politician, Collier, were nothing more than a short-cut – something we had hoped would be a simpler and quicker way for us to achieve our goals.'

'A short-cut that's backfired on you?'

'So it seems. But all is not lost, I think. By tomorrow I shall be in a position to offer an arrangement that will keep you and Miss Washburn safe, and at the same time satisfy the needs of my employers.' He held up a hand to stop Driscoll interrupting. 'Let us wait until then before we go further. For the moment, I am waiting to hear where you wish to be taken.'

'Anywhere. The nearest decent hotel.' Driscoll had given up trying to second guess his way out of a situation that was becoming so murky that it was hard to believe that a few hours ago in The Black Swan he'd been foolish enough to think he was close to understanding it.

Feng was pushing buttons on a cell phone. 'If a hotel is satisfactory I shall arrange for someone to make the necessary reservation,' he said.

'Someone at your embassy?' Driscoll said.

Ignoring the remark, Feng spoke in to his phone while he traced out a route with his finger on the illuminated screen of the BMW's satellite navigation system.

By now Natalie had stopped shivering, but after her experiences of yesterday, the Fiesta's crash had left her badly shaken, and Driscoll could see she was barely coping.

'Who's Feng talking to,' he asked her.

'I don't know. He's just finding out the names of hotels in a place called Yeovil. How far away is that?'

'Not very. Ten or twelve miles maybe. Look, don't tell me I'm asking a stupid question. I know I am, but you are OK, aren't you?'

She nodded. 'I'll be better when we're out of this car and away from these people. Do you believe what Feng said about the Russian?'

'I can't see why he'd lie. If Energex needed a hard man to do their dirty work, there are plenty of them around in Russia.'

Feng turned round again. 'You wish for separate rooms?' he asked.

'No.' Natalie answered without looking at him. 'What's going to happen about my rental car?'

'It is of no importance. You should worry more about Melinkov – although by tomorrow I am confident you will agree to a proposal which will make it difficult for him to find you.'

Which sounded as though the Chinese had yet to learn about Rebecca Wilson, Driscoll thought. In which case their intention to carry on using westerners in the game they were playing was going to be trickier than they imagined. Keeping their pawns ahead of Energex was one thing: keeping them ahead of the police would be a different matter.

Resisting the temptation to ask more questions, he checked on Natalie again, hoping she might have stopped biting her lip.

She had, responding to his concern by reaching out to squeeze his hand while she pretended not to listen to the arrangements that were being made for them.

Feng had completed his phone call. 'It is done,' he said. 'At the Waverley Hotel in Yeovil, a room has been booked for you in the names of Mr and Mrs Graham Evans. We shall be there soon.'

'You know we'll be contacting Collier right away, don't you?' Driscoll said.

'Of course. You must tell him of your fortunate escape tonight.'

The man was pretty damn smooth, Driscoll thought, someone accustomed to being ten steps ahead of everyone else, and flexible enough to adapt his plans to a new set of circumstances.

So what were the Chinese going to do, Driscoll wondered? Now Energex had spoiled their short-cut for them, were he and Natalie simply going to be recycled and incorporated in to Beijing's original plan – this time Feng offering them protection in exchange for access to Johnathon Collier? Was that it – a means for the Chinese to make their demands for compensation with no diplomatic strings attached – a communication channel so unlikely that if news of it was ever to leak out, its existence could be easily denied?

Worried that, if he'd guessed correctly, he and Natalie were facing a

disturbingly uncertain future, he spent the rest of the journey endeavouring to think his way out of the mess they were in, and was still
wrestling with the problem when Feng dropped them off in the rain
outside the entrance to the Waverley.

It wasn't until they'd finished checking in and had been shown to
their room that the feeling of being trapped began to leave him.

Their accommodation had been chosen well. Located on the top
floor of an unpretentious Victorian building in the high street, their
room had been recently refurbished to a standard that couldn't have
been more comfortable, nor more of a welcome sight – particularly to
Natalie who, without removing her shoes or bothering to brush out the
lingering traces of powder from her hair, had thrown herself down on
one of the beds.

'This is all your fault,' she said. 'I was having a nice holiday in Paris
before you phoned me.'

'You didn't have to come to England.' Driscoll smiled at her. 'That
was your idea, not mine.'

'I wasn't expecting to see someone shot. And I didn't expect to have
my rental car written off for me.'

'Think of the great story you've got now. If you'd stayed in France,
you wouldn't have met Comrade Feng.'

'I wouldn't have met Johnathon Collier either. When are you going
to phone him?'

'You do it,' Driscoll said. 'He likes you.'

'How do you know that?'

'He noticed how people stared at you in The Black Swan.'

'Oh.' She flushed slightly. 'That doesn't mean anything. It's because
I'm half Chinese.'

'You make the call anyway.' Driscoll headed for the bathroom. 'I'm
going to take a shower. Tell him what's happened and say we need to
see him again as soon as he can make it.'

'We don't know where he is. He had to drive back to London, and
he mightn't have gone straight home.'

Driscoll handed her Collier's business card. 'His mobile number's on
that. Say we're fairly sure it was someone called Victor Melinkov who
killed Rebecca Wilson, and don't forget to tell him that Feng's supposed
to be offering us some kind of deal tomorrow.'

She sat up on the bed. 'I don't understand why the Chinese wanted
to use us to begin with. If they've known what Energex have been doing

for as long as they say they have, why didn't they just leak the story to the international press? They could've gone to any of the big papers in the US, or in England – or even Russia.'

'And show them what? A bunch of coloured flags stuck on a map of their Tarim Basin oil fields? What were they going to accuse Energex of when not a single one of their wells turned out to be dry? That's why they needed you and me and Collier. All they had to do was find the right way to motivate us.'

'I don't feel very motivated any more.' She took a deep breath. 'I'm just scared.'

'No you're not. Look, we're a hell of a lot better off than we were yesterday. You get hold of Collier, then we'll come up with our own plan. How does that sound?'

'Patronizing.' She studied the business card. 'Don't be long in the bathroom. I need a shower more than you do.'

He left her to make the call, wondering again why he often found himself staring at her when he shouldn't have been, and wishing she'd stop being prickly when she had no reason to be.

His shower was a wasted effort. Instead of the water helping to scour away the images of Charles Collier's face and the back of Rebecca Wilson's head, the longer he stayed in the cubicle the more vivid they became, and the more difficult it was for him to pretend he could still walk away from this if he wanted to.

Not that walking away was going to solve much, Driscoll decided, an outside possibility, and an option that seemed to be wholly unrealistic once he'd finished in the bathroom and rejoined the young woman who was waiting for him in the other room.

She'd finished making her phone call, but was still lying on the bed, her eyes closed and with her head propped up on a pillow.

'I'm not asleep,' she said. 'I'm only trying to make myself relax.'

'Is it working?'

'No. We've got some help though.'

'Collier?' He sat down beside her.

'Mm. He said he'd got in touch with his secretary before he left Dorchester, so he must have taken us seriously.'

'Did you tell him everything that's just happened?'

'Everything I could remember.' She opened her eyes. 'He's busy tomorrow and it's his son's funeral on the 16th. That means he can't meet us until Friday, so he's asked his secretary to work all night.'

'To see what she can dig up on Energex?'

'He doesn't think she'll be able to find out much at such short notice, but he wants us to have as much information as we can get before tomorrow. He's getting his secretary to email us.'

'Have you hooked up your laptop?'

'It was easy.' She pointed. 'All the rooms have LAN ports. And I've set up a rule too, so we'll know as soon as she sends us anything.'

Driscoll couldn't help grinning. 'You're not happy unless you're on-line and all connected up, are you?'

'I don't fly planes for a living like you do. I deal in information. If I can't access stuff quickly, my Shanghai mortgage doesn't get paid because someone else is going to write the story I ought to have written.'

'Get to the bottom of this one and you'll be able to pay off your mortgage overnight,' Driscoll said.

'If it isn't too dangerous to print. It depends if we're doing the right thing trusting Collier. He's already been to see Energex twice. For all we know he's a friend of Sir Oliver Fox.'

'You have to trust someone.'

'I already do.' Leaning across the bed, she carefully pushed back his hair and kissed the bruise on his forehead. 'I'm sorry I've made things more complicated for you,' she said. 'I can't very well go back to Paris, but there are friends I could stay with in Shanghai. If I went back there, you wouldn't have to worry about me anymore, would you?'

'I'm not worried about you. I've just been trying to keep you in one piece.'

'If that was true you wouldn't have gone ahead and contacted Collier. You'd be back in Africa, or in South America, or somewhere. I haven't met anyone like you before, but I know how you think.'

'You don't know the first damn thing about me,' Driscoll said.

'Tell me then. What was it that happened to you in Africa? I know something did because you thought Gorman had told Collier about it. You said so this afternoon. I heard you.'

'Why would you care?'

'Well, seeing as this is the second night running I'll be sharing a room with you, I'd like to find out who I'm sharing it with.'

'You could have had your own room if you'd wanted.'

She compressed her lips. 'Are you going to tell me, or aren't you? Were you working for Energex when you were in Africa?'

'Not to start with. I had a job with an international aid organization that was operating out of Johannesburg. They were short of pilots who could fly in medical supplies to some of the rebel-held villages in parts of Namibia and Angola.'

'Was that dangerous?'

'It's OK if you know what you're doing,' Driscoll said. 'It only takes one trip to learn you don't fly in to places like that just to deliver medicine. You have to buy your way in and buy your way out.'

'How? With what?'

'Guns and ammunition mostly. Either that or heroin or cocaine. Depends on which rebel group you're doing business with.'

'So while you were delivering medicine you were running guns and trafficking drugs?'

Although there was no disapproval in her voice, he was wary of going into too much detail. 'It's pretty simple,' he said. 'If you want to get antibiotics to the villages that need them, you play by the rules of the people who buy the guns.'

'How long were you doing that for?'

'On and off for about eighteen months – until Energex came along and offered me an aerial survey job up in Botswana. They'd got themselves a big contract from a multi-national mineral company who wanted them to look for the gravity signatures of diamond pipes. Diamond pipes are tubes of volcanic kimberlite that cough up diamonds from deposits that can be a couple of kilometres underground.'

'And you can find out where they are by flying over them?'

'An airborne gravity gradiometer is a pretty good way to locate kimberlite. It's usually around ten per cent less dense than the surrounding rock.' Driscoll stopped talking. 'You don't want to hear this.'

'Yes I do. Did you find any diamonds?'

'I don't know. I found plenty of kimberlite, but I had a couple of crashes too. No one in Botswana has any idea of how to maintain light aircraft, and half the aviation fuel is contaminated or full of dirt and rubbish. Things sort of started going wrong for me from there. The guy who'd been supplying me with cocaine asked Energex if they could get me to deliver a shipment of the stuff to Ghanzi for him and then someone told the South African government I'd been selling guns to Namibian terrorists.' Driscoll decided not to go on. 'Are you happy now?'

'It'll do until I've had my shower.' She got off the bed. 'When I come back you can tell me why Energex sent you to the Tarim Basin.'

'Forget about the Tarim Basin. We have to think about how we're going to handle Feng tomorrow.'

'We'll have our email from Collier's secretary by then. See what there is in the mini-bar. I'll only be five minutes.'

Her five minutes turned out to be more than twenty minutes, by which time Driscoll was on his second Scotch, and the sparkling wine he'd poured for her had lost much of its sparkle.

She returned looking freshly scrubbed, and with a towel wrapped round her head. 'I hate having to put on the same clothes after a shower,' she said. 'I brought a change of things from Paris, but I left them back in the car.'

He handed her the glass of wine. 'You can go shopping in the morning. Feng said he won't be getting here until after ten thirty, so you'll have plenty of time. I've got cash if you haven't.'

'I can use my credit card.' She started to dry her hair. 'I've got bruises all over – a big one on my left shoulder and another one here.' She drew her hand down between her breasts.

'Seat belt,' Driscoll said. 'You didn't have a steering wheel to hang on to. Do you want me to have a look?'

'No, thank you. I want you to carry on from where you left off.'

It hadn't been the right time before, and it wasn't the right time now, he decided, particularly if something he told her about himself was to end up in one of her articles.

'I know what you're thinking.' She looked at him over the rim of her glass. 'If you weren't so suspicious of everyone, you wouldn't be such a lonely person.'

'I'm not lonely.' Because he could smell the freshness of her hair, he'd become uncomfortably conscious of her, half-hoping she wasn't aware of how close to him she was standing and half-hoping she was about to give him one of her broken smiles.

For the rest of the evening he refused to let her direct their conversation, using more Scotch to dull his senses while he attempted to convince himself that by tomorrow morning the information they were expecting from Collier would help clear the clutter from his mind.

He was asleep when the blaring of what sounded like a toy trumpet announced the arrival of their email.

Natalie had been asleep as well, but she was already seated at her keyboard when he went to read the incoming message over her shoulder:

FROM: The Office of the Rt Hon Johnathon Collier MP.
SENT: Tuesday, 16 Feb. at 1.17 a.m.
TO: Mr Peter Driscoll and Ms Natalie Washburn.
SUBJECT: Energex Corporation.

Good morning Mr Driscoll and Ms Washburn. In the last ten minutes I have been talking to Mr Collier on the telephone and have received his approval to communicate with you directly (yes, I woke him up).

At his request, my examination of official and non-official records, memos and documents has been restricted to those which refer only to the funding Energex has received from government and federal sources. Please note: data from Russia is scant and may be unreliable. Data obtained from US sources should be regarded as confidential, and should not, therefore, be disclosed to any third party.

Where I have been able to access documents that are theoretically in the public domain (some of which are buried so deeply that only the most determined of researchers would find them) I have included relevant statements from them as appendices. However, the following summary will, I trust, be adequate for your purposes:

ENERGEX CORPORATION

1. BACKGROUND:
Initially a privately owned company established in 2002 to exploit military technology first developed for the US Defence Department by Lockheed Martin. In its military configuration, gravity gradiometer technology was designed to allow US nuclear submarines to negotiate underwater mountain ranges without alerting enemies to their presence (previously not the case because of easily detectable sonar pings).

Equipment was subsequently adapted for civilian use as an airborne method of detecting minute changes in the Earth's gravitational field generated by geological formations associated with diamonds and other minerals. Later employed with considerable commercial success to identify deposits of oil and gas from surveys carried out by light aircraft in various remote regions of the world.

In 2003 the company was expanded and renamed Energex (a combination of the words Energy and Exploration). The directors are:
- Senator Gilbert McCloskey (USA)
- Vladimir Yukos (Russia)
- Sir Oliver Fox (UK)

In mid 2004, when it became apparent that the economies of developing countries (China in particular) were starting to consume a disproportionate percentage of the world's dwindling oil reserves, Energex was formally recognized as being of strategic national importance to the governments of Russia, the United States and Britain.

As a result of this recognition, in the last two years Energex has been able to secure survey contracts in fourteen different countries. For the same reason it has been the recipient of numerous government grants from the UK, a substantial interest-free federal loan from the US and has received exploration fees from the Russian government that can only be described as generous (see below).

2. INTERNATIONAL FUNDING:
- Nov 04: £7.3 million UK Regional Selective Assistance Grant.
- Jan 05: £130 million UK Scientific Discovery Grant.
- Dec 05: US$1.2 billion 0% interest loan from the US Federal Reserve Bank. Paid in three instalments over a two-year period.
- Feb 06: £145 million UK Technologies Development Grant.
- April 06: Rumoured US$600 million payment for a 16-week aerial exploration of Russian-owned oil fields in Kazakhstan

and Kyrgyzstan. Made up of US$1.5 million paid by Russian government for each of 400 data packages.
- June 06: £17 million UK Technology Strategy Programme Grant.

I hope this is of some help to you. I will send more information as I come across it. In the meantime, Mr Collier has said it would be helpful if you could perhaps obtain a photograph of the Chinese gentleman you are scheduled to meet later this morning, and also record the number plate of his car if that would be at all possible. I assume you understand the reason for this request.

Yours sincerely
Sheila Stanton
(Personal Secretary to Johnathon Collier)
Appendices 1-8 follow

Driscoll's familiarity with the company's history had allowed him to skip through the first part of the email, but no sooner had he done so and started on the second section than the implications hit him like a hammer.

The truth had been staring him in the face all along, he realized, a scenario so chilling that only politicians could have ever thought it up, and one so ambitious that only governments could have ever hoped to fund it and pull it off.

'Not just Energex by themselves,' he said slowly. 'It's never just been them. Three of the most powerful countries in the world are paying Energex to choke off China's oil supplies, and now the Chinese have guessed what's going on, we've been made to stick our noses in to the middle of it. And we were too damn stupid to have worked it out.'

Natalie stopped scrolling through the first of the appendices. 'We haven't been that stupid,' she said. 'Collier hadn't figured it out either.'

'It's you and me Energex are hunting down. No one's trying to put a bullet through Collier's head.'

She pushed her laptop away from her. 'He's a politician. What if he's part of it?'

It was like asking whether keeping their appointment with Feng was still a good idea, Driscoll thought, questions to which they somehow had to find the answers, because if they couldn't, instead of them facing an uncertain future, they'd be lucky to have a future of any kind at all.

CHAPTER 9

The contractors who had refurbished the Waverley had done their best to modernize the reception area, but even on a weekday as cheerless as this one, it was still too small to accommodate the number of guests that were coming and going.

Hoping Natalie was hidden among them somewhere with her camera, but being careful not to look, Driscoll walked over to the bank of house phones where his visitor was waiting for him.

'Good morning.' Feng bowed slightly. 'Miss Washburn is unable to join us?'

'She'll be down in a minute. She's not feeling too good after the accident. I said we'll be having coffee in the restaurant, so she knows where to find us.'

'But you are ready to talk?'

'Depends what we're going to talk about.' Driscoll headed off across the foyer. 'I'm not much interested in hearing what someone like you has to say.'

'Then I think you will have not yet seen the newspaper in which you and Miss Washburn are named.'

Driscoll stopped in the doorway of the restaurant. 'Rebecca Wilson,' he said.

'Why did you not tell me?'

'Why would I? What difference does it make to you?' Driscoll followed one of the waitresses over to a corner table where Feng sat down facing the door with his briefcase positioned carefully in front of him.

'Your room is satisfactory?' he asked.

'It's fine. Did you bring the paper?'

Feng took a copy from his case. 'The death of the woman is reported on page four.'

Driscoll had just found it when Feng stood up to greet Natalie.

'I am sorry you are unwell,' he said.

'It's only a headache.' She sat down and looked at Driscoll. 'Is there something in the morning paper?'

'Yep. Listen.' Keeping his voice down he read the article to her out loud.

' "*Police are anxious to trace the whereabouts of two people in connection with an overnight murder in Wiltshire. The body of Rebecca Wilson, 32, was discovered in a Mere house shortly before 11.00 p.m. after she failed to answer repeated phone calls from her army husband, David, who at the time was away from home. Neighbours report seeing two vehicles parked outside the house during the day: a red Ford Fiesta yet to be found, hired from Heathrow in the name of Natalie Washburn, a Shanghai-based journalist who is believed to be visiting the UK from France. The other car has been seized by the Dorset police, also a rental, hired by Mr Peter Driscoll in whose brother's home the body was found. Driscoll is a commercial pilot who until recently was working for the Energex Corporation in a remote region of north-west China where he has been implicated in the trafficking of drugs, and suspected of deliberately causing the death of Charles Collier, son of prominent MP, Johnathon Collier. As of this morning, Mr Collier has not been available for comment.*" '

Natalie's expression was more of surprise than concern. 'How did they find out so much so quickly?' she said. 'How could anyone know I came from France?'

'It's pretty easy since the London bombings. You can trace anybody from anywhere nowadays. I didn't have any trouble getting hold of you, and this guy Melinkov didn't either.'

Feng handed Natalie a photograph. 'This is the best picture we have of the Russian,' he said. 'I am glad you have come to understand the danger he poses. From now on, you must watch for him.'

'How do you know he works for Energex?' Driscoll took a look at the photo. It was in black and white, showing a stocky man of about 30 standing on the platform of a railway station somewhere. He had close-cropped hair, an unusually thick neck and was wearing a soiled leather jacket.

'You are familiar with the corporate structure of Energex, I think,' Feng said. 'While the American office in New York is responsible for marketing and for the commercial development of the gradiometer technology, the London office pretends to concentrate on the legitimate business of aerial surveying.'

'But that's not all London do?' Driscoll said.

'It is from them we receive the distorted data for our oil fields.'

Natalie lay the photograph of Melinkov on the table. 'Where does he fit?'

'Ah.' Feng smiled. 'The activities of the Moscow office are a different matter. They spend much of their time employing the Energex technology for themselves in order to open up oil fields in the countries of the old Soviet Union. But they also run a covert division that does not officially exist. The division is called *Red-Ops*. We know little about it except that it is behind the sabotaging of many of our overseas wells, and that the Russian is associated with it.'

'Who told you?' Driscoll asked.

'It is an interesting story.' Feng beckoned to the waitress. 'We should ask for our coffee first.'

The break in conversation gave Driscoll the chance to glance at Natalie. Since there had been no indication she'd been successful with the little Minolta they'd bought this morning, he was beginning to wonder if he should fabricate an excuse so she could try again.

'How's the headache?' he asked.

'Better, thank you.'

'You don't need to get yourself another aspirin?'

'No. I'm all right.' She waited for Feng to finish ordering their coffee before asking him if they could keep the photo of Melinkov.

'Of course. I bring it for you. He is a man we first learn of four years ago, after one of our foreign wells is destroyed by explosives in the Darfur region of the Sudan. For us, the loss of the well was not good, but in another way it was what the Americans call a lucky break.'

'Because you caught Melinkov red-handed?' Driscoll said.

'No, no.' Feng shook his head. 'From twenty kilometres away, Chinese workers at another rig were the first to see the smoke, but it takes them more than one hour to drive there, by which time the saboteur is gone.'

'But you were pretty sure it was him?'

'Not to begin with. When the workers arrive, they find the well is burning. They also find four children who have starved to death and two Darfurian women who have been shot in the head. There is nothing to be done for these people, but before the men leave they try to identify the bodies and discover one of the children is still alive. He is a young boy, too weak to speak, but in the sand he is able to scratch the word Nissan and write down the figures he has seen on its number plate.

'Once the men pass on this information to our office in Khartoum by satellite phone, the Nissan is traced to a businessman who had rented it in the name of Victor Melinkov. It is the name the Russian often uses, but we doubt it is his real one.'

'What happened to the boy?' Natalie asked.

'The men give him a little water and some food, but he dies on the journey they make back to their camp. Life in the Sudan is cheap. In Darfur alone, more than fifty thousand have been killed by the *Janjaweed* militia.'

'What made you connect Melinkov with Energex?' Driscoll was becoming increasingly intrigued. 'Did the Sudanese do it for you?'

'They had no cause to. The rig workers could offer no proof of sabotage or suggest who had done the shooting. But in such parts of the world, money can buy many things. Before he leaves his hotel in Khartoum, we are able to intercept two faxes he sends to Moscow.'

'To Energex?' Driscoll said. 'To this *Red-Ops* division?'

Feng nodded. 'It is from this we start to understand how our enemies are acting to prevent China from becoming a world power.' He stopped talking while the waitress delivered their coffee. 'Despite this threat to China's economy, it is not possible for us to respond in an aggressive way,' he said. 'If we ignore America's incursions into Afghanistan and Iraq, western imperialism is as dead as the Maoist version of Communism is in my country. Today, like everywhere else, China's future relies less on military might than it does on diplomacy, international trade and the removal of tariff barriers in those countries where we do our business. China cannot afford to be seen to be operating outside internationally accepted conventions, nor can we behave in a manner that would serve to isolate us from our export markets.'

'Have you finished?' Driscoll said. 'Is that it?'

'You think I speak like a politician?'

'Why don't you just cut out the crap? What is it you want from us?'

'Is that not clear? Do you not see how the murder of the Wilson woman has made things more difficult for you? According to the newspaper, the British authorities wish to interview you, and Energex will be expecting you to start searching harder for the answers you and Collier have been trying to find. They will not call off the Russian now.'

'So you're here to help us, right?' Driscoll made no attempt to keep the sarcasm out of his voice.

'I am here to explain how we may help each other. You must understand that, just as China has not the evidence to accuse the governments of Russia, Britain and America of acting secretly, so China wishes to communicate its wishes to these governments in a way that cannot affect our good relations with them.'

'By using us as a private pipeline through to Collier,' Driscoll said. 'No diplomats involved.'

'Already you have established contact with him. As a politician he will appreciate that unofficial channels have much to commend them, and he is well placed to pass on our demands to London, Washington and Moscow.'

'While you look after us?'

'Within four days I can have fresh passports for you, together with airline tickets to Hong Kong, Beijing or Shanghai – whichever you prefer. I can also guarantee accommodation arrangements to suit your needs. Extradition treaties do not exist between China and Britain, or between China and the US, so once you have new names and a new address, you will be much safer. In return you must agree only to contact Collier by telephone or email whenever you are asked to do so.'

'Until you're done with us, you mean?' Driscoll said. 'Then we'll be on our own. You're full of shit, Feng. If you think Natalie and I are going back to China, you can piss off now. We'd be safer staying right here where we are.'

'Another country, then? Somewhere in Europe, perhaps?'

In between picking out the fish hooks from Feng's proposal, Driscoll was trying to guess what leverage the Chinese could possibly apply to the last three governments in the world who were likely to respond to threats in anything other than a thoroughly hostile way.

'Look,' he said. 'You don't need us. I can give you a list of all the money that's being funnelled into Energex from Moscow, Washington and London. Use that instead.'

'I trust you are not suggesting our delegation to the United Nations should stand up and claim government funding is proof of an international conspiracy against China. They would be laughed at. All governments subsidize the industries that keep them in power, but communist regimes are a hundred times more guilty of it than the governments who are funding Energex.'

Driscoll changed direction. 'OK,' he said. 'What do you want us to tell Collier?'

'Simply that the Chinese People's Republic seeks reparation for the loss of oil production caused by the activities of Energex in the Tarim Basin and elsewhere. You should explain that this request comes from a man known to you only as Feng Shan who has no traceable connection with the Chinese government in Beijing and who is not associated with any Chinese terrorist organization.'

'What kind of reparation?' Driscoll asked.

'China's demands are straightforward. First we must receive the correctly processed data acquired by Energex from their surveys of the Tarim Basin. Second, Moscow will approve the construction of a new pipeline between Russia's eastern oil fields and China's domestic distribution network. Third, as compensation for the oil China has been unable to access, we require a one-off payment of sixty billion US dollars.

'How much?' Driscoll was staggered.

'Sixty billion US dollars.'

'You're crazy. No government is going to sign a cheque for that kind of money. Who the hell dreamed that up?'

'I show you.' Taking a pen from his pocket, Feng began writing numbers on a paper table napkin. 'Over the last three years, Energex has cost us an estimated loss of one million barrels of oil a day,' he said. 'Our total loss is therefore one million barrels of oil per day multiplied by, let us say, one thousand days, which equals one billion barrels. To put a dollar value on this, what average world price for crude would you suggest?' He looked at Natalie.

'It's been higher than seventy dollars a barrel,' she said, 'but that's unrealistic over the long term.'

'We have chosen forty. You are happy with such a figure?'

She nodded.

'Then the value of the oil that rightfully belongs to China, but that we have been prevented from retrieving is one billion barrels at a price of forty dollars per barrel, which gives us a total of forty billion.' Feng displayed his calculation. 'By itself, of course, this does not take account of the lost profit from export goods we would have manufactured with this oil, nor does it reimburse us for the survey fees we have paid Energex, or compensate us for the industrial expansion we have been stopped from undertaking.'

'So you thought you'd rack up the forty billion to sixty billion,' Driscoll said.

Feng shrugged. 'For rich countries like Britain, Russia and the US, twenty billion each is not so much compared with the cost of disasters like the hurricane flooding of New Orleans that sometimes can occur.'

Had he been listening less carefully, Driscoll would have missed the inflection in Feng's voice. 'Meaning what?' he said.

'You are familiar with the wreck of the USS *Richard Montgomery*? It is a ship that lies submerged in the River Thames.'

Driscoll had never heard of it, and Natalie was shaking her head.

'Perhaps Miss Washburn has some knowledge of the SAFOD project at Parkfield in California.'

She shook her head again.

'I see.' Feng crumpled up the table napkin and tossed it into his case. 'Then I doubt either of you know how it is the Russians transport nuclear waste to their processing plant at Chelyabinsk.'

'Where?' Driscoll asked.

'You may find out more about these things for yourselves, but for the purposes of our discussions this morning, permit me to give you a short history lesson.'

Somewhere inside Driscoll's head a warning bell had started ringing. He hadn't been expecting this any more than he'd been expecting Feng to reveal details of the ambitious reparation programme the Chinese had been working on.

Feng finished his coffee before leaning back in his chair. 'The USS *Richard Montgomery* was an American-built Liberty Ship,' he said. 'It was constructed in Florida in 1943 as part of the war effort, and in 1944 carrying six thousand tons of munitions sailed from Philadelphia to join a convoy of vessels bound for the United Kingdom and Cherbourg. On the night of 20 August, after arriving in the Thames Estuary, she dragged her anchor in shallow water and grounded on a mud-bank near the Isle of Grain where her plates quickly began to crack open.

'Salvage work to save the cargo was stopped in September after a storm had broken the hull in two. She sank with an estimated one thousand to three thousand tons of munitions still on board – high explosives that all too easily can be detonated by fuses which are known to be unstable, because for more than sixty years, seawater has been corroding them away.'

Natalie had been too busy listening to drink her coffee. Now she put down the cup she'd been holding. 'Why hasn't anything been done about it?' she asked.

'It is too dangerous. So great is the threat of the wreck exploding, and so unstable are the fuses that the British Admiralty will not permit ships or divers to go near it.' Feng placed his hands palms down on the table. 'For the public the problem is most serious. In the event of an accident it is said the blast would be one of the biggest non-nuclear explosions the world has seen.'

A chill was creeping over Driscoll. It had started in his stomach, gradually spreading out all over him while Feng had been speaking. 'An accident?' he said.

'We must hope it will not occur, but since it is the British who have allowed the situation to deteriorate for more than half a century, should such an accident take place, it would, of course, be no one's fault but their own.'

Driscoll had no idea what to say, too stunned to think beyond the destruction and loss of life that could result from an explosion so powerful that the effects were almost impossible to imagine.

Natalie was as shocked as he was, but handling the news better – maybe because she'd grown up in China, he thought, a country where people were accustomed to large-scale natural or man-made disasters of one kind or another.

'Is the SAFOD project a ship as well?' she asked.

'No, no.' Feng shook his head. 'SAFOD stands for San Andreas Fault Observatory at Depth. It is a research project run by the US National Science Foundation in central California.'

'To do what?' Driscoll asked.

'To study earthquakes. For many years, American scientists have been tracing the origins of tremors along the San Andreas fault. In 1990 they discovered that the most intense of these begins from a small hundred-metre-square zone some three kilometres below the surface between San Francisco and Los Angeles near the small town of Parkfield.

'Because the Americans wish to understand the physics of what happens before and during these quakes, they decide it will be a good idea to drill deep holes into this zone so they may install seismometers and other instruments.' Feng paused. 'It is clear to you why they do this?'

'Sure.' Driscoll wanted to hear the rest. 'How far have they got?'

'As an experiment, first they drill a pilot hole to a depth of two kilo-metres. Later, in 2005 they drill another. This one is three kilometres deep before it is made to change direction and go off at a steep angle. From the bottom of it, like branches on a tree, many two hundred and fifty-metre-long holes are used to penetrate into the heart of the fault itself.' Feng glanced at Natalie. 'From your knowledge of the oil indus-try, you understand how it is possible to drill holes which are horizon-tal?'

She nodded. 'It's not that difficult. Why are you telling us?'

'You disappoint me. It seems you are not one of those people who believe drilling such holes is extremely unwise and very dangerous. Just as the fuses on the *Richard Montgomery* are unstable, clearly so is the Parkfield zone of the San Andreas fault.'

This time Driscoll had recognized the potential for disaster before Natalie had started to ask her question. 'You've planted explosives,' he said. 'Explosives and some kind of electronic trigger – the same kind of trigger you've got sitting on top of the *Richard Montgomery*. Is that it?'

'In the drillings there has been room to introduce only a small quan-tity of high-explosive, so there can be no guarantee an accident can be made to happen. But the US may prefer to avoid the risk of a major earthquake when it is their scientists who will be blamed for destabiliz-ing the fault by foolishly interfering with nature in this way.'

'A risk the Americans won't have to take as long as they pay Beijing a cool twenty billion,' Driscoll said.

'Unless they are able to disarm a device which is designed to self-detonate under conditions of interference.'

With two-thirds of Beijing's so-called programme out in the open, Driscoll hardly needed to ask about the threat to Russia. He let Natalie do it, endeavouring to get his mind off the *Richard Montgomery* and the San Andreas fault as Feng launched into a description of a single-track railway line that travelled through part of the world where Driscoll had never been nor had the urge to go.

'Waste from Russia's nuclear submarines is treated at their floating Landysh plant,' Feng said. 'It is a barge moored off the Zvezda Far Eastern Shipyard near Vladivostok. But a quantity of waste from other sources is still taken by special trains to their Chelyabinsk nuclear facil-ity for reprocessing.'

Driscoll couldn't help himself. 'How about this?' he said. 'Unless

Moscow comes to the party, a trainload of radioactive waste is going to wind up being spread across the Russian countryside when a bridge it's on collapses – an old Soviet-era bridge, maybe, one they'd always been worried about, but hadn't got around to fixing – an accident they won't be able to blame on anyone else even if they want to. How close am I?'

Feng's expression had changed. 'You think this is a joke?'

'No, of course he doesn't.' Natalie was quick to interrupt. 'It's just that if you're expecting us to tell Collier, we need to know exactly what it is we're supposed to say.'

'You may explain that in early spring it is common for the special line from Troick to Chelyabinsk to be blocked by snow and landslips. Should wagons carrying waste be derailed by one of these in the wrong place, even hardened containers will not withstand the shock of falling many metres on to the rocks below.' Feng closed his briefcase. 'In the event our demands are not to be met, in the same way we cannot prove China's economy is under threat, so will it be impossible to prove these accidents are anything other than unfortunate acts of God. You have forty-eight hours to advise Collier and to decide whether or not you wish to be relocated.'

'Otherwise what?' Driscoll said.

'Otherwise Energex and the British authorities will be told how and where they may find you. It is a choice you must make for yourselves.'

Some choice, Driscoll thought. 'Why would you need me and Natalie after we've told Collier what you've just told us?' he said.

'You have the answer already. You will be our private communication channel – the route for negotiations which must follow. But let us hope I will not be instructed to initiate the triggering of our devices. Instead, I think it will be better for everyone if I am asked to permanently deactivate them. Then perhaps we can all leave this unpleasantness behind us.'

In the context of what they'd been discussing, it was beyond Driscoll how anybody could use the word unpleasant to describe deliberately staged accidents so appalling that, if they were ever to occur, the consequences would be unthinkable – horrifying scenarios politically charged to the point where no government in the world would admit to having indirectly brought the disasters upon themselves.

For the next day and a half, this would be the thought that would occupy him more than any other as, hour after hour, he and Natalie struggled to find a way out of the trap that, right from the start, had been so insidious that for them to escape from it now would either be impossible or too dangerous to attempt.

Not until they received Collier's blessing on the morning of the second day were they able to finalize their plans, made easier in part because by then Natalie had declared her own position to be non-negotiable, and in so doing had forced Driscoll to take the only course of action that would buy them some time, and perhaps help Collier to prevent the unthinkable from ever happening.

CHAPTER 10

On days like this, when the Aegean was unobscured by mist or rain, so complete was the island's separation from reality that it seemed to inhabit a dimension of its own, floating on a painted sea, or suspended by invisible threads beneath a sky that stretched away forever without any discernible horizon.

According to the owner of the local store, the weather had been kind to them during the two and a half weeks they'd been here, but this morning it was truly spectacular without a hint of wind, and with sunshine that was far less watery than it had been on some of the other mornings.

Viewed from the villa's terrace where Driscoll was standing, the whole of Santorini appeared to be bathed in light, there wasn't a cloud in the sky and, at the foot of the cliffs, a turquoise-coloured sea was being marked by hardly a ripple.

It was too pretty, he decided, picture-postcard scenery that brought tourists to the Greek Islands from all over the world, but where, for a few precious months every winter, as long as you could forget why you'd come here, you could pretend you were part of a community where life went on much as it always had done.

For Natalie and for him, forgetting had proved to be the hard part. Irrespective of how scenic the surroundings were, and no matter how bright the sunshine was, the reason for them being on Santorini was with them for every minute of every day – reinforced at increasingly frequent intervals by the emails they were receiving from either Collier or Feng now negotiations were reaching a more crucial stage.

Still, Driscoll thought, the island was as good a place as any for them to be, a temporarily safe haven that would have to do until they could see how things developed from now on.

It was Natalie who'd chosen Santorini, just as it had been Natalie who'd taken the responsibility of co-ordinating the provision of their new identities, using her laptop to communicate with Feng until their new passports and travel documents had been delivered to the Waverley Hotel by courier on 21 February.

They'd left England the following morning, arriving at the little villa after an uneventful day-long journey that had left them wondering why they'd ever imagined it would have been anything but uneventful.

Since then, apart from them fulfilling their obligations as email intermediaries, the days had passed one after another without incident – mostly cool, and mostly sun-filled days during which Driscoll had been careful to keep his thoughts about Natalie to himself.

Today, though, he suspected things were going to be different – partly because Collier was scheduled to visit them later on, which meant this would be their last opportunity to refine their plan, but also because, unless he was mistaken, the signals coming from Natalie were becoming less mixed than they had been.

Over the past three or four days she'd either been avoiding eye contact altogether, or had started accompanying him wherever he went, except for yesterday evening which she'd spent alone at a window staring out into the dark before choosing to say goodnight by kissing him on the lips for rather too long.

Without him knowing, she'd come to join him on the terrace.

'Here.' She handed him a glass of orange juice. 'This really is a special place, isn't it?'

'Better view than the one from my flat in Kensington.'

'You haven't told me about your flat.' She shielded her eyes from the sun. 'How often do you go there?'

'When I'm not somewhere else.' He didn't want to talk about it. 'Are you OK about today?'

'Except for the photo. It would be all right if we hadn't sent Collier the one I took of Feng's car, but I don't think he believes what we've told him about the shot of Feng being no good.'

'He can believe whatever he wants. It's our insurance. Except for you and me, and maybe the waitress who served us coffee that morning in the Waverley, no one in the States or Britain or Russia has any idea what Feng looks like. Right now, we're the only two people who can identify the bastard. If we hand over our photo of him to Collier, we lose the only edge we've got.'

'I know that. I'm just not sure it makes us as valuable as you think it does.'

'If it's Comrade Feng who's being paid to push the buttons, how is anyone going to find him and stop him if we don't give them a hand?'

'You're oversimplifying things.' She walked to the corner of the terrace and leaned back against one of the stone pillars. 'We might not be that important any more – not now we've told everyone what Feng wanted us to tell them.'

'So why is Collier taking the trouble to come and see us this after-noon, and why are we still being used as a clearing house for emails?'

'I don't know. I just wish none of this had happened.'

'If it hadn't, you and I wouldn't have met each other.' Putting down his glass of juice, he went over and placed his hands on her shoulders. 'Look,' he said, 'before Collier gets here, there's something we ought to sort out between us.'

'You could've done that last night.' She made no attempt to meet his eyes. 'Well, you could've done if there was anything that needed sorting out.'

'There is. Stop pretending you don't know what I mean.'

'It's not my fault. If you weren't thinking about shipwrecks, earth-quakes and trains all the time, I wouldn't have to pretend.' She stopped staring out to sea. 'Are you going to keep on talking, or are you going to kiss me?'

Of all the decisions he'd made of late, this was the only easy one. It was also the most rewarding.

Because he hadn't been alone in his anticipation, she was as eager as he was, kissing him open-mouthed, holding him to her while she pressed her breasts against his chest and used the tip of her tongue to show him what she wanted him to know, releasing him just long enough to look at him before smothering him with a flurry of kisses that left her breathless.

For Driscoll, adrift for several minutes in a world where the fragrance of her perfume and the touch of her lips were more real than the threats he'd been trying not to worry about, the experience had elimi-nated one uncertainty, but in so doing had created a situation that was now going to be more difficult to resolve than it had been before.

'We didn't time this too well,' he said.

'That's not my fault either. For someone who flies planes and drives like you do, you're really slow at some things.' She reached up and drew her finger across his lips. 'It's not that late yet. Collier's flight doesn't leave Athens until nine o'clock, and then he's got to find a taxi.'

'Suppose he gets here early? It's nearly ten already.'

'I didn't say anything about what he might interrupt.' She was disappointed. 'What do you think he's been doing in Athens?'

'Who knows? All his email said was that he was scheduled to meet someone there last night. It might have nothing to do with the Chinese programme.'

'It's not a programme. It's extortion.' She wriggled free and headed off towards the French doors. 'Are you going to have breakfast with me, or are you going to stay out here worrying that Collier's already noticed how you look at me sometimes?'

Driscoll didn't much care what Collier had noticed. He was concerned about her – just as he had been all along, except that things had suddenly become more personal and even more difficult to handle.

Instead of disappearing inside, she'd remained standing in the doorway waiting for him. No longer so self-conscious about her smile, and with the sunlight exaggerating the colour of her skin against the clothes she was wearing, she was looking as desirable as he'd ever seen her.

She'd bought the halter top and the skirt from a little shop in Fira yesterday, happy to use some of the 100,000 yuan that Driscoll had transferred from his Shanghai bank – money that couldn't have been better spent, he thought – repayment in a form he'd never expected for all the damn trouble it had caused.

'Are you coming, or not?' she called.

'Yeah, I'm coming.' He followed her into the villa, but before she reached the morning room, couldn't stop himself from grabbing her by the waist and spinning her round.

She was ready to carry on from where they'd left off, but this time he was more careful, breaking off their embrace as soon as he felt things starting to get out of hand.

'What was that all about?' she asked.

'Just checking.'

'You don't have to check. If I hadn't wanted this to happen, I wouldn't have come to Santorini with you.'

'Yes you would.' Driscoll grinned at her. 'You chose it.'

'Only because you were a free ticket to a place I've always wanted to see. If you're going to go through the emails again like you said, you can do it by yourself while I fix breakfast. I'm tired of reading them.

They're under my laptop on the bureau.'

'OK.' Although much of Driscoll's motivation had gone as well, he went to get them anyway, spreading out the copies in sequence on the floor.

There were two kinds: those they'd received from Feng, which they'd been instructed to forward on to Collier, and the replies from Collier that they'd duly sent back to Feng. It had been Natalie's idea to print off copies for themselves – a precaution against precisely what he wasn't sure – but now he came to study them again, the strategy behind them seemed to be leading in one direction only.

Despite the messages being couched in language so diplomatically obscure that it was often difficult to be certain what the intentions of them really were, one thing was clear, he decided. Unlike the British and the Americans, who were requesting more time to consider their response to the Chinese demands, the Russians were being characteristically blunt, falling short of refusing to negotiate, but making it fairly plain that, having had a gun put to their heads, they were unlikely to be offering financial compensation of any kind, and even less likely to be approving the construction of a pipeline from their eastern oil fields.

Or was something else going on, Driscoll wondered? To combat the threats, had Moscow, London and Washington joined forces? Were they working together, or acting individually to protect their national interests and insulate themselves in whatever way they thought would work?

Believing that Natalie might be better at reading between the lines, after they'd finished breakfast he persuaded her to try, keeping his own opinions to himself until she gave up, confessing that she was no more able to cut through the rhetoric and diplomatic-speak than he had been.

'So what have we decided?' she asked.

'Nothing. Do you want to have another go before Collier gets here?'

'No.' She'd been kneeling on the floor, but the sound of a car pulling up outside gave her the excuse to get to her feet. 'That could be him.'

'If it is, go and say hello while I get these out of the way.' Driscoll began gathering up the pieces of paper. 'Be nice.'

'I thought that's what I'd been doing.'

'To him.' Driscoll grinned. 'You don't have to overdo it.' He refolded the printouts before he took them to the bedroom and was in the process of hiding them in the wardrobe when he heard her scream out his name.

He reached the hall in less than a second, arriving in time to stop her tripping over as she backed away from the open front door.

She had both hands clamped over her mouth, frightened half to death, not by the sight of Johnathon Collier standing on the step outside, but by the presence of the man beside him.

It was Melinkov, the Russian in the photo Feng had given them – Rebecca Wilson's executioner, and the man Energex had hired to kill them.

CHAPTER 11

Collier was making things worse. In a half-hearted attempt to conceal Melinkov from view, the MP had begun moving in front of him.

'That'll do,' Driscoll yelled. 'One more step and I'll blow your fucking head off.'

The bluff had been unconvincing, but it had served its purpose, stopping Collier in his tracks. He stayed where he was framed in the doorway, holding out his palms either to ward off an imaginary bullet or as a gesture of reassurance.

'Easy there,' he said. 'You've misunderstood.'

Driscoll hadn't misunderstood anything, nor was he reassured, gripping Natalie so tightly that she was struggling to free herself.

'You're hurting me,' she whispered. 'If they'd wanted to surprise us, they wouldn't have come to the front door.'

Collier lowered his hands. 'I really am most sorry,' he said. 'This is entirely my fault. I should've telephoned you, but it was only last night that I decided I should bring Mr Melinkov with me.'

'And you figured that would be OK, did you?' Driscoll remained wary. 'Either he's out of here in the next ten seconds, or half the world's press agencies are going to be discovering where Energex are getting their money from and what they're doing with it.'

Melinkov had been keeping his own hands in the open, carefully watching Driscoll and being equally careful not to move too quickly. 'You have no gun,' he said. 'I also bring no gun with me. Perhaps if you will permit us to come in, Mr Collier can explain why it is I accompany him.'

'Save your breath,' Driscoll said. 'If you think Natalie and I want to hear some kind of crazy explanation from you or Collier, you've either got shit for brains or you've been told the wrong story about us. We know who you are, we know who you work for and we know what you do.'

'Things are not always how they seem to be. Mr Collier has said you do not understand. It is you who should listen.'

Unable to determine whether the Russian posed a threat or not, Driscoll switched his attention back to Collier. 'Have you been to see Energex again?'

'I've been to see a great many people in the last week. That's why I'm here.' Sensing an easing of the tension, the MP showed no inclination to leave. 'Given your position, I imagine I'd feel much the same as you do,' he said. 'But don't you think you're being hasty? After all, I'd hardly have brought Mr Melinkov without good reason, would I?'

'Depends what kind of a deal you've sewn up for yourself with him or Sir Oliver.'

'You're letting cynicism cloud your judgement. The situation is well beyond anyone making deals. From now on, Energex will be doing what they're told to do.'

'Which is?'

'Following a very different agenda from the one they had before. They've been given a new initiative.'

'Passed on to them by you?'

'Well.' Collier cleared his throat. 'Yes, I suppose you could say that.'

The picture wasn't getting any clearer, Driscoll thought. 'And you've been despatched to Greece to give us our new instructions – right?' he said.

'More a request for your continuing assistance – something I'm not willing to discuss from the steps of your front door.'

Driscoll wasn't sure he wanted to discuss anything that required Melinkov to be present. Wisely, the Russian had been keeping quiet, occasionally letting his eyes wander over Natalie whose suspicion had given way to undisguised hostility. She seemed prepared to accept what Collier had been saying, but showed little sign of allowing Melinkov to enter the villa, let alone get any closer to her.

Not that they were in much of a position to stop the bastard, Driscoll thought. The Russian wasn't just thickset and well built, he was a bull of a man, a foot shorter than Collier, but wide enough to be occupying most of the doorway by himself.

'Well?' Collier asked. 'Will you hear me out, or not?'

'We'll see how it goes. Close the door behind you.' Giving Natalie no opportunity to protest, Driscoll began towing her back in to the morning-room.

'You're mad,' she whispered. 'I'm not going to stay in the same room as the man who shot Rebecca Wilson.'

'You didn't mind being in the same room as Feng, and he's the guy who had Charles Collier burned to death.'

'Feng hasn't been trying to kill me: Melinkov has.' She made Driscoll let her go. 'What's the matter with you?'

Collier had overheard. He'd followed them ahead of the Russian and was clearly anxious to settle things down. 'The British police are still working on the Wilson case,' he said. 'But I understand there's no evidence that points in any one direction.'

So evasive was the statement that not even Collier had managed to make it sound convincing. But there was more to it, Driscoll realized. Collier wasn't stupid. By pretending there could be an element of doubt, he was asking for time – hoping for a chance to explain whatever the hell it was he wanted to explain.

He was going to have to hurry. It wasn't only Natalie who was uncomfortable. Melinkov was equally ill at ease, glancing first at the ceiling, then kneeling down to inspect the underside of the coffee table on which the phone was standing.

'You have checked for listening devices?' he said.

The precaution hadn't occurred to Driscoll. 'Why would Feng have planted bugs?' he asked.

Apparently unwilling to say more until he'd completed his search, the Russian went out on to the terrace where he began upending potted plants and combing his fingers through the flower beds.

'A cautious man.' Collier was watching him. 'If you can get past his surliness, he's more engaging than he looks.'

'For God's sake.' Natalie was furious. 'He shoots people. He's a contract killer.'

'He's also our best hope of averting three major world disasters.' Collier kept his voice down. 'Perhaps it would be more advisable for us to speak outside. It seems a shame to waste the sunshine on such a nice day, don't you think?'

For Driscoll, the Santorini sunshine had lost much of its magic. The Aegean was as calm as it had been before, there was still no wind, and the sky was still the same colour, but the feeling of tranquillity had gone, and with it had gone the sense of unreality that had been as temporary as his sense of well-being.

Not expecting to recapture his mood, he accompanied Natalie over to the same stone pillar where, twenty minutes ago, she'd been able to make both of them forget what had brought them to Santorini to begin with.

Collier's appreciation of the surroundings was more limited. Ignoring Melinkov, and too preoccupied to notice the view, he came over to speak to them by himself.

'I'm sorry all this has been so rushed,' he said, 'but I'm sure you understand we can't afford to waste any time. Had your efforts to photograph Feng been successful we'd have more options and longer to consider them. But never mind. That's the least of our worries now.'

'Did the photo of his car tell you anything?' Driscoll asked.

'It's one of four vehicles registered to the Chinese Embassy. No real surprises there, although it does remove any doubts we had about his credibility. However, that's not what I've come to see you about.'

Driscoll hadn't thought it was. 'Are you going to pay off the Chinese, or not?' he said.

'The British have no immediate intention of doing so, nor do the Americans or the Russians — but that's not the impression we wish to give Beijing. As things stand, we're being forced to exploit the only window of opportunity we have.' Collier paused. 'Which means we need your help.'

Driscoll kept his thoughts to himself, wondering how accurate his guesses would turn out to be.

Collier waved Melinkov away to prevent him interrupting. 'In one of the phone conversations we had before you left England, you mentioned an important point,' he said. 'If I recall correctly, Feng made the mistake of telling you he'd be responsible for triggering the explosives.'

Driscoll nodded. 'He's the guy Beijing are paying to do their dirty work.'

'And he also said he'd be responsible for deactivating all three explosive devices in the event of Beijing being paid the compensation they're demanding. That is right, isn't it?'

'Yep.' Driscoll was trying to remember the exact words when Natalie decided she'd heard enough. Like him, she'd realized where the conversation was leading and was ready to put an end to it.

'Why ask us for help?' she said.

Collier smiled at her. 'Well, first of all because no one except the two of you are in a position to identify Feng, and because I imagine you'd prefer not to endanger the lives of thousands of people.'

'You've missed something,' she said. 'Nobody's lives have to be in danger if Russia, America and Britain pay up the sixty billion dollars. So why don't they?'

'Miss Washburn, I know very well you're not as naïve as you're pretending to be. It's one thing for governments to subsidize corporations like Energex with grants and loans, but there's not a government in the world that could get away with handing over billions and billions of tax payers' money to a foreign power without explaining why.'

'So make them explain.'

Collier attempted another smile. 'I promise you that politicians aren't going to risk their careers by incriminating themselves in a conspiracy to withhold oil from the Chinese People's Republic. A confession of that kind has never been made before, and it certainly isn't going to happen now.'

'So what's happening instead?' Driscoll asked.

'Provided Beijing permits the US and the UK to witness the disarming of the explosive devices that Feng claims are in place for the *Richard Montgomery* and in the SAFOD project, London and Washington will be offering Beijing ex gratia payments of two billion each. They'll also guarantee to increase import quotas for selected Chinese-manufactured goods – things like sports apparel, running shoes and top-end mobile phones.'

'A bunch of T-shirts and two billion from the US and two billion from the UK,' Driscoll said. 'A tenth of what Beijing's asking for.'

'It's a starting point. We need to prolong negotiations for as long as we possibly can. I've brought the details of the offer with me. It's on a disk in your names, so you can send it straight on to Feng in the usual way.'

By now, Driscoll was fairly certain his hunch had been right. 'But there's no offer from Russia,' he said, 'because they're going to play hardball, are they?'

'That's what everyone wants Beijing to think.' Collier looked out to sea. 'The idea is to provoke the Chinese. By forcing their hand in Russia, with your assistance we hope to get our hands on Feng, which in turn will give us an opportunity to stop what could occur later on in the UK and the US.'

'What did London and Washington have to give Moscow for that?' Driscoll said drily.

'If you'd bothered to analyse the differences in the threats, you wouldn't need to ask.'

'What differences?'

'The munitions on board the *Richard Montgomery* can almost certainly be detonated remotely at any time, so can explosives that have the potential to cause a shift in the San Andreas fault. But the same isn't true of the situation in Russia. Derailing a train requires a much greater level of hands-on intervention.'

'Because trains are moving targets,' Natalie said. 'The Chinese will have to have someone on site there – otherwise they won't be able to trigger their landslide at the right moment.'

Collier nodded. 'In this case, the someone being Feng or one of his companions – or so we must hope. But that's not the only reason for the strategy. There's little that can be done about the instability of the *Richard Montgomery*, and even less that anyone can do to prevent the possibility of an earthquake in California, but there's plenty the Russians can do about the trains that carry their nuclear waste.'

Driscoll didn't need to have it spelled out. 'They can choose when to send them,' he said. 'And the wagons don't necessarily have to be carrying radioactive material. They only have to look as though they are.'

'Indeed. So now you understand why you've become an essential part of the operation, and why I was asked to bring Mr Melinkov to meet you.'

Driscoll only partly understood. 'Where does someone like him fit in to this?'

'Where do you think? Months before London, Washington and Moscow set out to starve the Chinese economy of oil, they knew how politically unwise it would be to deploy conventional intelligence organizations to do the job for them. Too many people would've asked too many questions. Their solution, of course, was to utilize Energex. Since then, the Chinese have reached a similar conclusion and have realized it's diplomatically safer for them to act through someone like Feng. The result of all this is that London, Washington and Moscow find themselves with their backs against a wall – so, to get out of the mess they're in, they've elected to use the resources of Energex again.' Collier paused to allow the information to sink in. 'And, as you already know,

Mr Melinkov is an Energex employee.'

Driscoll had no idea what to say. 'You don't really think we're going to buy in to this, do you?' he said. 'You can't.'

'I've already explained.' Collier's expression remained the same. 'I'm not the free agent you seem to think I am: I'm simply passing on a request.'

'If you're expecting us to work with Melinkov, you're crazy.' Driscoll glanced at the Russian who was busy lighting a cigarette from the stub of the one he'd just finished. 'Find someone else. Natalie and I aren't going anywhere with a sick bastard like him.'

'Miss Washburn won't be going anywhere with anyone. To maintain our communication channel through Feng, I'm afraid she'll be remaining here on Santorini. I'm not talking about her; I'm talking about you.' Collier's eyes were on a tiny fishing boat that was crawling north towards one of the other islands. 'The British are providing discreet intelligence,' he said. 'And the Americans are arranging covert satellite coverage of the terrain flanking the railroad between Troick and Chelyabinsk. Melinkov will be in charge of operations on the ground.'

'How much are Energex paying him for that?' Driscoll said.

The MP pretended not to have heard. 'Your own contribution will be nominal,' he said. 'As soon as Feng has been captured and identified, you'll be free to return here while he's persuaded to provide information about the supposed underground explosives at Parkfield and the underwater explosives in the Thames Estuary.'

'That's it, is it? That's the master plan.'

'Unless you and Miss Washburn can suggest an alternative. I suppose I should've asked you.'

'You don't know what you're doing.' Driscoll was searching for a way out. 'If you think Natalie's going to stay here by herself, you've wasted your time.'

'If she'd care to invite a friend to join her, I'll be happy to make the necessary arrangements. Instead of answering for her, perhaps you should ask her what she thinks.'

Driscoll had no opportunity to do so. Before Collier had finished speaking she'd marched from the terrace. A minute later, from somewhere inside the villa there was the sound of a door slamming.

It was a signal for Melinkov to extinguish his cigarette. Until now, as though unwilling to participate in the proceedings, he'd been sitting in one of the canvas chairs, but with Natalie gone he had a message for Driscoll.

'Your friend is foolish,' he said. 'If she is angry because you do not permit her to speak for herself, you should tell her why it is she cannot accompany us. At this time of year, the mountains and forests in my country are at their coldest. They are not places where a girl can do what you and I must do there.'

Driscoll didn't need to be told, and he sure as hell didn't need any advice from Melinkov – nor was he happy with the assumption that he'd agreed to something he had no intention of agreeing to.

'Tell Energex to find another way,' he said. 'Or can't you twist their arms any further?'

Collier frowned. 'It hasn't been a question of arm twisting. The Energex directors understand their situation. They're under no illusion about the personal consequences should the worst come to the worst.'

Driscoll was under no illusion either. 'Tough break for them,' he said. 'Still, better than governments or politicians carrying the can for acts of God that don't actually turn out to be acts of God at all. Or am I being cynical again?'

'I'm afraid that's how things work.' Collier was continuing to watch the fishing boat. 'A country's stability and prosperity relies on a public perception of high governmental integrity. Take that away and you end up with a Zimbabwe. Anyway, I've told you. Energex understand their position very well. What we're trying to establish is how well you understand yours.'

Although no specific penalty for his non-co-operation had been spelled out, there wasn't a shortage of possibilities, Driscoll thought. His newly acquired reputation as a drug trafficker wasn't going to help, and with the supposed accident to the Cessna still unexplained, and with Rebecca Wilson's death not yet out of the news, Collier had plenty of options to choose from.

'I need to talk to Natalie,' he said. 'Help yourself to a drink. There's beer in the fridge and half a bottle of Scotch lying around somewhere.'

She was in the front bedroom, seated at the dressing table examining the photo she'd taken of Feng.

'Give them this.' She handed it to him. 'Then they'll go away and leave us alone.'

'They'll go away, but they're not going to leave us alone – not now. We're too dangerous. If Collier's plan misfires, and Beijing gets offside with Moscow and with Washington and London, who's going to trust us to keep our mouths shut?'

'I don't care. We can go somewhere else – just you and me. If we split up now, you'll forget about me.'

'No I won't.'

'Promise me then.' Instead of turning to face him, she studied his reflection in the mirror. 'Say it.'

'OK. I promise.'

He'd made the commitment in good faith, but two days later, ankle deep in snow on the outskirts of Chelyabinsk and numb from the cold of a Russian winter's morning, all he could remember was the lost look in her eyes when she'd kissed him goodbye, and how hard she'd been trying to mend her smile before he'd walked away and left her.

CHAPTER 12

At the airstrip in the Tarim Basin, sometimes so cold had been the mornings that the very air itself had seemed to be frozen. But it was colder here.

In the industrial wasteland behind the razor-wire fence on the other side of the road, the only things that weren't frozen solid or smothered in overnight snow were the floodlit reservoirs and holding tanks of the Chelyabinsk Mayak Chemical Combine Plant, ugly squat cylinders and vats containing warm radioactive waste that was awaiting vitrification and further processing.

According to Melinkov, at this very moment the plant could be storing anything up to half a million cubic metres of solid waste and another half a million cubic metres of liquid waste – enough to poison the whole of Russia and most of the rest of the world as well, Driscoll thought, the legacy of a nuclear programme in such disarray that it was spewing out toxic waste a hundred times faster than it could be disposed of.

'So, now you see where it is the train will come,' Melinkov said. 'Soon a new vitrification kiln will be commissioned here. It will allow Russia to accept shipments of waste from other countries which will make much money for the Duma. Already, a contract has been signed to process fifteen hundred tons of spent nuclear fuel rods from Hungary alone.'

'What happens after the stuff's been vitrified?' Driscoll wasn't sure he wanted to know.

'The glass capsules are sealed in steel containers before they are buried in trenches or stored at a safe place above ground. It is better than dumping them in the Techna River or in Lake Karachay which was formerly how it was done. You have heard about the disasters here?'

Driscoll shook his head.

'In the first of these, after a tank of nitrate acetate is permitted to run dry, one day in 1957 there is a big explosion. Then ten years later, a hot summer evaporates the water in the lake, and a big wind blows radioactive dust and sediment over the country. It is said more than two hundred thousand people are exposed to high levels of radiation, but the danger is covered up by the Soviet government and kept secret for twenty years.'

'How safe is it around here now?'

Melinkov shrugged. 'For myself I would not live near Chelyabinsk, but others do not have this choice. There are many factories here that pay good wages.' He glanced at Driscoll. 'Energex have given you those gloves, a fur coat and good Russian boots, but still you shiver?'

'I'm bloody freezing.'

'Then we shall return to the car and go to see if the snow-plough is ready for us.'

Although it was apparently standard procedure to clear the track from the north before any trainload of waste was despatched from the marshalling yard at Troick for its journey here, Driscoll doubted that they were going to learn much by accompanying the driver of the plough today.

With this much snow about, identifying places where a landslide could be made to happen would be difficult enough from the air, he thought. Trying to do it from the cab of a diesel-electric snow-plough seemed to be an exercise in futility – an unlikely way of guessing where the Chinese might have buried their explosives, let alone a means of deciding if and where Feng could be preparing to detonate them.

Because the snow was even deeper on their drive from the Mayak plant to the rail siding where Melinkov had arranged for his rendezvous with the plough, Driscoll found himself becoming increasingly pessimistic.

'How far did you say it is between Chelyabinsk and Troick?' he asked.

'A hundred and thirty-six kilometres.' Melinkov kept his eyes on the road. 'As long as there is no trouble, our rail journey to Troick will take us less than three hours.'

'What the hell are we going to see from the cab of a moving snow-plough?'

Melinkov smiled. 'You must understand how it is we will counter the

111

Chinese threat. For more than one week now, seven of our nuclear sites
have been sending only what appear to be tanks of waste for assembly
in the yard at Troick. They do this because the State Nuclear Safety
Inspectorate is told of a possible attack by Chechen terrorists. By
tomorrow eighteen railcars carrying more than fifty casks will have
been assembled – enough of them to form a train. If the Chinese have
been watching, they will be ready. And if their intelligence is good, they
will know the despatch of the plough today is proof that the train will
soon be leaving.'

'The tanks are empty, are they?'

'They are marked with the usual nuclear sign, but for the locomotive
to sound as though it is pulling a heavy load, they have been filled with
sand.'

'I can't see that helping us much,' Driscoll said, 'not with so much
line to worry about.'

'It is not so hard.' Melinkov cracked open his window and lit a cigarette. 'Landslips, avalanches and rock slides have been known to block
the track in three places only. For a derailment to look like an accident,
it will be at one of these where Feng will do his work.'

'And that's where you figure we'll find him?'

Melinkov shook his head. 'He will think it too dangerous. Perhaps
more than a month ago on a dark night he has put his charges in position, but tomorrow, if the wind is in the wrong direction for him, he will
not wish to be so close to what he believes are broken containers of
radioactive material.'

'So how's he going to do it?'

'He has three choices. He can sit on a mountain-top five kilometres
away with good binoculars and send a radio signal to his detonators
when he sees the train is at the right place for him, or after the plough
has done its job this morning, he can fix a pressure switch to the rails so
it will transmit a similar signal when the train runs over it tomorrow.'

'Which won't work if it snows tonight and the plough has to make
another pass,' Driscoll said. 'If that happens, all he's going to do is
derail a snow-plough.'

'You have not permitted me to explain the third choice he will have.
It is the one I myself would use in a situation of this kind.'

Aware that he was listening to someone who made a living by sabotaging oil wells, Driscoll waited to hear what it was.

'Although it has disadvantages, sometimes it is an easy way.'

Melinkov blew a mouthful of smoke out his window. 'You need only a small package in which you put a pre-programmed GPS unit and a mobile telephone. Once this has been hidden on board the train, your job is done.'

'Because when the GPS unit senses it's reached the right co-ordinates, it'll tell the phone to make a call, and that'll fire the detonators up on a cliff somewhere? Is that how it works?'

'For anything moving which can vary its speed throughout its journey, the system is more accurate than a timer. It is much used by Palestinians and Iraqis, and more reliable than a suicide bomber who can change his mind.'

Melinkov would know, Driscoll thought. Like Feng, the Russian was a man of contrasts. As well as appearing to be as well educated as he was well mannered, just as Collier had said, his surliness was superficial, apparently reserved for situations in which he was uncomfortable or when he was in the presence of people he mistrusted or disliked.

In between worrying about Natalie, Driscoll had spent much of the commercial leg of his flight from Athens reconsidering the wisdom of agreeing to work alongside Melinkov at all. But after being met in Moscow by an efficient young woman from the local Energex office who, in the company of an equally efficient Russian immigration official, had escorted him to a waiting Energex corporate jet that had whisked him to Chelyabinsk, he'd begun to appreciate the scale of what he was involved in and come to realize that, in a game with stakes this high, Melinkov and Collier were as much pawns as he and Natalie had become.

Whichever way you looked at it, the whole thing was still sick, he thought. After Energex had been paid to do the dirty work in China, now they were being paid to do the dirty work again, but this time with even greater backing from governments and politicians who were so anxious to save their skins in the event of the public learning the truth, that they'd given the Energex directors the equivalent of a blank cheque.

'We are here.' Melinkov slowed the car at the entrance of a small rail siding. 'You like the machine?'

It was hard not to. Freshly painted and emblazoned with the RZhD insignia of the Russian Railways, in addition to being twice the size of any ordinary snow-plough, it looked and sounded enormously powerful, growling to itself and belching smoke from its twin exhausts now the driver had gunned his diesel to show he'd seen them coming.

Melinkov parked the car and went to unload his leather satchel from the boot while he waited for Driscoll to get out. 'Soon you will be warmer,' he said. 'In the cab there will be good heaters and, if we are lucky, the driver will have coffee for us.'

The heaters were better than good. With the outside temperature hovering between twenty and thirty degrees below zero, the heat in the cab came as something of a shock.

So did the coffee – a scalding, thick black liquid drawn off from an urn clamped to the floor beside the driver. He was an older man with startlingly blue eyes set in a face that looked as though it was made from worn-out folded leather.

'His name is Yuri,' Melinkov explained. 'He has little English, but wishes to say he is pleased to have your company today.'

Driscoll smiled. 'Thank him for the coffee. Tell him it's a bit stronger than the stuff I had served up to me at my hotel this morning.'

Yuri was amused, speaking briefly to Melinkov before checking his instruments and easing the big plough out of the siding to commence his run.

Inside the cab there was more noise and more vibration than Driscoll had expected, although once they'd gathered speed and were properly underway, the plough seemed to settle down, clearing the occasional drift without effort despite the snow becoming a good deal deeper now they were leaving the southern outskirts of the city.

To begin with, the track ran alongside the M36, the main highway from Yekaterinburg to Kustanaj, but soon there were fewer glimpses of the road and they were in open country, travelling south at nearly sixty kilometres an hour, the plough throwing up graceful arcs of snow from each side of its burnished prow.

They were about fifty kilometres into their journey when the driver reduced his speed and muttered something to Melinkov who pointed to a large drift that lay ahead.

'He is afraid there may be rocks hidden in the snow,' Melinkov said. 'They come from the steep slope to our left.'

Driscoll was more interested in the eighty-foot drop on the right hand side of the track. How many rocks or boulders could be lying at the bottom he couldn't tell, but for anyone wanting to push a train over the edge, this looked to be as good a place as any.

Today, the drift was either free of rocks, or those that had come down since the plough had been here last were too small to impede its progress.

'You think Feng can create his landslide here?' Melinkov asked.

'Depends how much Semtex the bastard's got buried at the top.' Driscoll was endeavouring to judge the angle of the slope. 'Better mark it on the map anyway.'

Yuri had understood part of the conversation and was anxious to contribute. Taking the map, he placed a finger on a point further along the line and began to gabble.

Melinkov waited for him to finish before providing a summarized translation. 'He says this track was constructed many years ago for the transport of timber and minerals from the Ural Mountains. But always it has suffered from landslips and rock slides which is why the new fast line from Troick to Chelyabinsk was built, and why this one is used no more than once a month for trains carrying nuclear waste to the Mayak plant.'

'So what?' Driscoll said.

'According to him, the slope we have just seen is not such a big worry, but before we pass under the road bridge to Jeman□elinsk he can show us a more dangerous place where, when the thaw comes, the track is often blocked or damaged.'

Irrespective of the time of year or how infrequently the trains were scheduled, transporting radioactive waste on a line like this was always going to be a risky business, Driscoll thought, a typically Russian out of sight out of mind approach to a problem they wished they didn't have.

Viewed through the windshield of the plough, Yuri's dangerous place was an accident waiting to happen. After the diesel had started working harder on an incline that had taken it around the base of a shallow hill, the track had started to twist and turn in all directions, winding its way first through a series of valleys and ravines and then, in order to avoid what appeared to be the vestiges of an ancient river-bed a hundred feet below, out on to a narrow shelf that had been dynamited into the side of a mountain.

Here, above the track, the rock-face was almost sheer, as high as the drop on the other side, and too steep to have retained the snow which had accumulated on the line in front of them.

Yuri had reduced his speed again and was being careful to keep his hand on the throttle, but sufficiently confident to grin at Driscoll before they hit the drift head on.

Rising up like a wave, a torrent of snow cascaded over the cab and across the roof. But the snow was dry and gone just as quickly, allowing another glimpse of the boulder-strewn river-bed below.

It had been impossible to gauge if Yuri had been showing off or whether experience had told him the line was free of rocks, but of one thing Driscoll was certain: this would be the place, he thought, which meant that if Feng wasn't bluffing, somewhere high above them, right now, explosive charges were awaiting the signal that would dislodge several hundred thousand tons of granite.

Melinkov was of the same opinion. 'Although we have some way still to go, I think we may need to look no further,' he said. 'Had I myself been asked to cause such an accident, finding anywhere better would not be easy.'

In case there was somewhere, once they'd passed under the Jeman□elinsk road bridge and had again drawn closer to the afternoon traffic on the M36, Driscoll continued to watch the countryside unfold, discounting the suitability of other sites as they came across them, and only bothering to question Yuri about the frequency of landslips at a small cutting they encountered shortly before the plough pulled in to the marshalling yards at Troick.

In this region of Russia at this time of year, when the sun rose at ten and disappeared at three, so few were the hours of daylight that, like the Mayak processing plant, the yards were illuminated by floodlamps, half of which were either broken or without bulbs.

But here and there enough of them were working for Driscoll to see what was going on. On a separate siding along the east edge of the yard a number of flat-bed railcars were being shunted into position, each of them carrying three large stainless-steel casks bearing the distinctive three-petalled nuclear hazard sign.

Once the plough had come to a standstill, and after shaking hands with Yuri to thank him for the trip, Melinkov had a warning for Driscoll.

'Because we spend our journey here in the warm, when I open the door you will find it cold outside,' he said.

It wasn't just cold, it was so unimaginably cold that, despite having taken the precaution of pulling up his hood, he was only halfway down the steps when his eyes started watering and he felt his nose block up with ice.

'You will become accustomed to it.' Melinkov lit a cigarette before marching off to inspect a railcar that was awaiting collection.

They looked vulnerable, Driscoll thought. And there were plenty of them. Worse still, once the train began its journey, they'd all be coupled together – a nice soft target compared with a submerged shipwreck or a three kilometre-deep hole somewhere in California.

'So what's the plan?' he asked.

'If I am correct about the method Feng will use, it will be necessary for him to conceal his trigger somewhere on the train while it is stationary. If I am wrong, and instead he watches and waits tomorrow from what he believes is a safe distance, then it will be harder for us to catch him.'

'If he's going to try and plant a transmitter on the train tonight, why don't we make it easy for him?' Driscoll had noticed the soldiers. There were dozens of them – fresh-faced young recruits standing beside each of the railcars with their rifles at the ready while they stamped their feet against the cold.

Melinkov shook his head. 'Feng will expect the shipment to be well-guarded here, just as he will be expecting guards to accompany it to the Mayak railhead. By showing him we are careful, we will not risk frightening him away because we are doing what he expects us to do. When it becomes darker, the soldiers will be told to maintain a small presence, but to allow an intruder to penetrate the perimeter fence so he can be apprehended before he can make his escape.'

'If he doesn't get himself shot first. Feng isn't going to be much use to anyone if one of these guys gets over-excited.'

'They have no ammunition in their guns. You think we have not considered these things?'

'I don't know what you've considered and what you haven't. What if he's sitting on a hilltop tomorrow? How are we going to grab him then?'

'Russia has some satellite coverage of its own, but I am told the Americans are offering infrared feed which is supposed to be good on a cloudy day. Also, while you and I keep pace with the train by driving north on the M36 so we will always be close to it, Energex are to have two fixed-wing aircraft and five of their survey helicopters on standby. As long as Feng and his team have not been warned off, they will not get away.'

'Warned off how?'

'We talk about it later.' Melinkov used his boot to grind the embers of his cigarette in to the snow. 'For now we should familiarize ourselves with the layout of this place so we can see where it is we think a trespasser will come in. First, though, we should get something to eat.'

Doubting that anywhere so freezing cold and filthy dirty could provide a warm drink let alone a meal, Driscoll was more interested in having a leak and getting warm.

He followed Melinkov along a path of packed-down snow, stepping over sections of rusty track and piles of rotting sleepers until they entered an open-fronted building where two men were using sledge-hammers to remove a bogey from a damaged wagon.

At the far end of the building a group of soldiers were laughing and exchanging cigarettes outside a wooden door that had the word *Kafe* burned into it.

'We are here.' Melinkov held the door open for Driscoll. 'If you would care to tell me what you prefer, I will order for you.'

The atmosphere inside was as hot and stuffy as it had been in the cab of the snow-plough, but instead of being filled with diesel fumes, the air was thick with smoke and smelt powerfully of bortsch, stale sweat and burning fat.

Of the dozen or so men seated at the tables, a few were railway workers, but the majority were young soldiers relaxing with their boots unlaced and with their fur jackets piled up on the floor beside their rifles.

Propped up on the serving counter, behind which a large-breasted woman was taking orders and handing out plates of food, a blackboard covered in unreadable Cyrillic displayed the menu for today.

'I'll have what you're having,' Driscoll said. 'Where's the can?'

'There.' Melinkov pointed. 'I think you will not enjoy *salo* and black bread, so I shall get us *kolbasa* and *galushky*.'

So efficient was the kitchen of the marshalling yard *Kafe* that by the time Driscoll returned, Melinkov was already ferrying their order to a vacant corner table, balancing a platter of smoked sausages on his arm and carrying a plate of freshly boiled dumplings.

'You will have beer?' he asked.

'Not if we're going to be hanging around outside all night.' Driscoll sat down. 'What did you mean about Feng being warned off?'

'I say only that it is possible.' As though unwilling to elaborate, the Russian chewed the end off a sausage before helping himself to dumplings. 'It is not important.'

'Look,' Driscoll said. 'I've worked with some nasty bastards in some tough places, so I can handle working with you for as long as I have to. But the minute I find out you're not telling me the whole story, I'm out of here. If a bunch of politicians want to use Energex to screw the Chinese all over again, that's fine by me, but if you even start to screw me around, you'll be identifying Feng all by yourself. Have you got that?'

'It is not necessary for us to be enemies. You and I are not so different. When you know no more about me than I know about you, a man of your experience should choose his words with greater care.' Reaching into his pocket, the Russian took a small photograph from his wallet. 'This is a picture of my daughter,' he said. 'I show it to you so you can see how young she is. Her name is Catherine, but she will not live to see her tenth birthday unless I can earn much money for the surgery she must have.'

Driscoll couldn't muster up much sympathy. Having heard variations of the story more times than he could remember – usually from street-corner junkies or alcoholics – Melinkov's version lacked a certain originality.

'You do not believe me?' the Russian put the photo back in his wallet.

'I didn't ask you about your daughter; I asked you who could've warned off Feng. Are you going to answer my question, or not?'

'You must understand it is not me, but Collier who has these suspicions. I learn of them only after he talks to me in Athens.'

Driscoll waited.

'It is the girl – the half Chinese girl who Collier thinks will have opened her legs for you in Santorini.'

In Driscoll's mouth a piece of dumpling had become suddenly uneatable.

'You have not considered this?' Melinkov looked at him.

He couldn't reply.

'I myself do not know of everything that has gone before, but would it not explain why, after your aircraft is destroyed, the Chinese fly you back to Shanghai where she was told she must contact you?'

Driscoll said nothing.

'According to Collier, it is the girl who decides she will travel from France to see you again in England. Is that correct?'

'More or less.'

'And when together with her you first meet Collier, it is she who suggests Energex have falsified the Chinese oil-field data – yes?'

'I guess. Yeah, it was her theory. She came up with it first.'

'I see.' The Russian looked uncomfortable. 'Do not blame yourself,' he said. 'For any man, distrusting such a pretty girl is not so easy.'

Driscoll was feeling nauseous, cursing himself for not realizing Collier could have suspected her all along, and no more willing to believe she could be part of the original set-up than he was able to believe that, for all this time, she'd been playing him for a fool.

'You must eat.' Melinkov thrust the platter of sausages in front of him. 'With an empty stomach you will not keep warm tonight.'

'I don't want anything. Collier's got it all figured out, has he? If Feng doesn't show, it'll be because Natalie's told her handlers we'll be waiting for him?'

Melinkov shrugged. 'On the flight to Santorini, Collier says only that he wishes our plan to be discussed in front of her.'

'So if she's working for Beijing, she'll pass the information on to Feng.'

'Collier is more devious than you think he is. Should Feng not come to Russia because of her, she will have proved her guilt, so then she can be taken for questioning instead of him. That is why while you and I are here, Collier has arranged for her communications from the villa to be monitored and recorded.'

By now, Driscoll was endeavouring to recall everything Natalie had ever said to him, remembering their initial meeting in Shanghai when, in response to his questions, she'd seemed unusually willing to talk about herself and divulge her family history. Or was that just the way she was, he wondered? Was it really possible that her Paris holiday had been more than a lucky coincidence – one that had placed her conveniently in France while he had been in England? He didn't know, but he was sure as hell going to find out.

'Where's your sat phone?' he said. 'I'm going to call her.'

'No.' Melinkov shook his head. 'You must wait. If Collier is right, we will know soon enough.'

'Why in God's name didn't he tell me instead of telling you?'

'You would not have listened to him, and it would have spoiled his little game. If you wish to check her out for yourself, why not telephone Ji Sui-kai at the Energex office in Shanghai? Ji will not guess why you ask for such a favour, and she will be able to discover if the girl is the journalist she claims to be.'

'Does Ji know what's going on?'

'She knows nothing. I give you this suggestion only in case Collier is wrong. Do not be deceived by his politeness. He is a driven man who seeks to avenge the death of his son by working to his own agenda.'

Driscoll didn't care. In a world gone mad where everyone had their own agenda, all that mattered was the truth – something that had become so murky and so obscure that whether Natalie was who he'd believed her to be depended on whether or not Charles Collier's killer was at this very moment making ready to sabotage a freight train in the middle of central Russia.

Unable to eat, and reinforced against the night air with nothing more substantial than two steaming mugs of *chai* – black tea that was even stronger than the coffee Yuri had supplied them with this morning – Driscoll wasted the next few hours trying not to think the worst, only half-listening to Melinkov's briefing of the local troop commander before accompanying the Russian on what seemed like a never-ending and worthless reconnoitre of the rail yard.

By 11.30, having lost all feeling in his feet, and with his bladder close to bursting, he was again in urgent need of warmth. He amused Melinkov by stating he had no intention of risking frostbite by unzipping his fly, then used the pretext to return to the *Kafe* toilet.

He was on his way out again when he saw the international pay-phone on the wall – an invitation to make the one call that would put an end to the uncertainty that was eating away at him and, at the same time, tell him if there was any point in going on with this.

Several minutes spent trying to communicate with the woman at the counter saw him armed with instructions and the necessary phone card, and he was as ready as he was going to be.

Wondering whether he'd be getting Natalie out of bed, he keyed in the Santorini number and waited.

But after letting it ring for what seemed like an eternity, and as his hopes slowly began to drain away, he knew she was never going to answer because, for reasons of her own, she'd already gone.

CHAPTER 13

The intruder came at exactly three minutes before five o'clock. Driscoll knew it was exactly three minutes before five o'clock because of the deadline he'd set for himself.

Having spent most of the night holding his doubts at bay while he stood behind a stack of oil drums in the north east corner of the railyard, he'd chosen five o'clock as his cut-off point, the time at which he'd decided his blood would have stopped circulating altogether and he'd be leaving Melinkov to carry on alone.

The Russian was sixty feet away, crouched alongside one of the piles of sleepers. Despite his line of sight being partially blocked by the remains of a derelict shunting engine, he'd seen the intruder too, although so far he hadn't used his radio to alert either Driscoll or the few half-frozen soldiers who'd stayed on guard.

Because he wasn't sure yet, Driscoll wondered? Or because he was waiting?

Whoever it was moving in the shadows wasn't being particularly cautious. The man was avoiding pools of light from the odd floodlamp, but his actions were not overtly furtive, and he was making little attempt to hurry.

From this distance it was impossible to tell whether it was Feng or not. He was tall enough, but wearing bulky clothes and had his hood pulled up. It was equally difficult to know where he could have come from. He'd appeared suddenly – presumably after cutting through the fence or by climbing over it somewhere.

His attitude was one of confidence, Driscoll thought – someone who knew where they were and what they were doing, or were about to do.

Walking more quickly now, the man was skirting the row of assembled railcars, heading for the RZhD locomotive that had been coupled up overnight ready for its north-bound haul later this morning.

While Driscoll was trying to get a better look, the intruder changed direction. It had happened as the man had been stepping over a sleeper at the front of the railcar nearest the locomotive, a slight deviation that had taken him closer to the track than he needed to be, and closer to it than he'd been a moment ago.

After twice trying to press the transmit button on his radio with fingers that were too numb to work, Driscoll was removing his glove when a muzzle flash and the crack of a rifle told him he didn't have to bother.

It had been Melinkov who'd fired. Responding to the same telltale signs, he'd acted without compunction, using a rifle that Driscoll had never seen nor knew he had.

The Russian was standing up now, peering across the yard as if hoping to discover how effective his shot had been.

'Are you out of your fucking mind?' Driscoll yelled. 'If Feng's dead you've blown everything.'

'He is not dead.' Melinkov started walking, methodically disassembling his rifle as he went. 'We go so you can see.'

Until they'd pushed through the circle of soldiers that had gathered around a crumpled figure on the ground, it was impossible to determine whether the intruder was alive or not.

He was – moaning and clutching his leg, trying to stem the flow of blood that was soaking into his trousers.

'Ah.' Melinkov was disappointed. 'I do not believe this is Comrade Feng.'

Driscoll had seen the man before. He was an RZhD employee, one of the workers who'd been removing the bogey from the damaged wagon. The bullet had caught him just above the knee, disabling him and causing a good deal of pain.

Waving the soldiers away, Melinkov handed Driscoll a flashlight. 'If you would care to retrieve what our friend has placed on the train I will stay here and ask him some questions.' He planted his boot on the man's injured leg. 'He will soon tell us who he is and who he is working for.'

Driscoll didn't doubt it. Leaving Melinkov to handle the interrogation, he walked over to the first of the railcars and began his search, using the flashlight to scan beneath the casks before carrying out a more thorough inspection of the steel deck and the chassis.

The transmitter was easy to find. It was at the end of the cross-member on which the coupling was mounted, an innocuous-looking box clamped to the beam by what he guessed were magnetic strips.

Half the size of a loaf of bread, the box was made of dark-coloured rigid plastic, and remarkably difficult to remove. Although there was no reason why it should contain explosives, Driscoll was cautious, taking care to keep it upright while he gingerly prised it off.

He was examining it when Melinkov came to see.

The Russian had a cigarette hanging from his mouth, and was looking unhappy.

'Problem?' Driscoll said.

'At the time I think it best to shoot so there can be no chance of the man escaping, but my idea is not so good.'

'It wasn't ever a good idea,' Driscoll said. 'You've been working overseas too long. Why the hell didn't you tell me you had a gun?'

'Because what I carry with me is my business.' Melinkov patted the satchel he never seemed to be without. 'And because you would not have trusted me to shoot straight in the dark.'

It was an unwarranted assumption. Driscoll hadn't forgotten how precisely centred the hole in Rebecca Wilson's forehead had been. Nor was he likely to forget how that had been another of Melinkov's mistakes. 'So you've screwed up again,' he said.

'The man is of no use to us. He believes the box contains a thousand ecstasy tablets for delivery to a dealer who works at the Mayak Chemical Combine Plant. To conceal it on the train, the man I shoot is paid five thousand roubles yesterday afternoon, and is promised another five thousand after he confirms he has done what he has been asked to do.'

'Confirm to who?'

'A stranger who speaks with him in a bar in Troick yesterday afternoon – a Chinese man who tonight has been waiting to pass him the second payment through the fence.' Melinkov spat out his cigarette. 'It seems we have been close to Feng, but my gunshot has spoiled our chances of finding him in the dark. It is my fault.'

The information was making Driscoll think more about Natalie than the missed opportunity. 'He wasn't warned off, then,' he said.

'We cannot be certain of it. If he has been told of our trap, maybe that is why he pays the railway worker to take the risk for him. Until you learn more, it is unwise to believe the girl is as innocent as you would like her to be.'

Resisting the temptation to mention his phone call to the villa, Driscoll gave the box to Melinkov. 'We need to have a look inside,' he said. 'Right now, it's all we've got.'

'We do it where we have more light. The army commander will be at home in bed so we can use his office.'

'What about that poor bastard with the hole in his leg? You're going to leave him to bleed to death, are you?'

Melinkov was uninterested. 'The soldiers can attend to him. For you and I there is more important business.'

The commander's office was located on a mezzanine floor above the *Kafe*, a stuffy windowless room lit with a single bulb and heated partly by the pungent fumes rising from the kitchen below and partly by an early twentieth century radiator that was standing by the wall in a puddle of hot water.

Melinkov placed the box on the desk. 'Which of us is the bravest, I wonder?' he said. 'You would like to open it?'

Driscoll wasn't about to volunteer. 'I couldn't open a door right now. I haven't got any feeling in my hands.'

'You use the cold as an excuse, I think.' Unconcerned about the possibility of there being a booby trap, the Russian turned the box upside down and studied several rows of screw-heads before reaching in to his satchel for a knife.

'That's a *Red-Ops* survival kit you carry around with you, is it?' Driscoll said.

Melinkov smiled. 'Except for binoculars and the AR-7 take-down rifle you have seen, I bring only my favourite handgun which has been made especially for me in Pakistan. It is based on the action from a .357 calibre Glock, and very nice. You would like to see it?'

'Another time.' Now that the Russian was using his knife to remove the screws, Driscoll had become aware of a vaguely familiar smell emanating from the box.

With two screws left to go, Melinkov stopped work. 'Something is the matter?' he enquired. 'You believe it contains a detonator and some C4?'

'No.' Driscoll couldn't recall where he'd encountered the smell before. 'Carry on. I don't think there's anything dangerous inside.'

There wasn't. The box was three quarters empty. Nestled together at the end furthest from the magnetic strips, a hand-held Garmin GPS unit and a Nokia mobile phone were wired to a small, encapsulated printed circuit board.

'Ah.' Melinkov was pleased. 'It is as I say it will be.' Using his knife again, he started teasing apart two of the wires.

'I wouldn't do that if I were you,' Driscoll said.

'You are worried that if I touch the wrong wire the phone will make its call and I shall start a landslide fifty kilometres away from here?'

'Why take the risk?' Now the smell was stronger, Driscoll had been able to locate the source. It was coming from blobs of adhesive that had been used to hold the phone and GPS unit in place – some kind of glue from which residual solvents were evaporating now the box had been brought into a heated room and opened up.

'So,' Melinkov said. 'We must decide whether we have frightened Feng away, or whether we have not.'

'We've already decided. That's why we didn't bother looking for him outside the fence.'

'No. No. I mean for tomorrow.'

'It's already tomorrow.' Driscoll checked his watch. 'It'll be daylight in a few hours. Anyway, he's not going to be stupid enough to try again, is he?'

'Stupid, no: determined, yes. Perhaps to give himself a better opportunity at another time, he allows us to find this transmitter because it is a decoy.'

'One of these days you're going to out-think yourself.' Driscoll was tired of the speculation and the manoeuvring. 'If he turns up somewhere later, that's fine. We're not going to get anywhere trying to cover everything when we haven't any idea what he might do and what he mightn't.'

'You are sour from too long outside in the cold. Until it is time for us to follow the train, you should stay here and get some sleep.' Melinkov picked up the box and headed for the door. 'I myself have something else to do.'

'What?'

'It is necessary for me to make my report to Mr Yukos. He is the director of Energex in Moscow – a difficult man who will not be pleased to learn of our failure tonight.'

'Speak for yourself,' Driscoll said. 'I didn't shoot anyone. You did. Tell him it's his fault for sending a mad bastard like you.'

Melinkov grinned. 'I will see what he says. In the meantime there is something personal I wish you to know.'

'Which is?'

'I understand your problem with Miss Washburn, but I must tell you that no good can come from you thinking of a girl who all men would like to enjoy in bed. There are many pretty Chinese girls with nice tits and long legs whom you could trust more easily, so if you are to have any peace, you must forget about her.'

Besides it being unwanted advice, it turned out to be the best possible way of ensuring that, try as he might over the next hour and a half, Driscoll would be unable to think of anything else.

At seven o'clock, having abandoned any idea of sleeping, he went downstairs to use the *Kafe* phone again, this time placing a call not to Santorini, but to Paris.

It was answered by the same woman who'd answered the call he'd made from England a month ago.

'Hi, this is Peter Driscoll.' He made himself sound positive. 'Is Natalie there?'

'I am sorry. She is not.'

'You don't happen to know where I can get hold of her, do you?'

'You could perhaps try her office in Shanghai.'

The news caught Driscoll wrong-footed. 'You don't mean Santorini, do you?' he said.

'She is no longer on the island. Last week she phones to say I will receive an airline ticket so I may join her there for a holiday. The ticket comes to me by courier, but before I can use it, she calls again to say she must return to China on important business. I tell her she works too hard, but like all girls of today, she will not listen to her mother. If you will give me your number, when next I hear from her I can ask her to contact you.'

'Thanks anyway, but I don't know where I'll be.' For several minutes after he'd said goodbye and ended the call he maintained his grip on the receiver, trying to crush it in his hand, realizing how thoroughly he'd been deluding himself and knowing that because of the roller-coaster ride he'd been suckered into taking, he'd wound up no further ahead than when he'd started.

Melinkov had been right, he thought; never trust a pretty girl – a fundamental truth from someone who not long ago had thought no more about trying to put a bullet through Natalie's head than he had about shooting the railway worker in the leg tonight.

*

By Russian standards, the morning traffic on the M36 was reasonably heavy, consisting mostly of trucks of varying sizes mixed with the odd car here and there. Only on the outskirts of villages was there any congestion, caused more often than not by horse-drawn carts or peasant farmers pushing barrowloads of produce or manure along the road.

From the passenger seat of the Lexus it was easy to gain the wrong impression of the countryside. The snow made everything look fresh, but Driscoll had spent long enough in the streets of Chelyabinsk to know that, underneath it all, the rural communities they were passing through would be as depressingly grim and dirty as the poorer areas of the cities.

The Lexus belonged to Energex, a two year-old, high-mileage car that had suffered from too many winter trips across the Urals, and from the long hauls it had made to the oil fields in Kazakhstan.

The ENX logos on the mud-streaked doors were all but unrecognizable, and the windshield had been so badly damaged by stone chips and abraded by windblown sand that it would've been almost impossible to see through it on a sunny day.

Today there was no sun. Nor were there any clouds. Instead, in all directions, the sky was uniformly overcast and dull, a dreary combination that had done little to provide a lift to Driscoll's spirits.

The delayed departure of the train hadn't helped either. At Melinkov's insistence, once there had been sufficient light, a squad of soldiers had been instructed to conduct a comprehensive inspection of the locomotive, the railcars and a wagon that had been coupled up overnight to the rear of the train.

They'd found nothing, but the search had taken so long that Driscoll had soon lost interest, bitter after his phone call, and too disillusioned to worry about the possible presence of a second trigger.

But that had been then – before they'd set out on their drive in the comfort of the Lexus, and before he'd considered the risk to the soldiers who were travelling on board the train.

Three armed men were accompanying the driver in the locomotive, and six more were in the wagon – all carrying assault rifles, but with not a round of ammunition between them – recruits who'd been told they were guarding a shipment of radioactive waste when in reality they were little more than window dressing.

The subterfuge was pretty thin, Driscoll thought, and not entirely without risk. If Feng had a workable fallback plan, and if he wasn't already halfway back to China, there was a chance of every one of these young men losing their lives.

'What happens if we hear a satellite's picked up a thermal image of a snowmobile parked on the edge of our rock-face?' he asked.

Melinkov was temporarily too busy to reply. For the last twenty minutes, when he hadn't been puffing on a cigarette, he'd either been receiving information over the speaker of the car phone or using his radio or his mobile, cursing alternately in Russian or English whenever he lost reception or when other vehicles were slow to let him overtake.

'If there is such a snowmobile, we should be happy,' he said. 'We shall proceed to the nearest bar where we can celebrate while others do our work for us.'

'As long as it's Feng and not someone else he's paid to do the job.'

Melinkov grinned. 'Whoever is there, this time I promise not to shoot them.'

Unlike Driscoll, the Russian was in a good mood. He'd been in a good mood since before daybreak, presumably because his obligatory phone call to Vladimir Yukos had gone better than he'd expected, or maybe just because he was glad to be on the move again.

During the last half hour, the M36 had swung more to the west, and they were gradually travelling further and further away from the railway line along the edge of a forest.

Driscoll had seen some of the Ural forests from the air, vast tracts of pine, larch and Russian birch covering the lower slopes of the foothills for hundreds of square miles – densely wooded regions that would provide the perfect escape route for a potential saboteur, although so far there had been no confirmed sightings of anyone suspicious.

According to Melinkov's communications centre, the train was making good progress, maintaining a higher than usual average speed, and with the driver reporting nothing out of the ordinary over his radio.

The situation was to be short-lived.

While Melinkov was squeezing the Lexus past a truck that had finally pulled over to let them by, his mobile began to ring, and messages started flooding in over the radio and the car phone.

'Good news or bad news?' The only words Driscoll had been able to recognize were satellite, kilometre and American.

'Wait.' Melinkov held up a hand. He answered one of the calls, issuing what sounded like a series of terse instructions, then put his foot down.

'Well?' Driscoll said.

'Two men Energex have stationed near the turning to Jeman□elinsk say that in the last minute a car has stopped somewhere on the bridge.'

'Have the Americans got it on satellite?'

'On a day like this, their cloud-penetrating technology seems to have some limitations. I am told they have an infrared signature of what they believe is a stationary vehicle, but they are not yet sure where it may be parked. The geospatial data is being worked on now.'

'How far away are the men from the bridge?'

'They say they first see the car with binoculars, so I think they are not so close.' Melinkov held down his horn button to frighten the driver of a slow-moving van. 'But it will not matter. If it is Feng on the bridge, they will have time enough to get him. He has to watch and wait for the train to reach the rock-face before he can detonate his charges.'

'No he doesn't.' Driscoll had remembered something. 'How long before it goes under the bridge?'

'I have not enquired. One or two minutes perhaps. By then we shall be close enough to see for ourselves.'

'Radio the driver,' Driscoll said. 'Now. Tell him to jam on every brake he has.'

'For what reason? There is no danger. Feng may be in position and ready to push a button, but by having to stay on the bridge until he sees the railcars are in the right place, he makes a big mistake.'

'For Christ's sake,' Driscoll shouted. 'Radio the fucking driver. Feng doesn't have to stay or wait. He's going to drop one of his GPS phone transmitters on to the train. He'll be gone before your men get anywhere near him.'

'He would not be so foolish. To aim between metal casks that are travelling at seventy kilometres an hour is not possible. He will know that any object would at once bounce off.'

Realizing the futility of grabbing the radio and yelling out a warning of his own in English, Driscoll forced himself to remain calm. 'Listen to me,' he said. 'Remember that smell from the box we opened up? It was coming from the stuff on the outside of a sticky bomb. I've smelt it before – when I was in Angola.'

'I see.' Melinkov's expression changed. 'I am not so familiar with

these weapons. Sticky bombs are those devices much favoured by guer-
rillas for attacking armoured vehicles at close quarters, are they not?'

'Yep. The adhesive comes from an armament factory in
Czechoslovakia. Bury a fuse and handful of Semtex in the middle of a
blob of the stuff and it'll stick to anything you throw it at. You can't
touch it with your fingers or you'll never get it off again.'

'I am sorry.' The Russian glanced at his watch. 'Had I been quicker
to understand, we would have more time.' Speaking in to his phone
again, he began relaying what Driscoll hoped were urgent instructions,
not just to his communication centre and the locomotive driver, but to
whoever was in charge of the nine unwitting soldiers.

Melinkov was driving faster, holding the Lexus in third gear and
braking late, using all the road on bends which he judged were free of
ice and increasing his speed at every opportunity.

He was taking risks as well, twice scattering oncoming traffic when
he'd refused to back off during overtaking moves and, now he'd caught
sight of the Jeman□elinsk junction, putting the car into a slide to slow it
down before they had to make the turn.

'How far's the bridge?' Driscoll braced himself for a collision.

'I am not certain.' Melinkov swore as the car rebounded off a bank
of packed-down snow. 'Please to get my rifle from the satchel on the
seat behind you. Since I cannot assemble it while I drive, you must do
it for me.'

There wasn't time. No sooner had Driscoll got his hand on the
satchel than he saw the bridge.

There was no car parked on it. Instead, the bodies of two men lay
sprawled on the road in pools of blood, while 500 yards up the line,
with sparks coming from every wheel, the train was approaching the
rock-face at an alarming rate.

'Keep going,' Driscoll yelled. 'Feng thinks he has to drive downwind.
We can catch him up.'

'It is not necessary.' Melinkov brought the car to a standstill on the
centre of the bridge. 'If roadblocks fail, the helicopters will drop road-
spikes from the air, and they have men on board who can use gas canis-
ters, stun grenades and tasers. We stay here to see what happens.'

Driscoll already knew what was going to happen. No matter how
fiercely the train's brakes had been applied, at seventy kilometres an
hour, an emergency stop for several hundred tons of locomotive, railcars and sand-filled casks was always going to take too long.

131

Leaving Melinkov to warn the driver and the soldiers of an imminent disaster, he got out and went over to the bridge rail.

The train was decelerating, but as though in slow motion – losing speed at a rate that was agonizingly slow to watch.

So where was the damn trigger, he wondered? Where the hell was it? Halfway along, or stuck to the roof of the locomotive – the worst possible place for a GPS unit that at any minute was going to wake up and transmit a fatal message to the phone beside it?

Melinkov was coming to watch as well. Evidently more fascinated than dismayed, he stepped over one of the bodies and joined Driscoll at the rail, using his binoculars to scan along each of the railcars. 'I have told the driver and soldiers they must jump,' he said. 'But I think they are frightened because until now the train has been travelling too fast.'

It wasn't travelling fast any more. It had nearly stopped – not before it had reached the rock-face, but immediately beneath it.

In spite of the wagon being nearly a kilometre away, Driscoll didn't need binoculars to see men beginning to spill out of it.

Leaving their companions to follow, three of them had dropped their rifles and had started running back along the track, stumbling over snow-covered sleepers in their haste and endeavouring to keep well away from the hundred foot drop on the right hand side.

But they'd left their run too late, and they were never going to make it.

High above them, a billowing white wall had erupted skywards. For a moment it seemed to hang there, then, as the shock wave and the thud from the explosion reached the bridge, the entire wall darkened and began to fall, collapsing downwards in a swirling avalanche of boulders, giant rocks and snow to engulf the locomotive and five of the leading railcars.

A second later, swept away like a caterpillar in a rainstorm, the whole of the train was gone.

CHAPTER 14

Melinkov was impressed. Appearing to be no more concerned by the loss of the train and soldiers than he was by the presence of the two bloodstained bodies lying in the gutter of the bridge, he was continuing to use his binoculars, watching as the billowing cloud of snow finally started to disperse and settle into the ravine.

'So Energex have failed,' he said. 'Beijing will be pleased with their work today.'

'They won't be pleased for long.' Driscoll was endeavouring to get a grip on his own feelings. 'They're going to be pissed off when they hear the casks were filled with sand.'

'They will not find out.' Melinkov lowered his binoculars. 'Moscow will be anxious to prevent another of these deliberate accidents from taking place on Russian soil, so already they will be working on the wording of a press statement, and if they are clever, soon they will start evacuating the neighbouring towns and villages.'

'That's not going to help London and Washington much, is it? If your people don't get hold of Feng in the next few minutes he'll have disappeared into one of those forests. If he gets that far, he's gone.'

'I shall check to see if his position has been determined.'

Instead of going back to the Lexus with Melinkov, Driscoll remained standing where he was in the cold, wondering what he was going to do now and considering if there was anything to be gained by telling the Russian about his wasted phone calls to Paris and Santorini.

On balance there wasn't, he decided. To Melinkov, Natalie was just another player in the international fight for oil, no more important to anyone than Charles Collier, Rebecca Wilson and the soldiers on the train had been. In a brave new world where economic survival was everything, and people counted for nothing, nobody gave a shit about who was working for who as long as the oil kept flowing in the right direction.

The thought was depressing, made worse by the unwanted memory of his last morning alone with Natalie on the island where, for a few brief hours, he'd been foolish enough to believe he'd got a fix on things.

The expression on Melinkov's face when he returned from the car showed that he didn't have much of a fix on anything either.

'Well?' Driscoll said.

'The Americans think Feng is somewhere on the road to Kolejga.' The Russian stopped to answer a call on the radio he'd brought with him, shouting angrily into it before holding it high above his head to allow whoever was listening to hear the throbbing from a rapidly approaching helicopter.

The chopper was coming from the north, the pilot flying low and following the railway line until he reached the scene of the accident and elected to hover in order to inspect the landslide.

By shouting into his radio again, Melinkov made sure the pilot didn't hover long.

The helicopter was one of the seven survey aircraft that Energex had ready to put into the skies today, its company insignia visible on the underside of the fuselage now it was sweeping towards the bridge and beginning to turn west, the pilot responding quickly to the commands he was receiving from Melinkov, or perhaps to those he was getting from the control centre that was supposed to be co-ordinating today's surveillance.

'If this is the best we can do, we do not deserve to capture Feng.' Melinkov was still annoyed. 'First we permit him to kill two of our men here on the bridge, then after allowing him to detonate his explosives, we are slow to pursue his car. When Energex cannot organize something as simple as this, is it any wonder the Chinese were suspicious of the survey data they were given?'

'Are the Americans sure they're tracking Feng's car, or do they only think it's his?' Driscoll was conscious of his own frustration.

Melinkov shrugged. 'I understand the road passes through valleys in areas of heavy forest, and that the US satellite is not ideally positioned to cover this region of the country.'

'What about the Russian satellites?'

'For political reasons, sometimes Moscow pretends that Russian technology is better than it is. You wish to stay here? Or shall we ourselves proceed towards Kolejga so we may be closer to Feng when he is apprehended?' Recognizing that his attempt at optimism had fallen flat, Melinkov busied himself by lighting a cigarette.

'I'd start thinking of some good excuses if I were you,' Driscoll said. 'If this turns out to be another screw up, you know who's going to be carrying the can, don't you? You've got nine soldiers buried up there on the line along with eighteen railcars, fifty-four casks, a locomotive and a driver. And you've got these poor bastards here.'

'It is not me but Energex who will take the blame. It will be their fault.' Melinkov blew out a stream of smoke. 'But they will not care. Over the years when things were going well for them, they have been paid enough for what they do.'

'Like you,' Driscoll said.

'I work hard for my money.'

'Yeah. Sure you do.' Overlaying Driscoll's frustration and sense of anti-climax was the realization that he was freezing. His feet were numb again, and now the breeze was freshening, for all the protection his fur-lined jacket was providing, he could have been wearing a summer shirt.

Further to the north, where the same breeze was carrying away the last vestiges of airborne dust and snow, the resting place of the train should have been easier to see by now. Instead, there was nothing but two black pencil lines of track disappearing into a mountainous pile of ice and rubble.

Strike one to Beijing, he thought – or it would have been if the veil of particles had been as lethal as it was supposed to be.

'Ah. We have news.' Melinkov had been listening to his radio again. 'Men from the helicopter are making ready to stop the car.'

'How are they going to do that?'

'They are to land on the road in front of it. Unless Feng is quick to reverse his vehicle, there is nowhere he can go.' Melinkov threw away his cigarette and headed off back to the Lexus again. 'We should hurry so you can be there to identify him.'

'What about these bodies?'

'Already I have asked for them to be collected, but I shall issue a reminder.'

There was no opportunity for him to do so. Before either of them had reached the car, calls started flooding in – firstly over Melinkov's mobile, then over his radio and finally over the phone in the car itself.

The Russian answered them one by one, this time keeping his voice level for the most part, and swearing only twice when whoever he was speaking to apparently refused to answer the string of questions he was asking.

Although it was evident that some kind of problem had arisen, not until Melinkov slammed the door of the Lexus and went to toss his cell phone and radio off the bridge could Driscoll be certain that whatever had been in the process of going wrong had already gone wrong.

'*Kuda delsja etot ublyudok.*' Melinkov watched as his phone and radio shattered into pieces on the rails below.

'What?' Driscoll said.

'The driver of the car is a simple farmer from Jeman□elinsk who earlier this morning has loaded his truck with cabbages for delivery to the market at Plast. While he is travelling through a valley he is over-taken by a car that stops on the road in front of him. When the farmer gets out to see what is happening, he is pistol-whipped by the driver who then takes over his truck and tells him that if he wishes to stay alive, he must drive the man's car on to Kolejga by himself.'

'Feng?'

'Perhaps. It is not possible to know.' Melinkov leaned over the bridge to spit. 'According to the report I receive, the farmer has said only that the man was warmly dressed and of Asian descent.'

In spite of fearing the worst, Driscoll hadn't expected the bad news quite so quickly. 'How far has the truck got?' he asked.

'It is one of many vehicles on the road that were not being tracked so closely. Without computers, the Americans say they can follow only a certain number of thermal images on their screens. On such a cloudy day, I think they are fortunate to get images of any kind.'

'Which means Feng's either been smart enough to make his move in the right place at the right time, or he's just a lucky bastard. Why can't the Americans tell the difference between the image of a car and a vegetable truck?'

Melinkov spread his hands. 'Ask me how best to blow up a wellhead in the desert and I will give you a good answer. But the only satellite picture I have seen was not of vehicles travelling on a road, but of the coast line of East Africa.' The Russian paused for a moment. 'Since there is nothing more we can do here, you are ready to go?'

'What are the chances of running down Feng after this?'

'They are poor. Energex are deploying their fixed-wing aircraft, and they have other helicopters in the air, but with every minute that passes, they have more and more roads to search.'

Last ditch effort, Driscoll thought, and one that was never going to work now. Feng had only to change vehicles again by pulling off the same stunt, and no one was ever going to find him.

'OK.' He was ready to leave, unsurprised by the outcome of an operation that had proved as fruitless as the one last night had been, and finding that already his thoughts were beginning to turn elsewhere – not to what might yet happen to a geological fault in California, or beneath the muddy waters of the Thames, but to the need to discover whether Feng had been able to elude them for reasons that had less to do with luck, and more to do with the young woman who'd kissed Driscoll goodbye at the airport on that last morning they'd spent together in Santorini.

During the drive back to Chelyabinsk, of all the memories he had of her, the one at the airport had proved to be the hardest to forget. Why that should have been, he wasn't sure. All he knew was that it had taken some hours for the memory to fade, and not until he'd come down here to wait for Melinkov in the busy hotel bar had he been able to rid himself of it altogether.

Watching a bunch of noisy Russians enjoying themselves was probably the therapy he'd needed, he decided. After too many hours in the cockpit of the Cessna and too long spent considering how he'd managed to get himself mixed up in any of this, it was easy to become divorced from the real world in which ordinary people went about the business of leading ordinary lives.

So which world had Natalie Washburn come from, he wondered: the real one, or the one inhabited by men like Feng and Melinkov or Collier and Gorman?

Because the question was unanswerable, he was glad when Melinkov arrived to interrupt his thoughts.

The Russian was freshly shaved, and as well as having changed his shirt and trousers, seemed to have shrugged off the disappointment of the day.

'No news of our comrade,' Driscoll said.

'No. If indeed it was Feng, I think we can assume he is lost to us, but I have something else for you.' He handed Driscoll one of the sheets of paper he'd brought with him. 'While I order myself a vodka, please to tell me what you think.'

'What is it?'

'You can see what it is. It is an email from Ji Sui-kai. Last night when I suggest she could obtain information on the Washburn girl for you, I believe you are unwilling to ask her for it, so instead I do it for you as a favour.'

'Crap. You did it for yourself. You want to know who Beijing have working for them as much as I do.'

'You are quick to accuse me when you have not yet looked at what I give you.'

Placing the sheet of paper on the bar, Driscoll started reading, trying not to skip, but doubting that an overnight email was going to shed much light on anything:

From: Ji Sui-kai, Energex, Shanghai
Sent: 13 March
To: Mr Victor Melinkov
Subject: Natalie Washburn

The following information comes principally from the People's Republic Department of Records and from the Beijing offices of the American-owned agency of Associated Press, who were able to provide a copy of Miss Washburn's CV and those details of her career history that remain on file at their New York headquarters where, for nearly two years, she was employed by them as their China-based oil industry correspondent.

Full name: Natalie Washburn (no middle name)
Age: 26
Born: Shanghai, June 1981
Father's name: Lewis Christopher Washburn
Mother's maiden name: Kezeng Ding
  • Parents appear to be separated – no record of divorce
  • Mother is presently living in France
  • Father's whereabouts are unknown, but in 2006 was working as an architect in Rhode Island, USA
Communist Sympathies or Affiliations: None listed or found
Qualifications: Linguistic degrees in English and French
Experience and Credits: *Feb 2004 to Dec 2006* – journalist employed in Shanghai by Associated Press to report on the Chinese petro-chemical industry with emphasis on those

projects having a direct bearing on the international market for crude oil, petroleum, natural gas, plastics and other oil-based chemicals and products.

2006 to present – working out of Shanghai as a freelance journalist. Takes frequent trips abroad to Russia, the US and France, but is having fewer articles published overseas than was the case when Miss Washburn was working for A.P. She is best known for several highly regarded studies of the Chinese oil industry, one of which was published in the Chinese Economic Quarterly in 2006.

The data was worthless, Driscoll thought. Besides containing no useful information that he didn't know already, the email offered no clue as to whether or not Natalie was being controlled or manipulated by some shadowy figure in Beijing.

Melinkov had recognized the need for tact, voicing his own opinion only after he'd lit a cigarette and swallowed half a glass of vodka. 'So now you are going to tell me your friend in Santorini is just a pretty girl,' he said.

'She's not in Santorini – not any more.'

'You know this for certain?'

'She wasn't there when I phoned her last night from the *Kafe* in the rail yard and her mother in Paris says she'd gone back to China on business.'

'I see. Why did you not tell me of this earlier?'

'What difference would it have made? Anyway, why would I want to tell you anything? A month ago you were getting paid to kill her – or have you forgotten that?'

'You are angry because the email is of little value.' Melinkov downed the rest of his vodka. 'What I say to you before is true. I ask Ji to send it only in case it can be helpful.'

'I don't need any help from you. When I do, I'll let you know. What's that other piece of paper you keep looking at?'

'It is a press statement that is being issued worldwide by the ITAR-TASS agency. Mr Yukos sends me this copy less than one hour ago. I am told that CNN and the BBC World Service are promising to run the story on TV tonight, and that, by tomorrow morning, English language newspapers like *The Moscow Times* and the *St Petersburg Times* will have been provided with aerial photos they will be permitted to print.'

'Is that copy of yours in English?'

'You wish to see it?'

'Not really.' Driscoll had a fair idea of what it would contain. 'You can read it to me if you want.'

'Very well.' Melinkov stubbed out his cigarette. 'At the top there is a headline that says RUSSIAN LANDSLIDE DERAILS TRAIN CARRYING NUCLEAR WASTE.' He looked up. 'You understand, or course, that what follows is intended to give the Chinese the information they are expecting to hear.'

'Are you going to read it out, or aren't you?'

'I am sorry. This is what it says. *"Following an accident in the Urals twenty-five kilometres south of Chelyabinsk at 1300 hours today, a train transporting a quantity of the high-level isotope Cesium 137 for processing at the Mayak Chemical Combine Plant was lost in an avalanche along with the driver of the locomotive and an as yet undisclosed number of military personnel who were accompanying the shipment.*

"According to a spokesman from EMERCOM, the Russian Emergency Control Ministry, since the wreckage is buried under a deep layer of rock and winter snow, the radiation levels are expected to remain low in the short term.

"However, EMERCOM say this is likely to change once the spring thaw begins, when the danger from ionizing radiation and radiological dispersion will present a much greater hazard to public health.

"Plans to evacuate neighbouring towns and villages are on hold pending the results from an urgent study into the feasibility of permanently entombing the wreckage in a concrete sarcophagus – a hazardous, twenty-four hours a day, seven days a week operation that, as long as the track can be cleared and repaired in time, will require many thousands of tons of concrete to be poured from special railcars travelling down from Chelyabinsk.

"The Ministry of Internal Affairs regrets that efforts to recover bodies can neither be attempted nor considered." '

After Melinkov stopped reading he gave the sheet to Driscoll. 'I think you do not listen,' he said. 'So you may have that to read later.'

The Russian was only half right. Driscoll had paid more attention than Melinkov imagined. Moscow had been clever, he thought. Everything sounded perfectly believable, and by coming up with an excuse that allowed them to avoid the expense of a wide-scale evacuation, they'd still managed to pretend the country had suffered a major disaster, although how much time that was going to buy the British and Americans was another question.

'You are not drinking?' Melinkov said.

'I don't feel like it. What do you figure will happen now?'

'Near Tuapse on the coast of the Black Sea, Energex have a private cottage where sometimes certain employees are permitted to enjoy a short holiday at the company's expense. Twice in the summer I have taken my daughter Catherine to stay there. When later tonight I make my phone call to Mr Yukos, I shall ask if it is possible for you and I to use it for a while.'

Before Driscoll could suggest that after today's fiasco, Melinkov might be better off looking for another job, a young woman from reception came hurrying in to the bar.

'There is a Mr Driscoll here?' she enquired.

'Over here.' He stood up.

'Ah.' She smiled at him. 'There is an overseas phone call for you. It is from a Mr Johnathon Collier in England. If you wish to take the call here, I can transfer it for you.'

'No, it's OK. I'll take it in my room. Give me a couple of minutes to get there.'

Giving Melinkov no opportunity to interfere, Driscoll left at once, guessing that Collier had heard the news, but without any idea of why the MP was finding it necessary to telephone.

The explanation was not long coming. Within a minute of Driscoll picking up the receiver and saying hello, the prospect of spending a few days with Melinkov at the coast was sounding a good deal more attractive than the option Collier was proposing.

'Why the hell would I want to go to California?' Driscoll said.

'Because Washington want you there, and because I want you there. Energex will be responsible for flying you to Los Angeles, and they'll be looking after you and Melinkov while you're in the States.'

'Why's Melinkov going?'

'In view of the need to restrict the number of people who know what's going on, and if the SAFOD project is really under threat – and after the events of today, I believe we can assume it is – he's the most qualified person Energex have on their payroll.'

'To do what?'

'What do you think? He's an experienced explosives expert who should be able to recommend the best way to disarm any underground devices if in reality there are any.'

'So Washington have heard about the train, have they?'

'They're in something of a panic in case news about Parkfield gets leaked to the press. That's why they've been on the damn phone for the last two hours. You know how things are over there right now. I'm afraid it's what comes from having a US President who's frightened half of America into believing only he and God can save them from another 9/11.'

'What's that got to do with me?'

'Energex's office in the US have called in a favour and arranged for you to play with some new equipment that's under development by the FBI. I understand it's a computer system that should allow you to generate a three-dimensional likeness of Feng in full colour.'

'And that's going to solve everything, is it?' Driscoll made no effort to keep the sarcasm from his voice.

'It's not the only reason you're going. As far as I can make out, after a lot of soul searching, Washington have taken one of the SAFOD geophysicists into their confidence, and he's insisting on meeting you in person.'

'Why?'

'You'll have to ask him. I imagine he's after a first-hand account of precisely what it was Feng said to you about the Parkfield project.'

'Tell him to phone me.' Driscoll had already made his decision. 'I'll pass on the trip if it's all the same to you, thanks.'

'This isn't a request. You'll be picked up from your hotel at nine o'clock tomorrow morning and taken to the airport where Energex will have the plane ready for you. It's about time you understood your position.'

'Meaning what?'

'Meaning that since you're suspected of selling drugs at the airstrip in China where my son lost his life, it's not in your best interests to have more details of your past disclosed.'

'What are you talking about?' Driscoll became more guarded.

'You know very well what I'm talking about. In the event of Energex choosing to release the Johannesburg report they have about your drug trafficking and gun-running activities in Africa, it wouldn't be hard for the British police to connect Rebecca Wilson's death with a drug deal she had the misfortune to interrupt that night in your brother's home.'

'A drug deal that was going down between me and Natalie?'

'Why not? There's that photo Gorman has of a Chinese narcotics dealer leaving the Hotan hotel where you and my son were staying.

Then, of course, there's the peculiar coincidence of Miss Washburn following you all the way from Shanghai to a house in Wiltshire.'

'And she's half-Chinese.'

'Exactly. Which brings me to another thing. I suppose you don't happen to know where she is, do you? She's stopped replying to my emails, and she's not answering the phone at the villa either.'

Having decided that the wisest course of action was to say as little as possible, Driscoll kept his mouth shut.

'Are you still there?' By now Collier had stopped trying to conceal his irritation.

'Yeah, I'm here. How would I know where she is? For the last two days I've been freezing my balls off in the middle of Russia watching a train fall of a cliff.'

'So you're not concerned?'

'Should I be?'

'I don't know, but it seems to me that after their success today, Beijing may believe they have no further need for non-diplomatic manoeuvring. They've made their position clear by giving us a demonstration of the consequences should we continue to drag our feet or refuse to meet their demands. If that's the case, they may regard you and Miss Washburn as being surplus to their requirements, so to speak, an unwanted complication they need to deal with – especially as you both have the ability to identify their man Feng.'

This time Driscoll was keeping quiet for a different reason. Suspecting Natalie of betraying his trust was one thing; that she could be dead because he'd left her at the villa to fend for herself was a possibility he wasn't ready to consider, and certainly not something he was going to discuss with Collier.

The MP was being careful not to overplay his hand. He was waiting – expecting the satisfaction of a response that Driscoll had no intention of giving him.

'What about Melinkov?' Driscoll changed the subject. 'Does he know he's being sent to the States?'

'Not yet. Once you and I have reached agreement, he'll be receiving his instructions directly from Energex in Moscow. Now Beijing have started the ball rolling, we must assume they'll be directing their attention to London or California fairly swiftly, so can I take it you'll be on the plane tomorrow?'

'Not until I've spoken to someone else first. I'll call you back in an hour.' Driscoll replaced the receiver before Collier could reply, wishing there was someone he could talk to, but knowing that, with Natalie either dead or back under the control of whoever the hell she worked for or didn't work for, the only person from whom he could seek advice was the Russian he'd left drinking at the bar downstairs – the *Red-Ops* hard-man whose future now seemed to have become somehow or other inextricably interwoven with his own.

CHAPTER 15

After his unwelcome departure from Santorini, Driscoll had found himself in an environment that had been unremittingly depressing. Not once in Chelyabinsk or Troik had he seen the sun, and not once while he'd been there could he recall the temperature rising above freezing.

But that had been four days ago. This morning, in place of the leaden cloud-filled skies of Russia, the sky above California was filled with sunshine, and there wasn't a cloud in sight.

From inside the car, how warm the day might yet turn out to be was hard to tell, but because the Energex driver had started adjusting the air conditioning controls more frequently, Driscoll took it as a sign that the weather was going to be at least as warm as it had been yesterday, even though yesterday he hadn't seen much of it.

Unlike Melinkov who, within an hour of their arrival in LA, had been whisked away by helicopter to the Parkfield site, Driscoll had spent the bulk of the afternoon in Bakersfield, closeted in a stuffy downtown office in the company of a quick-witted young woman from the FBI.

In his briefcase were the fruits of her labour, colour copies of the identikit pictures he'd helped produce on her computer, and a CD that enabled any PC to display a rotating image of Feng's facial features – or what were supposed to be Feng's facial features.

Driscoll was pleased with the end result – not because he'd provided information to generate a false likeness, but because he hadn't. A week ago, while he'd still been trying to look after Natalie and protect himself, there had been reason enough to withhold her photograph of Feng, but now she'd disappeared and made it clear that she didn't need anyone to guard her back, Driscoll had more or less stopped caring about his own.

Not that the identikit picture was going to be of much damn use, he thought. Even if Feng had visited the SAFOD project under some pretext or other in the past, it was wishful thinking to believe that showing the picture to scientists at a busy geological research site like Parkfield was going to produce anything in the way of leads.

He was also beginning to doubt whether there was such a place as Parkfield.

Already the trip from Bakersfield had taken twenty minutes longer than the driver had said it would, and still there was no sign of anything resembling the kind of installation he was expecting to see.

After they'd turned off highway 466 at Cholame, for a while the countryside had started to look more promising, but since then, the only road signs they'd come across were warnings about wandering cattle.

In the last minute or two, the driver had slowed the car as though he was searching for an intersection.

'Do you know where we are?' Driscoll asked.

'No, but that's got to be it.' The driver pointed ahead to a dirt road and mud-spattered sign on which the letters NSF had been freshly painted.

'It hasn't got SAFOD written on it,' Driscoll said.

'It's the only goddamn road around here that might lead to someplace we want to go.' Swinging off the tarmac, the driver made the turn, reducing his speed still further now that, instead of having to worry about wandering cattle, he was having to avoid ruts and potholes that looked as though they'd been caused by the passage of too many heavy vehicles.

The vehicles themselves were parked at the end of the road. There were dozens of them, mostly army trucks lined up in neat rows alongside low-loaders and diesel bowsers, while further away, military bulldozers and scrapers were busy levelling a hundred yard-long strip of ground to allow the last section of an imposing perimeter fence to be erected.

Like the fence around the Mayak Chemical Combine Plant in Chelyabinsk, this one, too, had coiled razor-wire along its top, but it was four feet higher, and if the warning placards were to be believed, once it was finished it was going to be electrified.

After threading his way through a maze of giant concrete blocks, the driver pulled up at a pair of reinforced steel gates where he handed his authorization documents to a uniformed army sergeant.

The sergeant glanced inside the car. 'You're Peter Driscoll, right?'

'Nine-thirty scheduled meeting with a Doctor Goldberg,' Driscoll said. 'I'm a bit late.'

'OK. Look, sorry about this, but since last Tuesday, no civilian vehicles are being allowed inside. I'll try calling Goldberg. If he's in his office he can grab a Jeep and come and get you.'

'Is his office over there somewhere?' Driscoll pointed to a cluster of prefabricated buildings.

'C Block. First door on the right. Do you wanna walk?'

Only in America, Driscoll thought. The buildings were less than 150 yards away, standing on an island of poorly manicured lawn in the centre of a compound that was nothing like any drilling site he'd seen before.

He got out of the car while the soldier was opening one of the gates, then headed off towards the building complex, realizing that, despite the presence of a solitary unused derrick and the usual mess that drillers left behind them, he'd been wrong to imagine the place would have anything in common with the sites he was more used to encountering in the oil fields.

The sandy-haired young man who came to meet him was in his twenties, wearing leather work-boots and causally dressed in jeans and a blue open-necked shirt.

'Hi. I'm Dan Goldberg.' He smiled as he shook hands. 'They didn't shoot you at the gate, then?'

'I thought they might be waiting until I got inside,' Driscoll said. 'Why no visitors' cars?'

'God knows.' Goldberg smiled again. 'You'd need a bigger bomb than you can jam in a car to do any good around here, but it's a waste of time trying to tell the army anything. Same with that nice fence they're building. If the bad guys want to get in, a twelve-foot fence isn't going to stop them. Still, the National Science Foundation say they're going to give us floodlights and have the road fixed, so I guess we can put up with things for another couple of weeks.'

'Is that when the military are pulling out?' Driscoll said.

'So they say. Come on. You haven't driven out here to hear me complain. I've got good coffee in my office.'

Goldberg's office was as low-key as the young man himself, a cramped, windowless room overflowing with books, charts and computer printouts, and made even smaller by several unstable-looking racks of telemetry equipment that were bolted to the walls.

Goldberg had been right about the coffee. An army officer was having it delivered three times a day from a restaurant in the nearby Parkfield township, he explained, an arrangement that was unlikely to last, but to be taken advantage of for as long as it did.

'Is Melinkov here?' Driscoll asked.

'He's around, unless he's got bored looking at the site plans and the reports I gave him. When I saw him last thing yesterday, he said he's got plenty of questions, but I think he's been waiting for you to arrive.' Goldberg sipped at his coffee. 'You probably won't believe me, but a month ago this place was a sleepy hollow. You could sit in the sun, listen to the birds and think about earthquakes for hours on end without anyone coming to disturb you.'

'Then it all went wrong,' Driscoll said.

'Pretty much. The first thing we know, a bunch of your people from Energex are here, and a week later the army are crawling over everything. Are you going to tell me who this guy Melinkov is and what he's doing, or do I have to guess?'

'How much do you know?' Driscoll didn't know whether to be cautious or not.

'I know you both work for this Energex outfit, and I've more or less figured out what business Energex is in. And I've been told you're the guy who knows about some terrorist who's supposed to have slipped explosives in to a couple of our holes.'

'But you don't think it's happened?' Driscoll had sensed Goldberg's scepticism.

'I didn't say that.'

'Is it possible?'

'I don't know. Up until this security clampdown, I guess it wouldn't have been too hard to break in here the night before we were scheduled to install equipment in a drilling. If we were half asleep, we wouldn't necessarily have known if someone had stripped out the guts of a seismometer and replaced it with a chunk of high explosive.'

'So instead of terrorists having to plant the charges themselves, you'd have done it for them.' Driscoll said.

'Maybe, but that's not why a fence is being built out there, is it? Ask any of those military guys why the panic, and they'll all tell you the same thing. They think the Department of Homeland Security has picked up intelligence about an organization that's planning to flatten half of Los Angeles by smashing their way in here and detonating enough TNT to set off a 7.9 magnitude earthquake.'

'What if your Department of Homeland Security people are right?'

'They aren't. It isn't going to happen because it can't.' Goldberg pushed aside a sheaf of computer printouts and picked up a book. 'It's a question of shock transmission versus the inertia and the energy absorption of a zillion tons of rock that's been sitting where it is forever and doesn't want to move. I'll show you.'

Driscoll watched as he stood the book on end on the floor and propped it at an angle against the side of his desk, gradually increasing the slope until it was in danger of slipping over.

'OK.' Goldberg straightened up. 'One side of the book we've got the North American Tectonic Plate, and jammed up against it on the other side we've got the Pacific Plate. Because of Continental Drift, for the last couple of hundred years or so the pressure between the two has been building up. That's the San Andreas fault.'

'Which is ready to let go at any time,' Driscoll said.

'Mostly because of the Pacific Plate. Since the big San Francisco quake in 1906 it's been moving north-west at a rate of around two inches a year. That's why we're in a hurry to find out how much longer the rock in the fault zone can stand the strain, and why we're measuring things like strata deformation and the increase in fluid pressure, in case that's going to be the straw that breaks the camel's back.' He handed Driscoll a ballpoint pen. 'Try this,' he said. 'You're a hairy-arsed terrorist who's smashed his way through the gates. When you drop that pen on the top of my desk, it'll be the same as you detonating half a ton of TNT or setting off a mini-nuke from my office.'

Driscoll didn't drop the pen on the desk. Instead, he leaned over and dropped it on the top edge of the book.

There was a satisfying thunk as the book fell flat on the floor, but for all the affect it had on Goldberg, it could have remained where it was. 'How are you going to do that?' he said. 'Even if you were smart enough to feed explosives into the heart of the Parkfield fault zone, what are you going to use to detonate them when they're two miles down at the bottom of a capped drill-hole that's lined with steel casings?'

'I don't know. Radio signals maybe.'

'Good luck. You still won't get a jolt that's anything like strong enough to do what you want it to do.' Goldberg stuck his hands in his pockets and sat down on the edge of the desk. 'You're not going to tell me what this is really all about, are you?'

'No.'

'And you're not going to tell me why the hell the Pentagon and the NSA are allowing a private company like Energex to send a Russian and an Englishman to poke around a research station that's being run by the US National Science Foundation?'

'No.' Driscoll had been expecting the questions, uncertain of how best to fend them off, and not yet sure whether Goldberg's confidence was misplaced. So far the physicist had showed little sign of alarm, appearing to be as unconcerned at the prospect of an explosion occurring two miles underground as he was about one that could take place on the surface.

But was he guessing, Driscoll wondered? Did anyone know enough about the geology of the San Andreas fault to guarantee it couldn't be artificially destabilized? Or was Goldberg unconcerned simply because he was convinced that the explosives were nothing more than the figment of someone's imagination?

'What if you're wrong?' Driscoll said. 'How bad could it be?'

'I will tell you.' It was Melinkov who had answered the question. He'd arrived unannounced and had been listening at the door without Driscoll realizing he was there.

'It will be very bad.' The Russian came in and removed a core sample from a chair so he could sit down. 'From one of the reports Dr Goldberg has been kind enough to lend me, I learn that during the April 1906 earthquake in San Francisco more than three thousand people die, half the population are left homeless and twenty-eight thousand buildings are destroyed. But that was then. Today, in the Bay Area alone, instead of the eight hundred thousand people who lived there in 1906 now the number is seven million. So you can see how serious a powerful earthquake will be.'

'It's not just people and buildings,' Goldberg said. 'You're looking at the near total loss of a three hundred and fifty billion dollar economy and that's without worrying about collateral damage from firestorms, tsunamis and landslides. And if we're talking about LA instead of San Francisco, there'll be flooding from a whole bunch of old 1920s dams that you can bet your life are going to fail up in the San Gabriel mountains.' He paused for a moment. 'Then there are things like Valley Fever. It's a real nasty fungus infection that can kill people who breathe in the dust from landslides. We had over a thousand cases of it after the

1994 Northridge quake, and that was just a little one.'

'But you said nothing's going to happen.' Driscoll was still thinking.

Goldberg smiled. 'No I didn't. What I said is that terrorists aren't going to make it happen. Everybody knows the fault's going to unlock itself sooner or later. The trick is figuring out when. We get good shakes here round about every twenty-two years, but the Parkfield zone hasn't had one of those for a while.'

'What's a bad shake?' Driscoll asked.

'Magnitude six or greater. Before 1966 we had them in 1934, 1922, 1901, 1881 and in 1857, so they're kind of regular.'

'OK.' To bring the discussion back on track, Driscoll tried another angle. 'Suppose you're the hairy-arsed terrorist,' he said. 'How would you go about it?'

'I don't know.' Goldberg frowned. 'You'd better let me have a think about that. You guys can sort out whatever it is you have to sort out while I go for a walk. Help yourself to more coffee if you want.'

'Hang on. If you're going for a walk, see what you can do with this.' Driscoll opened his case and took out two copies of the computer-generated images of Feng, handing one to Goldberg and giving the other to Melinkov.

'I thought we were talking about terrorists?' Goldberg was studying the picture.

'We are.'

'This guy doesn't look like an Arab to me.'

'Right.'

'I should've known not to ask, shouldn't I?' Goldberg headed for the door. 'Is he North Korean?'

Driscoll grinned. 'Not as far as I know.'

'OK. I'll see if any of our technicians remember seeing him around.'

Melinkov was waiting to offer his own opinion about the identikit picture. 'This is a good likeness of Comrade Feng?' he asked.

Driscoll nodded. 'Yeah, it is. The software that put it together is pretty damn smart. The girl who was driving the computer said she could call up five billion different combinations of facial characteristics. That's everything; warts, moles, colour of teeth, eye pigmentation, skin texture, pore size, eyelash thickness – you name it, she could display it on her screen.'

'I think it will not help us.' Melinkov returned the picture. 'Since yesterday I have learned much which is of interest. I will tell you about it later, but you should know that the first SAFOD pilot hole was drilled here as long ago as 2002. That means Beijing have had many years in which to send someone to do their work for them.'

'Let's see how Goldberg gets on. You never know.' Driscoll wasn't optimistic either, but the feeling was to be short-lived.

Less than two minutes after the young physicist had left the office, he came hurrying back in.

'Have you had some luck with the picture?' Driscoll asked.

'I didn't get that far.' Goldberg was still holding it but he'd been using a felt-tipped pen to sketch something on the back.

'It's easy,' he said. 'Look.' He laid the sketch on his desk. 'Imagine this cylinder I've drawn is a canister of high explosive that's sitting at the bottom of a drill hole. Never mind how it got there for a minute.'

'Does it matter how long it's been sitting in the hole?' Driscoll asked.

'No. That's the clever bit.' Goldberg drew three small squares inside the cylinder. 'Inside this first box is a battery and an electronic clock,' he said. 'The clock can be real tiny – no bigger than your fingernail. The second box holds a timer and a switch that's connected to a detonator, and the third box has an accelerometer or a shock sensor in it. They can be pretty tiny too.' He looked at Melinkov. 'That's all you need.'

'I am afraid I am a little slow.' Melinkov was continuing to inspect the sketch. 'But I think it is too simple.'

'OK.' Goldberg picked up a spool of paper which he unrolled on the floor. 'Seismic chart,' he said. 'The wavy trace is a record of all the earthquakes we've picked up from the fault zone over the last month. You can see how many of them there have been. The little ones are so small nobody's known about them before – right down to minus two on the Richter scale. We get those five or six times a day.' He drew his finger along the trace. 'But we get these bigger quakes about once a month and a decent sized jolt more or less every six months.'

Like Melinkov, Driscoll had been struggling to understand how Goldberg's device was intended to operate. 'Is the shock sensor the trigger?' he asked. 'Is that it?'

'Right. The day before stick your bomb in the hole, or pay someone else to do it, you start your clock and adjust the timer so it'll arm the bomb for you at some time in the future; that can be anything from a couple of days to six months – whatever you like. Then all you have to do is set your shock sensor to detect a certain magnitude of earthquake that's going to trip the switch and fire the detonator.'

'And sit back and wait.' Driscoll said.

Goldberg nodded. 'You could've installed one of these way back in January when we had dozens of contract drillers here, but it isn't going to be dangerous until the timer arms it, and even after that, the charge won't go off until the sensor picks up the exact size of jolt you've chosen as a trigger for it.'

The idea was almost too good, Driscoll thought. If in reality Beijing had developed something like this, the resultant disaster wouldn't just bear the hallmarks of an accident, the seismic records would confirm it as being an accident – a case of a minor unpreventable earthquake setting off the Big One.

Melinkov, though, had an altogether different perspective. He grinned at Goldberg, then left his chair and went to light a cigarette at the door.

'Your design has a flaw,' he said, 'one that no good bomb maker would allow.'

'What's that?'

'If you are still the terrorist, what can you do if I offer you one million dollars to disarm your bomb? With your idea, there is nothing you can do. After it has armed itself and lays waiting to be brought to life by a little earthquake, it will be too dangerous to retrieve. One small shake and it will explode.'

Goldberg thought for a moment. 'How about this?' Using his felt-tipped pen, he modified his sketch, creating a depression in the top of the cylinder and pointing to a thin line which he drew across the middle of it. 'Short length of wire,' he said, 'an exposed part of the connection between the sensor switch and the detonator. Give me my million dollars and I'll tell you how to disarm the whole thing in five minutes.'

Melinkov was grinning again. 'This time I am quicker,' he said. 'You will instruct me to pour acid into the drillings to dissolve the piece of wire which in turn will break the connection to make the bomb safe.'

'It's pretty Mickey Mouse. There'll be a better way.' Goldberg appeared to be losing interest. 'Look, I don't know one end of a goddamn detonator from the other. I'm making this up as I go along. You don't need me to tell you what one of these things could look like. There are plenty of experts around: ask one of them.'

Driscoll, too, was tiring of the game, once again realizing how far out of his depth he was, and reluctant to waste any more time on guesses and theories.

Intending to get some fresh air he went to join Melinkov in the doorway, but for no good reason carried on walking out across the compound by himself, no longer so conscious of the sunny day, but of how unstable the ground beneath his feet had suddenly become.

CHAPTER 16

With the California sun not yet at its zenith, in London the day had long been over, and after a dull morning and an equally gloomy afternoon during which the sun had not been seen at all, a cold mist had settled over the Thames Embankment where three men had gathered for a meeting.

For a fourth man, the evening chill had gone unnoticed. Over the course of a political career that had consumed nearly two decades of his life, Johnathon Collier had grown indifferent to the weather, and in recent years, just as he'd learned to forget the passing of his first wife, so had he learned to ignore the passing of the seasons.

Tonight, though, because the poor lighting was making it difficult to read the faces of the men who had been summoned here to see him, he was rather wishing he'd arranged to conduct his affairs in more comfortable surroundings.

It had been his idea to meet the three Energex directors in the open air, a safety measure to guard against the possibility of their conversation being recorded or overheard – something to be avoided at all costs given the delicate nature of what he had to tell them, but a precaution that he thought had probably been unnecessary now he'd been able to gauge the extent of their willingness to co-operate.

If there was going to be a problem, it would come from Yukos, Collier decided. Since the Russians were claiming to have suffered a disaster in which tons of radioactive waste had spilled from the train, Yukos could be feeling secure enough to act accordingly.

Sir Oliver Fox, on the other hand, was likely to bluster, while, in the event of a showdown, Senator McCloskey would be expecting to receive the backing of his colleagues in Congress – support that Collier was confident would evaporate the minute Washington realized their integrity was being challenged.

Sir Oliver was the first to voice an opinion. 'I appreciate the government finds itself in something of a dilemma,' he said, 'but you have no understanding of the corporate world. There's a limit to the resources we can commit to finding this man Feng, whoever he is. I'm afraid Energex is neither a police force nor a government department that enjoys funding from the public purse.'

Collier smiled. 'I doubt the public would share your view about funding if the number of loans and grants you've been receiving was to be more widely known. But we can talk about that later. For the moment, all I wish to do is make it clear that should accidents occur in Britain or the US of the kind we've been threatened with, there will be no official suggestion of any Chinese involvement. Let me repeat that: the Chinese will not be implicated. The accidents will be accidents, and they will be reported as such. Privately, however, the US, Russian and British governments will be holding you responsible, and in the interests of maintaining political stability, Energex will become a sacrificial lamb. That means, as directors of the company, you will be arrested on what will appear to be unrelated charges, and at a later date after proper proceedings, you will be prosecuted and convicted of conspiring to defraud the China National Petroleum Corporation.'

Yukos had been listening in silence; now though his patience seemed to have run out. 'I have been brought all the way from Moscow to be told this?' he said.

'I haven't finished.' There was no emotion in Collier's voice. 'In case you're wondering, you should assume that any court ruling will include instructions for the break-up and disposal of all Energex assets, the proceeds of which will go towards a payment to compensate the Chinese for the regrettable loss of revenue from their oil reserves.'

'Along with a crap apology.' This time it was McCloskey who'd become impatient.

Unlike Vladimir Yukos, who was a thin-faced, aesthetic-looking man, the US Senator was someone who had long since given up the battle to control his weight. Even in the dim light of the embankment street lamps, it was easy to see the fleshiness of his face – a sign that he shared Sir Oliver's weakness for good living.

But that wasn't McCloskey's only problem, Collier realized. He was intellectually weak as well – a man who hid his ignorance behind a smokescreen of self-importance.

McCloskey stepped forward and jabbed a finger against Collier's chest. 'You listen to me,' he said. 'If you think I'm going to let some two-bit British politician lecture me about what I can do, and what I can't do, you're in for a big surprise. You don't speak for Washington. The minute they hear about this, you're finished.'

'Really.' Collier raised his eyebrows. 'I have no idea who you intend approaching when you get home, but you may care to check your position with the US Administration first. I think you'll find the White House has a rather definite preference about how they want this matter handled.'

'If the shit hits the fan we can go public.' McCloskey took away his finger. 'What are you going to do if we leak the truth?'

'What truth is that, exactly? Where will your evidence come from? Even if there was any – which you know very well there isn't – ask yourself this: in the wake of the Enron scandal and goodness knows what else, what credibility do you imagine you'd have? There's nothing particularly unusual or underhand about the government grants and loans Energex has been receiving. They may have been excessive, but they've all been perfectly legitimate. In those circumstances, I think the public and the media would be more than willing to believe you've been falsifying your survey data and destroying Chinese-owned oil wells in return for illicit payments from rival petrochemical companies. It's a shame how common that sort of thing has become in the world today.'

Sir Oliver looked as though he'd been on the point of saying something, but had changed his mind. 'Have you heard from Melinkov and Driscoll?' he asked.

'Not yet.'

'What about that Chinese girl you've got stationed in Greece?'

'What about her?' Collier's expression remained the same.

'Feng is still communicating through her, is he?'

'No. Some doubt has arisen about who she might be working for, but someone's already been sent to find out and take her place, so I see no reason for concern.'

Yukos had sensed an opening. 'For you, no reason perhaps,' he said. 'But if you have made a mistake with the girl, why should we trust who it is you send to Santorini now?'

'Because I can't afford to make as big a mistake at my end as you've just made in Russia. If I have, God only knows what we could be faced with next.' Before he'd finished speaking, Collier knew he'd revealed the level of his own apprehension and in so doing had temporarily undermined his position of authority.

In an attempt to recover it, over the next ten minutes he worked hard, avoiding any further mention of the penalty for failure, and deflecting questions as best he could, until he judged the time was right to end the discussion and leave the three Energex directors to formulate their plans alone.

Whether or not he'd timed his departure well, he found it hard to know, and it was harder still to know whether the outcome of this evening's meeting was likely to be successful. What Collier did know was that so great would be the real penalty for failure, it would unquestionably mark the end of his career.

How soon that might come to pass was made clear when he called in briefly at his office on his way home and found an email waiting for him.

It was from his secretary, a long message from Sheila Stanton outlining the progress she'd made at the end of her second full day on Santorini, and an attachment that Collier fervently wished he'd never seen.

After telephoning his wife to say he'd be with her in half an hour, he sat down at his desk, telling himself there was little to be gained by overreacting, and deliberately doing nothing for several minutes before he made the effort to read the message through more calmly:

FROM: Sheila Stanton, Santorini
SENT: 2345 hours, 16 March
TO: The Rt Hon. Johnathon Collier
SUBJECT: Communiqué as requested

Dear Mr Collier,
First things first: as you anticipated, obtaining passenger lists from any of the airlines operating out of here has proved most difficult. However, I can report that Natalie Washburn boarded an Olympic Airways flight to Athens at 0930 hours on the morning of 12 March.

Two and a half hours after her arrival in Athens she transferred to Olympic Airways flight 05 to Delhi where she had a pre-booked reservation on Air China flight 496 to Hong Kong. From there, I have been unable to discover where she could have gone.

With the exception of her laptop computer which was still on standby when I arrived here at the villa, none of her belongings remains, and I do not believe you should be expecting her to return at any time soon, if at all.

Her personal computer files have been deleted, but perhaps if I were to bring her laptop back to London, someone cleverer than I am would be able to retrieve at least part of the lost data.

The communication that follows was received on Miss Washburn's computer shortly before ten o'clock this morning. The contents are, of course, alarming, but in the light of new initiatives, overtures and concessions being offered to Beijing by the Americans, I suppose we should not be too surprised. In case you have been too busy to keep up with the news, the Chinese President, Hu Jintao, has been invited to visit the US again in August of next year.

According to CNN, on this occasion the visit is to be more than a photo-op and will include meetings, not just at the White House, but also at Camp David and the ranch of the US President.

Washington have also softened their rhetoric about Beijing's refusal to allow the Chinese currency to rise in value, and seem to be hinting at greater tariff reductions on Chinese imports than those offered privately through the Driscoll/Washburn/Feng communication channel.

In line with the emails you showed me before I left London, the one that came today was unsigned and addressed to no one, so it is difficult for me to verify its authenticity. Consequently I repro-duce it here exactly as it was received. In view of the contents, if you think I would be of more use to you back in the office, please let me know.
Sheila Stanton

Following the recent nuclear accident near Chelyabinsk, the greatest sympathy is extended to the Russian people. In an increasingly dangerous world where harmonious international relations have become essential, countries must help each other and work together if tragedies of a similar kind are to be avoided in the future.

When the governments of Britain and the United States are known to share this view, it is all the more perplexing why they should be so reluctant to acknowledge the right of others to seek reparation for wrongs inflicted on them.

In this regard, whether an event to highlight the need for co-operation will go ahead in Britain at the scheduled time of 2.00 p.m. on 27 March will be dependent on the maintenance of the goodwill that exists between the peoples and governments of all like-minded nations.

So much for the Special Relationship between the UK and the US, Collier thought. Predictably, by continuing to do what Washington had been doing since before the invasion of Iraq, the Americans had bought themselves a reprieve at Parkfield and had successfully shifted the emphasis to Britain where the *Richard Montgomery* time bomb had started ticking in earnest.

It was a lesson, Collier decided. For those of his peers who had been stupid enough and misguided enough to imagine they could stem the red tide of Chinese nationalism, this was the end game. And ten days from now, it would be because of them that England could be facing disaster on a scale not seen since the worst of the bombing in World War II.

This time when he reached for his phone, it was not to contact his wife; it was to arrange an emergency meeting with a colleague in the Ministry of Defence and to place an urgent call to the Energex office in Los Angeles.

CHAPTER 17

In Africa, and on more than one occasion while he'd been flying around the Chinese north-west desert, Driscoll had come across mysterious hidden villages and communities – places so otherworldly that he'd never quite got them out of his mind.

By the end of his second day back in England, he'd started to think that, in its own way, the Isle of Grain was equally unique, and by this morning now the rain had eased, and he was able to see out across the estuary properly for the first time, he was inclined to believe that this forgotten part of the country was one of the strangest places he'd ever been.

Even Gorman was conscious of the odd surroundings. During their return trip to inspect the power station and the container terminal, he'd started using the word weird to describe an atmosphere that was no less peculiar here on the waterfront of the Grain township than it had been along the mudflats and the more isolated stretches of coastline they'd just come from.

Gorman parked the car outside the house and went to unlock the front door. 'Either of you want a leak before we get down to business?' he asked.

Driscoll shook his head.

'I too am all right.' Melinkov pointed to what looked like a medieval fortress or a derelict tower block that seemed to be floating above the water 500 yards offshore. 'That is where we are to go this afternoon?'

'Last chance we'll get.' Gorman headed for the stairs. 'The army are closing it off tonight. I'll meet you in the briefing room. While you're waiting, you can take a look through those police reports Collier sent over.'

Unlike Driscoll, who had already reached the point where another hour in Gorman's company would be another hour too long, Melinkov was handling the situation better, by and large concealing his contempt of the man by patronizing him and only admitting to his frustration when he was alone with Driscoll.

'We cannot go on in this manner,' he said. 'If we continue to do only what Gorman thinks we should do, we will go nowhere and achieve nothing.'

'I know.' Driscoll made his way along the corridor and entered the room where Gorman had set up his Energex headquarters.

Although two electric heaters were switched on, as usual the room was cold and damp and, if anything, the all-pervading smell of the estuary mudflats was stronger in here than it was outside.

Not that Gorman would notice or care, Driscoll thought. With his job on the line, he would have jumped at the chance to rent any building in Grain, regardless of how long the place had been unoccupied or how damp and rundown it was.

Melinkov was glancing through the police reports. 'In English, when a man seeks foolishly to solve a problem you say he is seizing for straws, do you not?' he said.

'Grasping at straws,' Driscoll said. 'Is that what Collier's doing?'

'He is mistaken if he believes this information can assist us in our hunt for Feng. With so much crime in the Isle of Grain, if Feng is here or if he has been here, it is not possible to know for how much of it he has been responsible.'

'What are you talking about?'

The Russian kept a straight face. 'In the last six months alone there has been an arrest for disorderly behaviour, and a false report of a burglary that is made by a woman who tries to claim on her insurance. Then there is the case of a young boy who runs away and injures his leg after he is caught breaking into a warehouse, three minor car accidents and two brothers who are found drunk on the same night. Now I have read of these things, I think we should have stayed in America where it is much safer.'

Driscoll grinned. 'That's what you get with no cinema, no night clubs and only one pub. Goldberg said Parkfield used to be a sleepy hollow, but I guess he's never been to the Isle of Grain.'

'I am not surprised. When there are many pleasant parts of your country to visit and to live, why would a man wish to spend his time looking at mudflats and grey water in a place where no one comes?'

'I'll tell you,' Driscoll said. 'This isn't Russia. In England you can live wherever you want. The people here like it the way it is. They don't want anyone else coming to look at their mudflats.'

'Then they will be unhappy to have men from Energex and navy divers and soldiers in their streets. I think the people are not pleased to have their peace disturbed like this.'

'Fuck the people.' Gorman marched into the room. 'Unless we get a lucky break, it's going to get a hell of a lot worse than it is right now.'

'We're going to get a lucky break by sightseeing, are we?' Driscoll said.

'No.' Gorman went to stand behind his desk. 'Energex needs a legitimate reason for having their staff in town.'

'And us visiting a container terminal is a reason?'

'For Christ's sake Driscoll. Where were you yesterday? Weren't you listening?'

'All you said yesterday is that if anyone wants to know, Energex are carrying out a survey for British Petroleum. Who's going to believe that when the oil refinery BP had here was washed away in 1953?'

'The container business just happens to be sitting on land that's owned by BP. You're supposed to be part of a team that's looking at the potential of the site for redevelopment. Do you think you can remember that?'

The link between BP and Energex was tenuous at best, Driscoll thought, and one that was likely to backfire in Gorman's face if he wasn't careful.

'You got a better idea?' Gorman asked.

'How can we pretend to be surveying anything when the whole area around here has been declared a no-fly zone?'

'It's not the whole area; it's just a bit of it.' Gorman slapped a hand against the map that was pinned to the wall. 'Below thirty thousand feet, the airspace over the *Richard Montgomery* has always been a no-fly zone. If you'd read half the stuff in the file I gave you, you'd already know that. If you don't believe me, check with the Maritime and Coastguard Agency, then have a look at an Admiralty chart. Anything else you want to know is in the file – designation of the wreck under Section 2 of the British Protection of Wrecks Act 1973; exclusion zone co-ordinates for shipping; who's responsible for twenty-four hour surveillance of the wreck site; who maintains the warning buoys around it, and what happens to people like you who might get too close because they don't give two fucks about rules and regulations.'

'Sounds more like you than me,' Driscoll said. 'Who was it that didn't give two fucks about supplying the China National Petroleum Corporation with cooked-up survey data?'

'If you want to talk about that, ask Sir Oliver. I only do what I'm told.' Having failed to score any points, Gorman's temper was getting the better of him. 'Tell you what,' he said, 'if this is all too hard for you, why don't you just piss off?'

'OK. I'll let Collier know you don't need me anymore.'

Melinkov had anticipated Driscoll's response and had gone to block the door. 'This will not help to solve our problem,' he said. 'A man who acts in haste is a man who will have regrets. From what you have told me, if Collier wishes to do so, he can still make things difficult for you.'

'Screw him.' Driscoll wasn't in the mood for Russian proverbs. 'And screw you too. Get out of my way.'

'No, no.' Melinkov stayed where he was. 'If we are to discover whether Feng is here or if he has been here, we must put aside our differences. Only by working together will we have a chance to beat him.'

For Melinkov, that's all this was, Driscoll thought; a game to see who could beat who and find out who would be the winner. On the other hand, unlike Gorman who seemed to believe that by protecting Energex he was somehow safeguarding his own position, Melinkov was at least being honest in circumstances where honesty had been abandoned months ago by the other players of the game.

Driscoll remained halfway to the door. 'How long do you think it'll be before someone orders an evacuation?' he said.

Gorman shrugged. 'You tell me. If we can't find anything, and the army and navy can't find anything either, I guess the government could get themselves so shit scared they wouldn't have a choice. They're just keeping their legs crossed and hoping it doesn't come to that.'

'What's the military been told?'

'Same crap the Russian and American military were told.'

'About a suspected terrorist attack?'

Gorman nodded. 'British Intelligence are pretending to have picked up an increase in the Intel traffic coming from the Middle East, but they're playing the whole thing down. They're saying it's probably just a wet dream of some al-Qaeda crazy who woke up one morning with what he thought was a good idea.'

'Are the public buying it?'

'They don't have to. They've been fed a different story. They think the army and navy are looking for munitions that could've been dislodged from the wreck in a storm that hit the coast last week.' Gorman paused for a moment. 'I guess it doesn't matter who believes what – not when we could be looking at a bluff. According to you, Dan Goldberg's pretty sure there aren't any bombs in his holes at Parkfield.'

'In my country the threat to the train was real,' Melinkov said. 'Only a brave man would gamble on the *Richard Montgomery* being safe.'

Having decided that Driscoll wasn't leaving, or perhaps to prevent him from leaving, Gorman reached into a drawer and took out four photographs which he arranged in a neat row on his desk.

'Take a look at these,' he said. 'They're multibeam sonar images of the wreck. Twenty years ago, divers used to go down to carry out surveys, but it was as dangerous as hell, and trying to see anything underwater in this part of the estuary is like looking through soup because of the mud.'

Driscoll was astonished by the quality of the photos. They were extraordinarily clear – so much so that they could have been aerial photos of a ship that had been left stranded on a beach.

The rusting hulk of the USS *Richard Montgomery* was lying in two pieces on the estuary floor at some unknown depth beneath the surface. The individual sections of the hull were of similar size and close to each other, resting upright on their keels, and surrounded by huge irregularly-shaped depressions that tidal currents and the river flow had carved out of an enormous sculpted mud-bank on which the wreck was sitting.

Despite the ship being an old steel-hulled vessel with a broken back, the corrosion was not as advanced as Driscoll had expected it to be.

The rectangular outlines of hatches were still reasonably well-defined, and even after being submerged for more than half a century, the fractured edges of the deck plates were easy to see, as were a number of ominous-looking cracks that had spread out elsewhere across the superstructure.

Gorman went to peer out the window. 'Weather's holding,' he said. 'As long as our friendly tour guide remembers to turn up we ought to get a pretty fair view of the site from that tower we're going to have a look at.'

'What can you see of the wreck from there at low tide?' Driscoll asked.

'Probably not much more than the three mast-heads, but they stick out like dog's balls. You can't miss them. On a good day when it's not pissing down with rain you can see them from here.'

'How about the explosives? What do we know about them?'

'It's in your file.' Gorman picked up a sheet of paper. 'According to the Admiralty and the Ministry of Defence, before the ship split up and sank, most of the munitions were salvaged from the rear section, but there's no record of anyone ever having been inside a couple of big holds in the front bit. If that's right, it means there's something like twelve hundred to three thousand tons of TNT waiting to go up. All we've got to go by is the manifest that lists what the ship had on board when it left Philadelphia in 1944.' He looked up. 'I suppose you want to know what that was.'

'You're going to show us anyway, aren't you?' Driscoll said.

Gorman ignored the remark and thrust the paper at them.

13,000 general purpose 250 lb bombs, 9,000 cases of fragmentation bombs, 7,000 semi-armour piercing bombs, 1,500 cases of fuses, 1,400 cases of phosphorus bombs, 1,400 cases of 100 lb demolition bombs; 800 cases of small-arms ammunition.

'How does that grab you?'

A month ago in the breakfast room of the Waverley Hotel, it had been Feng who had first mentioned the estimate of 1,000 to 3,000 tons of TNT. Driscoll could remember being alarmed at the time, but now he was actually within spitting distance of the wreck itself, the breakdown of the manifest had brought home the reality of what they were dealing with. He could almost taste the danger, and he had only to look outside to see how truly horrifying the result of any blast would be.

Melinkov could sense it too. 'There is much history here,' he said. 'In the days when German U-boats patrolled the North Atlantic, I think great courage would have been needed by men who sailed with such a cargo from America. But the explosion of a munitions ship at sea is not the same as the explosion of a ship in the estuary of the river Thames.'

'Bet your fucking life it's not.' Gorman was anxious to drive home his point. 'If the *Richard Montgomery* goes up, you can figure on the bang being a whole lot worse than the one in Nova Scotia when the *Mont-Blanc* blew itself to pieces outside Halifax in 1917. At low tide there's only about thirty feet of water covering the hull, so we're talking about a blast that'll be seven hundred times more powerful than the 1995 one in Oklahoma City.'

'Meaning what?' Driscoll said.

'The best estimate comes from a report that was issued back in 1970 by the government's Explosive Research and Development Establishment. They carried out a bunch of tests on some scale models.'

'Scale models of what?'

'The estuary.' Gorman went to the map again, this time placing his finger on the red rectangle that marked the position of the wreck. 'If you believe the experts, a three-thousand-foot diameter column of mud and water will shoot a couple of miles up into the sky, and a sixteen foot-high wave is going to travel out across the estuary and sink any ships that happen to be around.'

'Except there won't be any ships,' Driscoll said, 'not if the exclusion zone is enforced.'

'Forget the wave and forget the ships. It's the air blast and the ground shock that'll cause the damage. The bottom of the estuary is mostly clay, and clay is real good at transmitting shock.' Gorman moved his finger along the map until he reached the town of Sheerness on the north coast of Kent. 'If the divers and bomb squads come up with nothing, and we don't get a lead on Feng, Sheerness is one place you don't want to be after lunch on 27 March.'

'Along with where we are,' Driscoll said.

'You could evacuate every man and his dog from the Isle of Grain in less than an hour. Try moving twenty thousand people out of Sheerness and see how far you get. There'll be a whole lot of panic and a whole lot of questions afterwards that the government doesn't want anyone to ask.'

Melinkov went to inspect the map for himself. 'Sheerness is how far from the wreck?' he asked.

'Bit over a mile – close enough for the blast to shatter every window in the place and shower every street with shit and mud and unexploded bombs.'

The Russian smiled. 'Then you choose to base your headquarters here where we are also close because, like Dr Goldberg, you yourself believe there are no hidden charges for anyone to find?'

'We're going to know that one way or the other pretty soon, aren't we?' Gorman hesitated as though he was uncertain of how to proceed.

'What's it going to take?' he said. 'How hard would it be to set the whole lot off? You're the guy who's supposed to know.'

'The question is not so easy to answer. You must understand that the fuses are not just old, but of an old design. They contain lead azide which by itself is not a problem. Even if the fuses have corroded, and seawater has leaked inside the casings, the water will have simply washed away the chemical.'

'So the fuses aren't as dangerous as people think they are?'

'I did not say that. If you will permit me to finish, I will explain. If instead of water, the casings have been penetrated by water vapour, then hydrozoic acid will have formed which, in turn, will have reacted with the copper detonating caps to produce a material called copper azide.'

'And that's the dangerous stuff, is it?'

Melinkov shrugged. 'I myself have no direct experience with copper azide, but I think it will be so sensitive that the slightest knock will cause it to detonate – which, of course, in this case will initiate the chain reaction we all fear.'

Gorman seemed to have lost interest. Before Melinkov had finished speaking he'd started thumbing through his notes, either incapable of understanding the finer points of fuse design, or more likely because he resented the Russian's expertise and wanted no more to do with him than Driscoll did.

It would be hard to find three people who had less in common, Driscoll thought – an observation uncomfortably similar to one he remembered Natalie making in the little back room of the Black Swan when she'd first put forward her theory to explain the reasoning behind the Chinese plan.

At the time, partly because he'd been attracted to her, and partly because he'd believed she'd been after nothing more than a good story, not once had he questioned her motives – in hindsight an error of judgement that had cost Rebecca Wilson her life and delivered him in to the hands of governments whose relentless thirst for oil was about to determine the fate of three kilotons of sunken TNT.

So why was he still thinking about Natalie Washburn at all, Driscoll wondered? What had it been about her that made her so damn unforgettable? And why, after all of his mistakes and everything else that had happened, could he still recall the way she'd looked on that last day in Santorini?

Because that had been then, he told himself – before he'd suspected her of playing him for a fool, and before he'd come to realize how cleverly she'd used her broken smile to disguise what she'd known all along was going to be a broken promise.

CHAPTER 18

Gorman's friendly tour guide had turned out to be neither particularly friendly nor a tour guide. Instead, Gerald Mullen was a snappily dressed, weak-chinned real estate agent from central London, a busy man, so he claimed, who had other important matters to attend to, and who could ill-afford the time to assist Energex in their survey of the area, whether the survey was for British Petroleum or for anyone else.

On their drive to the causeway, because Gorman was making no effort to engage Mullen in conversation, the salesman had started asking questions.

'I don't understand why an oil company would be interested in the Martello Tower,' he said. 'They do realize it's a Registered National Monument, don't they?'

'I wouldn't know.' Gorman sounded uninterested. 'My brief is to have a look at it and find out whether it could be restored and made into some kind of tourist attraction. The way I see it, BP are looking to buy themselves a bucket of goodwill from the natives by throwing money at the place.'

The Texan was no better at lying than he was at anything else, Driscoll thought, although for the moment at least, Mullen seemed willing to accept the story and was looking less pained than he had been.

'What's the sale price?' Driscoll asked.

'Seven hundred thousand pounds. Spend another hundred thousand and it'd be a good investment for anyone. They're not making any more of these.' Instead of turning right on to Port Victoria Road, Mullen slowed the Range Rover and carried on down a short dead-end street that led to a flat area of tidal mud and gravel.

Leaving the engine running, he got out and went round to open the tailgate. 'Time to get changed,' he said. 'You'll need to put these on. Help yourself.'

Inside the rear of the Range Rover stood a row of gumboots and two cardboard boxes containing a selection of freshly laundered overalls. Mullen chose a set for himself and waited while Melinkov struggled in to the largest pair of overalls he could find.

'Where's the causeway?' Driscoll could see no sign of it.

'Right in front of you.' Mullen pointed. 'We're a bit early. Give the tide another half an hour and you'll be able to walk on it without getting your feet wet. Don't worry. I've been out to the tower when the water's been a lot deeper than this. All you have to do is drive in a straight line.'

From where Driscoll was standing, the Martello Tower was no less sinister and prison-like than it had seemed to be earlier in the day. It was utterly unappealing, a sombre-looking, flat-topped cylindrical building from which protruded a crude structure that could once have been some form of observation post and flanked by an equally ugly rectangular addition that was standing on mud-stained foundations made from cross-braced concrete piles.

'Is this the only way to get to it?' Driscoll asked.

Mullen nodded. 'Unless you want to try by boat, but getting off isn't that easy. There used to be a landing stage, but most of it's rotten. The only other way is through old underground tunnels. There's a whole network of them running out from somewhere underneath the village.'

The information should have been surprising. But it wasn't. It was just another incongruous aspect of the Isle of Grain, Driscoll decided, another peculiarity to add to the rest, and somehow no more surprising than the proximity of the *Richard Montgomery* and the bizarre-looking tower block they were about to visit.

'Why can't we use the tunnels?' he asked.

'They're sealed off. No one's allowed inside them.' Mullen got back in to the Range Rover. 'You ready?'

Driving out into the estuary was more like travelling by boat than by car. Although the tide was slack, and the causeway was submerged in only a few inches of discoloured water, the vehicle gave the impression of riding on the surface rather than on the ground beneath it, and once or twice before Mullen drew up alongside the tower itself, Driscoll had started to doubt the estate agent's ability to keep the car on course.

At close quarters, the building looked more primitive, and the age of it was easier to see.

The base was obviously the oldest part, made of granite blocks, and instead of being completely circular, it had flats on the east and north-west sides.

Recessed into the centre of the north-west flat was the main entrance, a doorway that had an 1855 date stone set above the lintel. By way of contrast, and because the steps leading up to the entrance had long ago disintegrated or been washed away, in their place today was a shiny aluminium ladder.

'Is 1855 when it was built?' Driscoll asked.

'About then.' Mullen repositioned the ladder. 'The locals will tell you it was more like 1866, but I don't know. A whole chain of these was built along the coasts of East Sussex, Kent, Essex and Suffolk in the 1800s. There were seventy-three of them at one time, but most of them have been demolished.'

Driscoll followed Mullen up the ladder and waited for Gorman and Melinkov to join him on a ledge outside the door. 'Are all the towers the same as this one?' he asked.

Mullen nodded. 'The design's based on an old fort in Corsica that put up some kind of heroic resistance against the British forces when they tried to storm it in 1793. That's why Whitehall decided they'd be an ideal defence against Napoleon. As it turned out, of course, they were more valuable during the two World Wars.' He pointed to the remains of an enormous chain that was wrapped around the base of the tower. 'That was used to string a net right across the mouth of the River Medway.'

Melinkov went to look at it. 'To stop the German U-boats, yes?' he said.

'And anything else.' Fastening the top button of his overalls, Mullen stepped inside. 'Come and have a look.'

The entrance opened into a cold, brick-lined lobby from which two sets of stairs led in different directions – one to a windowless chamber containing a slate water tank, the other to a smaller room that looked as though it could have served as a latrine.

But it was a large central column in the lobby that was attracting Driscoll's attention. Rising from the floor, it too was made of brick, flaring out at the top to form a remarkably graceful ceiling.

The walls surrounding the column were almost as imposing. To withstand the pounding from cannon, they were six or seven feet thick, and thicker still on the seaward side where the need for strength had been the greatest.

The whole impression of the place was one of strength – decaying perhaps, Driscoll thought, but not yet to the point where restoration would be impossible.

Except for the ground floor which was partly flooded, the rest of the building was damp and dripping in condensation, but otherwise not in too bad a condition. There were living quarters, an ablution block, a kitchen, an artillery store and a gun floor where, according to Mullen, until 1929 a pair of 4.7-inch guns used to be mounted.

On another floor near the top, a few threaded studs protruded from an old World War II searchlight platform, although the armoured shutters that had protected the light had rusted away to almost nothing.

Nearby, running along the west wall, a set of steel rails for ammunition trolleys had suffered a similar fate. The sole piece of equipment that was not in a state of advanced corrosion was a lift that had been designed to carry up ammunition from the magazine.

Unlike the mechanical fittings, the stonework had withstood the elements well, and only the ugly rectangular barrack block was beyond repair, a more modern part of the complex that had been largely stripped out, vandalized and left to fall to pieces by itself.

Most surprising of all was evidence of a rudimentary electricity supply.

Gorman had come across it first and was kneeling down to inspect a length of broken copper cable. 'Where the hell did the power come from?' he asked.

'There was a generator back on shore somewhere.' Mullen wiped a blob of mud off his face before leading the way out on to an east-facing parapet. 'I don't know whether the power lines came through the tunnels or whether they were overhead. In 1940 a couple of six-pounder QF guns were installed on one of the floors and, as far as I know, they couldn't have been operated without an electrical supply.' He smiled slightly. 'All mod cons.'

'You'd need them in a place like this,' Driscoll said. 'It's pretty bleak, isn't it?'

Mullen nodded. 'Sixty years ago, forty men used to be stationed here. How would you like to have spent a winter in a Martello Tower?'

Gorman had been looking out across the estuary. 'That's the wreck, right?' He pointed into the distance where the receding tide had exposed more of the *Richard Montgomery*'s masts.

'BP will know all about that.' Mullen sounded unconcerned. 'It's been lying there for longer than most of the people in Grain or Sheerness have been alive. If it was going to blow up, it would've blown up long before now.'

'What about people who are thinking of buying this place?' Driscoll said. 'Don't they care about the wreck, or do you just happen not to mention it?'

'They mostly already know. I've got a young American couple on my books who look on it as an added attraction. They're thinking of converting ex-commercial ships into houseboats or live-aboards and mooring them along the mud-bank. Whoever buys the tower gets a two thousand foot-long frontage of freehold riverbed for their money, and the Americans had worked out you could berth up to thirty vessels on the property.'

'They're not going to be so keen after they hear the story about munitions being washed out of the wreck,' Driscoll said.

'The fuss will die down. It always does. Whenever there's a bad storm, or there's a new sonar survey, the locals get themselves excited, then they forget about it again. Having a wreck this close to the tower is almost as good a selling point as the address.'

'Why?' It was hard enough for Driscoll to imagine anyone being happy to overlook several thousand tons of unexploded bombs, let alone understand why they'd be interested in the address of a property that was half underwater at high tide. 'What's so good about the address?'

'Number One, The Thames.' Mullen smiled. 'It's the Asian buyers who like it. If I can find myself another one of those, I might even be able to put up the price a bit – you know, by getting them to bid against each other.'

It had been a throwaway remark, made so casually that Driscoll was still thinking about it when Melinkov interrupted.

The Russian had been maintaining his customary low profile, but he'd suddenly become more interested. 'You have one such client already?' he asked.

'Potential client. You know what Asians are like. You can't really tell how serious they are.'

'I see.' Melinkov took his time lighting a cigarette. 'And this is how you learn the value of the address?'

'I know it sounds crazy, but having Number One on your letterbox is a big deal to the Chinese. It's a sign of honour or leadership, or symbol of constancy, or something.'

'So if British Petroleum wishes to purchase your nice Martello Tower, they must compete not only with the American couple you mention, but offer more than your Chinese buyer?'

'It's not exactly an offer,' Mullen said. 'Well, not yet it isn't.'

Melinkov smiled. 'I think it is not necessary for BP to know that. But we should make it clear they will not be the only bidder. If the information is not too sensitive, it is possible for you to say how firm the Chinese interest is and from where it comes?'

'It's not a secret. The enquiry came from a Hong Kong businessman. He must have been out here for two or three hours taking photographs and asking questions.'

By now Gorman had woken up and had his own questions to ask. 'When the hell was this?' he said.

'I can't remember exactly. A month or so ago, I suppose. Why?'

'What did he look like?'

Mullen was uncomfortable. 'Why do you want to know?'

'Did you get his name? Why would a Chinese businessman from Hong Kong be interested in buying a rat hole like this?'

'His name was Jun, and he was representing a group of Chinese investors who are acquiring properties of historical value right across Western Europe.' Mullen's unease was being replaced with suspicion. 'You're not working on behalf of British Petroleum, are you?' he said. 'You're something to do with what's going on in Grain and along the coast.'

'Wrong.' Gorman turned to Driscoll. 'Where's that identikit picture of yours?'

'Where do you think it is? It's back at the house.' Now Gorman had managed to undermine a cover story that only a hungry real estate agent would have believed in the first place, Driscoll could guess what the result was going to be.

'Well.' Mullen inspected his watch. 'If you've seen everything you need to see, I think it's probably time for me to drive you back. You can always phone if you have more queries or if you'd like me to bring you out again one day. In the meantime, I'm afraid I have another appointment.'

'Hold on there for a second.' Gorman took Driscoll aside. 'What did I tell you about us getting a break?' he said. 'Now listen. So there's no mistake, I'll get Mullen to take a look at the identikit picture when he drops me back at the village. Soon as I've got his confirmation I'll call Sir Oliver with the good news so he can pass it on. After that it'll be up to the government to do whatever they want to do.'

'I'd better call Collier too,' Driscoll said. 'I need to talk to him anyway.'

'You won't be talking to anyone. You and Melinkov are staying right here.'

'Mullen isn't going to like that.'

'Leave the prick to me.' Gorman lowered his voice. 'If Energex winds up having to fix this instead of the military, we need to be ready. That means you've got yourself a new job. I don't care how long it takes, but if this tower has half-a-dozen launch positions for a short-range missile, you'd better find every one of them before the tide comes in, otherwise you'll be in for a swim or the pair of you are going to be stuck here all fucking night. Have you got that?'

'Yeah, I've got that.' Instead of pushing Gorman off the parapet, Driscoll adopted Melinkov's strategy of treating him as though he was retarded. 'Why don't you show Feng's picture to Mullen on your computer screen?' he said. 'The disk's in my case.'

'Won't need to. We've got this pretty much nailed already.' Gorman went back to speak to Mullen, talking him down when he started to protest and endeavouring to mollify him by promising to return Melinkov's and Driscoll's overalls and boots at a later date.

Mullen wasn't buying any of it. Irritated by Gorman's attitude and child-like lack of subtlety, he was openly hostile and too annoyed to say goodbye before he left.

Not that it mattered, Driscoll thought. What did matter was whether or not Gorman had the intelligence to handle things tactfully from now on.

Melinkov had already decided he hadn't. 'The man is an idiot,' he said. 'We have fresh information to consider, yet he thinks we should waste our time searching more of this tower. What does he expect us to find?'

'How about a missile launcher? That's what he's worried about.'

'Ah. Then I have misjudged him, and he is shrewder than I thought.' Melinkov was trying not to smile. 'It is good to know that if we watch carefully on the morning of the 27th, we will see Feng drive out here so he can fire a missile at the wreck from an upstairs window. For his sake we must hope these walls are thick enough to protect him from the blast.'

'He could come out and set up his launcher on the night before,' Driscoll said. 'All he'd need then is a timer programmed for two o'clock on the following day. That way he wouldn't have to hang around.'

'If he is intending to use a timer, there is an easier method.'

'What?'

'On a dark night, one week or one month before the 27th, he rows out to the wreck in a small boat. Then he fits his timer to a waterproof bomb which he drops overboard. Why would he not choose such a simple solution?'

'Because he couldn't.' Driscoll had already considered the possibility. 'You've forgotten about the radar surveillance and the shipping exclusion zone – the same way you couldn't drop anything out of an aircraft either – because of the no-fly zone. Anyway, according to the data in Gorman's files, no one's been over or under or near the wreck for over a year. I checked.'

'But this morning you tell Gorman you have not read the file.'

'I like winding him up. Forget Gorman. Think about Feng. He can't use a boat and he can't use an aircraft, but there's nothing to stop him using a missile. So, how would he get hold of one?'

'It would not be so difficult. In every country there is a black market for armaments. If he is willing to spend sufficient money, in England perhaps he could buy himself a British Javelin. It is a surface-to-air missile, with a range of up to four kilometres, but for it to be successful, I think he would have to target the exposed parts of the masts.'

'What about an anti-tank job?'

Melinkov shook his head. 'They have not the range. The wreck is close to us, but not close enough for a small anti-tank weapon that can be used by one man.'

'OK. What would you use?'

'It is the same question you ask Dr Goldberg in California.'

'I know. What's the answer?'

Melinkov thought for a moment. 'For myself I would choose a mortar. There is one called Merlin that fires an eighty-one millimetre terminally-guided, anti-armour bomb. It is British, it weighs no more than thirty or forty kilogrammes, and has a range of over five kilometres. If one of those was to be set up in the right place, I think it would be very dangerous for the *Richard Montgomery*.'

'Except you wouldn't get away with setting it up,' Driscoll said, 'not while every damn creek and every mud-bank along this part of the coast is being patrolled by the Coast Guard, the police, army bomb squads and God knows who else.'

Melinkov seemed to have become preoccupied by another possibility. Instead of staring out over the water as he had been, he'd gone over to the stairwell and was looking down at the floor below. 'I have just remembered something,' he said.

'What?'

'The tunnels.'

Driscoll had forgotten about them too – a wonderfully convenient route to the tower, he realized, underground access that would have allowed anyone to have checked it out as often as they'd liked, and a corridor through which any number of missiles, mortars and timers could be transported without them ever being seen.

Melinkov was still peering down the stairwell. 'In Russia, we learned that Feng is a resourceful man who does his research well,' he said. 'He will know of the tunnels.'

'Mullen said they're sealed off.'

'It would not have been a problem for him to locate a disused entrance where no one goes. On the Isle of Grain there is not a shortage of such places.'

'If it was Feng,' Driscoll said.

'It was. Mullen will identify him from the picture. I am as sure of it as I am sure he has explored the tunnels with the intention of using this tower for his attack.' Melinkov lit another cigarette. 'So our work is finished, is it not?'

If it was, what now, Driscoll wondered? Wait and see if Melinkov was right? Or disappear to somewhere away from all of this and leave it to Gorman to handle the problem by whatever means he thought was best?

During the last ten minutes the temperature had dropped, and now the sun was lower, the Martello Tower was casting a shadow out across the mud-bank where at the water's edge, a crisscross pattern of ripples showed that the tide was on the turn. Further out in the estuary, the rusted masts of the *Richard Montgomery* were throwing their own shadows – thin dark lines that were more like scratches on a painting someone had wanted to deface.

It was all very calm and very picturesque, Driscoll thought. And, as Melinkov had said, there was a sense of history here. But the sense of irony was greater.

For 150 years, a river fortress that had been built to repel the forces of Napoleon had served its purpose well, acting as a silent guardian of the Medway and the Thames for all that time. But now, almost overnight, the Martello Tower had become a menace – a possible launch site for an attack that, if it couldn't be prevented, would have consequences more far reaching and more devastating than anything the navies of France and Germany could have ever dreamed of.

The prospect was too disturbing to consider, Driscoll decided, a nightmare for which he was not responsible nor had ever been responsible.

But it was something else as well. With no one left to worry about except himself, it was a turning point. And if the threat to implicate him in the deaths of Charles Collier and Rebecca Wilson hadn't been a good enough reason for him to disappear – now he had a better one.

CHAPTER 19

By providing Driscoll with a high-mileage Renault from the Energex car pool and by arranging for him and Melinkov to stay in a less than comfortable hotel in Rochester, Gorman had done himself no favours.

For their daily trip to Grain, the car was satisfactory enough, and there was nothing particularly wrong with the hotel apart from its location. The building stood on the corner of a busy intersection not far from the town centre, but Driscoll had found the noise of traffic less intrusive than the light from a nearby travel agency that had seemed to be filled with customers whenever he'd driven past the place.

This morning he hadn't driven past it. Instead, he'd left Melinkov sitting in the car and come in to book his flight.

The girl behind the desk was still looking apologetic and had gone back to pressing buttons on her keyboard.

'I'm sorry,' she said. 'It's always like this in the mornings.'

'So there's only the South African Airways flight today – the one that's full?'

'You could try for standby.' She studied her screen. 'Other than that – if you want to go direct – the only other flight I have to Johannesburg is tomorrow, but you said the 27th is too late.'

'What time tomorrow?'

'Seventeen twenty. You'd need to check in about three o'clock.'

'How about first class on tonight's flight?'

'I've got an aisle seat in business class.' The girl smiled. 'Would that be all right?'

'Yeah, it would. That'll be fine.' Having finally decided what he was going to do, and with his hundred thousand yuan present from the Chinese government mostly still unspent, Driscoll didn't care where the seat was or how much it would cost.

Pleased to have got things settled, he paid for the ticket, promised the girl he wouldn't forget to pick it up from the SAA desk at Heathrow, then returned to the car to answer the inevitable questions Melinkov was going to ask.

To begin with the Russian was careful not to say anything at all, keeping his thoughts to himself until Driscoll had threaded the Renault through the downtown traffic and joined the northbound stream of cars on the A228 at Wainscot.

'So you are leaving,' Melinkov said.

'Seems like a good idea.'

'It is not my business.' The Russian's eyes remained on the road. 'But if it is because you are unwilling to see how successful Beijing will be, I think it is not so necessary. You and I cannot blame ourselves for this fight for oil. If tomorrow the worst is to happen, it will not be us but politicians who are at fault. Am I permitted to ask where it is you go?'

'Long as you keep it to yourself. There's a guy I know in Johannesburg. I'm hoping he might give me a job.'

'South Africa is where you fly planes for him before?'

'Angola and Namibia mostly. Anything's better than getting screwed around by Collier and Gorman for another two months.'

Melinkov smiled. 'I think it is Feng who has done the screwing. But for him you could still be enjoying yourself in the oil fields of the Tarim Basin.'

Driscoll could have done without a reminder of the Tarim Basin – a place that seemed a world away from where he was now, and a job that he'd never imagined would eventually lead him back to Africa.

Having decided he might as well have stayed in Africa all along, he spent the rest of the trip wondering if the last three years had really been worthwhile and promising himself that, one way or the other, at least the next three would be.

If he hadn't called in at the travel agents he would have been less confident about his future, but booking his flight had made a difference, and by the time they reached Grain and he was parking the Renault outside the house on the waterfront, he'd come to terms with what might or might not have been a wasted past, and was ready, if not exactly willing, to squander a few more hours helping Gorman refine the strategy for the day ahead.

The Texan was waiting for them in the briefing room. 'Where the

181

hell have you been?' he asked.

'Traffic,' Driscoll said. 'Nose to tail outside Lower Stoke. Anything happened here?'

'Not yet. It'll be later today or sometime tonight.'

'Have you told the military what Energex are doing?'

Gorman considered the question. 'Sir Oliver wants our own people to handle the tunnels,' he said. 'That way the army and the police can concentrate their resources on the shoreline and the causeway.'

Driscoll almost felt sorry for him. Ever since Mullen had confirmed Feng's identity and called back to provide the date on which his Chinese client had visited the tower, the pressure on Gorman had been so great that he'd lost sight of how cynically the Energex directors were manipulating him, and seemed to believe that he alone had become responsible for the safety of the *Richard Montgomery*.

'What about the tunnel entrances?' Driscoll asked. 'Have the army rechecked to see if they're sealed off?'

'What do you think? They're not stupid.'

'So they're not worried about them?'

'Why would they be? They haven't the first fucking idea who Feng is, they don't know he's been out to the tower and they sure as hell don't know anything about what's going on between Beijing and London. The military are either looking for a suicide bomber who's going to try and get out to the wreck in a boat, or for some sick bastard who thinks he can drive along the coast and launch a rocket off the roof of his car.'

Having explained how misguided the army commanders were, Gorman was getting in to his stride. 'Which means we've got the tunnels to ourselves,' he said. 'I've had our guys watching the entrances since the day before yesterday. Everyone's working in shifts, so if you two don't want to spend tonight playing with yourselves in the dark on a street corner, you'd better put in the hours today and make sure you're not this late getting back here tomorrow morning.'

The plan was no more foolproof than the Russian's plan for the railroad had been, Driscoll thought, and probably no more likely to be successful.

'So the idea is to stop Feng getting in to the tunnels, is it?' he asked.

'No.' Gorman was looking smug. 'If Feng's got some clever way to get inside them, that's where he's going to stay. The army aren't taking any chances; they've blocked off the ground floor of the tower.'

'So what?' Driscoll said.

'So we'll see him go in and be ready for him when he realizes he's in trouble and tries to get out again.' Gorman went to open the lid of a slender cardboard box that was sitting in the corner of the room. 'We'll have all the time we need to put this baby in place, and we're going to know exactly where to put it.'

The box contained a gas cylinder that was connected by a short length of braided hose to what appeared to be a solenoid valve and a battery-driven control unit.

Stencilled on the cylinder were two international poison signs and a row of Cyrillic writing that only Melinkov could read.

'Ah.' The Russian knelt down to inspect the cylinder more closely. 'Mr Yukos has sent this to you?'

'It came yesterday. What do you think?'

'I think that if we release this gas into the tunnel, Feng may be fortunate to survive.'

'What is it?' Driscoll was waiting for someone to tell him.

'It is a fentanyl derivative nerve gas – the kind that was used in Russia to subdue the Chechen separatists who took over the Moscow Theatre in October 2002. In confined spaces it can prove most dangerous. In Moscow, more than a hundred hostages died after breathing in too much of it.'

'Shame.' Gorman closed the lid of the box. 'Sounds like just the stuff.'

'Why do we not shoot him?' Melinkov said. 'It will be quicker, cleaner and easier.'

'Now why didn't I think of that?' Gorman injected as much sarcasm into his voice as he could manage. 'Tell you what. I'll issue all our guys with assault rifles. Then, when an army patrol trips over us and decides the village is full of terrorists, we can pretend we're in Baghdad and have one big fucking shoot-up.'

'You've been told to take Feng alive, have you?' Driscoll said.

Gorman nodded. 'McCloskey's been on the phone to Sir Oliver about it. The Americans figure Feng's the only guy who's going to tell them how worried they ought to be about an earthquake in California.'

In which case there was a good chance of the Americans being out of luck, Driscoll thought, to say nothing of the risk to Grain and Sheerness if, over the next twenty-four hours, there was still no sign of Feng or of anyone else Beijing could have despatched to do the job instead.

How high the risk might be, Driscoll was unsure, but as the day wore on without any fresh information coming in, he found it difficult to distance himself from the problem and by five o'clock not even the thought of his evening flight was keeping his doubts at bay.

By six o'clock, Melinkov too had become concerned, announcing his decision to spend the night in Grain instead of returning to the hotel to get some sleep, but changing his mind when Driscoll had shaken hands with him to say goodbye for the last time.

Since then, for the last ten minutes the Russian had been sitting in the passenger seat of the Renault with his mouth clamped shut as though unwilling to offer anything in the way of an explanation.

To find out if there was one, Driscoll opened the conversation himself. 'Have you had enough as well?' he asked.

'No, no, although if by midday tomorrow there is still no progress, I think I will telephone Mr Yukos to ask if it is OK for me to return to Russia.'

'So what's going on?'

'It is not so easy for me to say, but over these weeks we work together, we have come to respect each other, have we not?'

'I'm not your friend,' Driscoll said. 'I haven't been working with you because I want to.'

'You do not understand. I mention this because I wish to seek your opinion on something.'

'What?'

'It is just that since this afternoon I have come to believe I may be wrong about the Martello Tower.' Melinkov's expression showed how uncomfortable he was. 'According to the man Mullen, it is on 22 February that he takes Feng to visit the tower. When one hour ago I check this date, I see it is two days after Feng meets with you and Miss Washburn to explain how he will use you to communicate with Collier.'

'So what? All that means is he was hanging around in England for a while before he took off on his trip to Russia.'

'There is more. According to the police reports, it is the same week that, in the Isle of Grain, a twelve-year-old boy cuts open his leg when he is chased away from a warehouse he breaks into. The dates are close; from the 22nd to the 27th.'

'It's not Collier who's grasping at straws,' Driscoll said. 'It's you.'

'Yet you, yourself, have said it makes no sense for Feng to have made himself known to Mullen if it has always been his plan to use the

184

tunnels and the tower. Is it not possible that it is what he wishes us to believe?'

'So while everyone's watching the tunnels and the tower, he's going to be somewhere else? Is that what you're saying?'

Melinkov shrugged. 'In a job like mine, often you should listen to the little warnings in your head. For Russia, Feng had two plans, but we will never know which of them he favoured most.'

Although the road ahead was clear of traffic, instead of overtaking the car in front of him, Driscoll tucked the Renault in behind it. 'Have you got the police report with you?'

'You were too anxious to leave for me to fetch it. That is why I come with you – so I may speak with you privately about this matter.'

'Why the hell wait until now?' Driscoll said. 'What did Gorman say?'

'I have not told him. Until this evening, I myself could not believe these things can be connected, but even if they are, Gorman would not have listened.'

'But you thought I would?'

'What I think is that you are not a man who would wish to risk the lives of many innocent people.'

'Crap,' Driscoll said. 'It isn't that – not for you it isn't. You just want to win the game and get your hands on Feng.'

'If that is true, at least I am still trying.'

Against his better judgment, Driscoll pulled off on to the shoulder and stopped the car. 'What's in the police report?'

'It says only that the boy lives with his mother at a place called Worthing, and that for a few days in February he visits the Isle of Grain to see his uncle who at that time had temporary work there at the container terminal. One morning, after the boy steals a dinghy, he rows up a creek to the warehouse where he is chased by a man and falls through the rotten planks of an old jetty.'

'And got away?'

'The report says he runs along the side of the creek, but before he can reach the place where his uncle is staying, he loses much blood, and later must have stitches in his leg. That is why on the next day the police go to ask the man why he did not try to help the boy or tell someone.' Melinkov paused. 'By then, of course, the man is gone.'

'And there was nothing out of the ordinary inside the warehouse?'

'Nothing that is mentioned in the report. But perhaps we could go to see.'

185

'Tonight?'

'Or first thing in the morning.' Melinkov wound down his window before lighting a cigarette.

By pretending to have forgotten about Driscoll's flight, the Russian had managed to make the suggestion sound even more unreasonable. But how unreasonable was it, Driscoll wondered? Long shot or not, was there really a possibility of Gorman being wrong and Melinkov being right?

'We're not going to find out anything at the warehouse now, are we?' he said. 'We'd be better off showing Feng's picture to the boy.'

Melinkov blew a stream of smoke out of the window. 'What time is it that your plane departs?'

'Why?'

'Would it not be a good idea for you to talk with the boy on the tele-phone before you leave? The number is in the police report.'

'Which you didn't bring.' Had the car not been stationary, Driscoll would have carried on driving. As it was, he kept his foot on the brake, knowing it was crazy to even think of making the call, but failing to come up with a wholly convincing reason why he shouldn't.

'Listen,' he said, 'you don't need me, and you can bypass Gorman. Either get some help from Collier or follow this up yourself.'

Melinkov shook his head. 'You forget I am a foreigner in your coun-try. I do not have the skills for such work, so I think this is something we must do together. You will phone the boy, yes?'

All but certain he was about to make another big mistake, Driscoll waited for a gap in the traffic, then rammed the Renault into gear, executed a u-turn and set off back in the direction from which he'd come.

In the short time they'd been away, the streets of Grain had become deserted. Coaches that had brought home workers from their jobs else-where were parked nose to tail ready for the morning, and along the waterfront, most of the houses had their lights switched on and their curtains tightly drawn.

There were no lights shining from the windows of the Energex head-quarters – a sign that Gorman was either out rallying his troops or had been summoned to a final meeting with Sir Oliver.

Wherever he'd gone, at least he wasn't here, Driscoll thought, and as long as he stayed away they wouldn't have to explain anything or answer a barrage of stupid questions.

Inside the house, the residual warmth of the afternoon had leaked away, and when Melinkov handed him the police report in the briefing room, the sheet of paper was as damp as the furniture and the carpet.

Except for some names and addresses, the report itself was sketchy and seemed to have been written by someone who'd lost interest halfway through.

'You will do it now?' Melinkov said.

'Yeah, yeah. Stop pushing.' Spreading out the report on Gorman's desk, Driscoll picked up the phone and keyed in the number that was written at the bottom of the page.

The woman who answered sounded wary and slightly flustered.

'Is that Mrs Barnes?' Driscoll said.

'Who's that?'

'My name's O'Hara.' He used the first name that came into his head. 'I'm a detective inspector with the Kent police. I'm sorry to disturb your evening, but we're following up on the accident your son had back in February of this year.'

'He didn't do nothing wrong. Leave a boat like that lying around, and any kid's going to take it, aren't they? Dangerous I call it. Raymond's a good boy.'

'We know that,' Driscoll said. 'This isn't about him. We're just trying to find out more about the man who chased him. Is it all right if I speak to Raymond for a minute?'

'He's away at one of them orienteering camps. He don't like school trips – not usually – but he wanted to go on this one. What do you want to ask him?'

'We were hoping he might remember what he saw inside the building and we'd like him to have a look at a picture we have of the man.'

'There wasn't nothing in the building – leastways that's what Ray said – just a metal tank full of dirty water and some bits of plastic pipe and wooden crates that were being broken up and burned on a fire outside.'

'How about the man?' Driscoll said. 'Do you think Ray could give us a description?'

'He's already done that – while he was up in Grain staying with his uncle Reg. Mind you, he hadn't seen the video then.'

'What video's that?'

'One he watched over at Jimmy Rawlin's place the other day. Silly foreign film about men who can fly fighting each other with sticks in the

187

tops of trees. Raymond's still talking about it. He says one of the men looked just like the one he ran away from.'

It wasn't the telephone call that had been a big mistake, Driscoll realized; it had been his own scepticism, something that a moment ago had brought him frighteningly close to hanging up. '*Crouching Tiger, Hidden Dragon*,' he said slowly.

'I knows it was Chinese because I remember the dragon bit. I don't think there was no dragons in it, though. Raymond would've said if there was. Keen on dragons he is. Get a copy of the video, then you'll see.'

'I'll do that.' Driscoll glanced across the desk at Melinkov. 'I don't suppose there's any way we can contact your son tonight, is there?'

'He'll be home for lunch tomorrow. Mini-van's dropping him off. Do you want to come and show him that picture?'

'If it's all right with you.' Driscoll was endeavouring to keep his mind on the call. 'What would be a good time?'

'I don't know. Eleven or twelve.'

'You've really been most helpful,' Driscoll said. 'Thank you very much. I'll send someone down in the morning. You'll make sure Raymond understands he isn't in any kind of trouble, won't you?'

He said goodbye and replaced the receiver, wondering whether he'd been lucky or unlucky to get the information now it was too late for him to do anything about it.

'Feng,' Melinkov said. 'It was him.'

'Probably.'

'Yet you tell the woman it will not be you, but someone else who will speak with her son tomorrow.'

'I've got a plane to catch.' Driscoll slid the report across the desk. 'There's the address. You go.'

'There are other flights you can catch on other days, but I think there will not be another day like tomorrow. By leaving tonight you will prove only that you are not the man you think you are.'

The attempt to make him reconsider was as weak as it had been overstated, but at the same time it had touched a nerve, reminding Driscoll of his failure to save Charles Collier from the burning Cessna, and of how an earlier preoccupation with his own affairs had contributed to the deaths of nine young Russian soldiers and the driver of the train.

This was different, he told himself. It was different because it had to be – a conviction that over the next hour grew progressively harder to hold on to, because the more he tried to forget about tomorrow, the more impossible it became for him to do so.

CHAPTER 20

Driscoll's impression of Mary Barnes had been wrong. Over the phone she'd sounded a fairly ordinary young woman, but in person she was as bright and clear thinking as she was pleasant. She was also painfully thin, in her late twenties with a pale, angular face and the figure of a teenage boy.

While Driscoll and Melinkov had been waiting for the mini-bus to deliver her son back home, she'd made them tea and done her best to conceal her awkwardness at having to entertain guests in a flat that was almost bare of furniture and in serious need of redecorating.

Her son had proved to be equally smart, unconcerned to find two policeman in his living room, and in between eating his way through a packet of crisps and half a bar of chocolate, talking so much about his school trip that Driscoll had been barely able to get a word in.

Only in the last few minutes had the boy's mother been able to slow him down by explaining that the gentlemen hadn't come all this way to listen to him.

'It's all right.' Driscoll smiled. 'How's your leg now?'

Rolling down his sock, the boy displayed a row of faint marks where the stitches in his calf had been. 'Nurse promised me a scar,' he said. 'But it don't look like it. Are you going to catch that man?'

'We hope so.' Driscoll produced the identikit picture. 'Is this him?'

The boy studied the picture. 'Don't know. Don't look as much like him as that man in Jimmy's video.'

'Raymond.' His mother interrupted. 'Just answer the question.'

'I told you. I don't know. He was yelling at me and I was running.'

'Why do you think he was angry?' Driscoll said.

'Maybe because he never knew I was there – least, not until he came back in from the fire. All I wanted was something to use for a paddle because the oars were getting too heavy for me.'

'And there wasn't anything in the warehouse except for a water tank and some rubbish?'

'It weren't dirty rubbish – just bits of plastic pipe and planks he'd been smashing off some wooden crates. That's all I took – one little bloody plank.'

His mother had seen Melinkov glancing at his watch and decided to intervene. 'Raymond, love,' she said, 'tell Mr O'Hara what was stamped on the plank.'

'It weren't Chinese.'

'Tell me anyway,' Driscoll said.

'Just names; Johnson Motors, and another one – something like Mini Car or Mini Motor. Didn't make no sense to me.'

It didn't to Driscoll either – another piece of meaningless information that was another letdown, he thought, although not as big a letdown as the boy's inability to identify Feng.

He was finding it hard not to be discouraged, and having spent three hours last night rescheduling his flight, and after wasting three more driving here this morning, he was annoyed with himself for ever believing the trip could be worthwhile.

Mary Barnes had sensed that things were not going well and had gone to join her son on the settee. 'What about that sticky stuff?' she said. 'You haven't told Mr O'Hara about that.'

Before the boy could open his mouth, Melinkov was asking questions. 'The material is black?' he said. 'It smells of almonds and cloves, and if you have it on your hands, you cannot remove it?'

The boy was surprised. 'How did you know that?'

'It is not so difficult for me. Once before in another place I have come across what your mother has called this sticky stuff. You find much of it in the warehouse?'

'I only gets it on me from one of them pipe off-cuts – just a bit of it that was smeared around inside up one end.'

His mother offered her own opinion. 'Like grease gone hard it was,' she said. 'Been all right if Ray hadn't wiped his hands all over his clothes, or if his uncle and the people at the hospital hadn't tried to clean him up. I had to throw away his sweater and a good pair of jeans he was nowhere near grown out of.'

Unaware of the significance of the information, neither the boy nor his mother had noticed the effect it was having – not so much on

Melinkov who, although clearly glad to have had his suspicions confirmed, was still to reach the alarming conclusion that Driscoll had just reached.

'Raymond,' Driscoll said, 'you're not on the internet, are you?'

' 'Course. Computer's in my bedroom. Uncle Reg bought it for me. It's not a new one, though. Do you want to see?'

'In a minute.' Wary of getting ahead of himself, but conscious of how swiftly the time was passing, Driscoll apologized to the woman for his rudeness before asking if she minded Raymond spending a few minutes to help them out on his computer.

'He'd be on the silly thing already if you wasn't here.' She turned to her son. 'You do what these gentlemen ask you now – and leave that chocolate. You can have it when you come back.'

Driscoll was accompanying the boy to the bedroom when Melinkov stopped him at the door.

The Russian was anxious to find out what was going on. 'You have a new idea?' he said. 'Now we can both be certain it was Feng, you are also certain he will not try to use the Martello Tower?'

'I never thought he would to start with.'

'So, because in Russia he attaches his trigger to the train with the sticky bomb material, at two o'clock today you believe a timer in the warehouse will launch a missile that will attach itself to the wreck?'

'No. He'll know people have been through every damn building along the estuary, and why would he bother with a sticky warhead when he's got a nice stationary target this time?'

'So what is it you are thinking?'

'I'm not sure yet.' Driscoll carried on into the room and went to stand behind the boy who was already sitting at his PC waiting for instructions.

'Try this first,' Driscoll said. '*www.johnsonmotors.com.*'

The youngster was careful and deliberate, using two fingers to enter the address before he leaned forwards to inspect the display that had come up on his screen.

The web page was an advertisement for a range of outboard motors manufactured by the Johnson Company in Minnesota; a colourful mixture of pictures, product descriptions and brand names, one of which was Minn Kota – a name that was close enough to the one the boy remembered seeing.

The boy had been equally quick to recognize it and was already clicking on to the site.

The Minn Kota web page was more detailed, presenting better illus-
trations and a block of text explaining that Minn Kota was the world's
leading manufacturer of electrically-driven outboard motors – products apparently much in demand by fishermen and wildlife photogra-
phers who needed a silent means of propelling their boats along the
shorelines of lakes and rivers.

In Driscoll's head a warning bell was ringing – not because of the
silent running claim, but because, unlike petrol engines, electric motors
that used batteries as their source of power were as capable of operating underwater as they were on the surface.

'Raymond.' Driscoll made the boy turn round. 'How big was the
plastic pipe you saw? If a length of it had been lying on the floor, could
you have crawled inside?'

'Nah. Jimmy could've. He's skinnier than me.'

'OK. Now tell me about the creek and the jetty. Where was the tide?'

'Low. Couldn't have got out to the boat otherwise.'

'How much water was there in the creek?'

The youngster thought for a moment. 'It were deep – well, I could-
n't touch the bottom with me oars. I remember trying, but I couldn't.'

The last of Driscoll's doubts had gone. But with them had gone the
last of his confidence. Minute by minute it had been draining away
while he'd been thinking, leaving him with a peculiar hollow feeling in
his stomach.

Melinkov, though, had yet to catch up. 'You think one of these little
outboard motors will drive a boat that is to be launched by remote
control?' he said.

'What boat?'

'The one Feng has fitted with high explosives.'

Driscoll shook his head. 'It's not a boat. If it was, the Coast Guard
would blow it out of the water before it got halfway to the wreck, and
if it had been left floating in the creek, someone would've found it
before now.'

'Then for what reason do you look worried?'

'Because it's a bloody torpedo. Feng built it out of parts he knew he'd
be able to buy locally. That's what the plastic pipe was for, and why he's
using batteries and an electric motor. The water tank is where he did
his testing.'

At the mention of a torpedo the boy had become eager to join the conversation. He started to stand up, but thought better of it and decided to pretend he hadn't heard.

'It is a guess,' Melinkov said. 'You cannot be sure of this.'

'Remember that box we pulled off the railcar in Troik?'

'Of course. You think it is possible the torpedo is fitted with a GPS unit that Feng has programmed with the co-ordinates of the wreck as he did for the co-ordinates of the rock-face?'

'Why not? It worked fine for him last time. All he's had to add is some kind of guidance system and a warhead. The components are being held in place by the sticky bomb adhesive he used before, and it's perfect for sealing up something that had to be lying underwater for God knows how long.'

In order to consider the implications, Melinkov reached for his cigarettes, but remembered where he was and slipped the packet back in to his pocket. 'Perhaps it is not necessary to wonder how long this torpedo has been lying in the water,' he said. 'If what you believe is true, I think it has been in the creek since the end of February when Beijing has first instructed Feng to put it there.'

'Ready for today. All it's going to take is a timer or a radio signal to switch on the electronics and the motor. Once that's happened and the warhead's armed, the bloody thing's unstoppable. No one'll have any idea where it is because no one'll be able to see it.'

'Gorman can stop it. But we should phone him now so he has plenty of time to do what must be done.'

'I'll do it from here,' Driscoll said. 'You call Collier on my mobile. It's in the glove box of the car. We'll use him as a back up. Tell him I'm arranging for the mouth of the creek to be blocked off, but that he or Sir Oliver better double check to make certain Gorman doesn't screw up.'

Leaving the boy sitting at the computer, Driscoll went to find his mother.

She was in the kitchen washing dishes at the sink, but had heard him come in and had started drying her hands on her apron.

'Don't let me hold you up,' Driscoll said. 'Is it all right if I use your phone?'

'I'll show you where it is.'

'It's OK.' He'd seen it in the hallway. 'I'm sorry we're being a nuisance.'

She smiled. 'That Chinese man's in trouble, is he?'

'Not just him.' Driscoll made the effort to return her smile, then went to make his call, hoping Gorman would be on station at the house and being more than a little relieved when the Texan answered.

'It's me,' Driscoll said. 'Before you start asking where I am, did you find an Isle of Grain police report on your desk?'

'It was you who left it, was it?'

'Have you got it?'

'Yeah, it's here. Why the hell aren't you and Melinkov?'

'Long story.' Driscoll glanced at his watch. 'Now listen; it's already quarter to one, so you haven't got much time. You have to send a team out to the warehouse at the address on that report. It's in the Lees Marshes about a mile up the coast from where you are. There's a torpedo lying outside in the creek near a broken down jetty. If you can't find anything or you figure it's too dangerous to go fishing for it, get a bulldozer to fill in the mouth of the creek where it opens out into the estuary. If you can't do that, drive a truck or a couple of cars straight into the creek itself. Whatever you use, one way or the other you've got less than an hour to get it done.'

'What are you talking about?' Gorman sounded annoyed. 'What torpedo?'

'Feng's built one. It's there in the water.'

'According to who?'

'According to me.' Driscoll had been expecting some resistance, but the hostility in Gorman's voice was a warning of how difficult this was going to be.

'Hey,' Gorman said. 'Just get back here. I haven't got enough men watching the tunnels as it is, and I sure as hell haven't got time to worry about some dumb theory you and Melinkov have dreamed up overnight.'

'It's not a theory. You don't know what's been going on at the warehouse. You don't even know where it is. But the boy's been there. And so has Feng.'

'The boy recognized Feng from the picture, did he?'

'No.' Driscoll took a deep breath. 'Not exactly. It's what he saw inside – a testing tank, large diameter plastic pipe to house the guidance system and a warhead, crates that had electric outboard motors in them, and sticky bomb adhesive. It all stacks up.'

'Sure it does. You've got a twelve-year-old boy who hasn't the first idea whether it was Feng or not, but that's OK because everyone knows torpedoes use outboard motors and are held together with bits of string and sticky bomb adhesive whatever the hell that is. Are you out of your mind?'

Driscoll managed to stop himself from looking at his watch again, knowing he should have lied about Raymond's failure to identify Feng, but still staggered by Gorman's frightening inability to understand the danger.

To recover lost ground, Driscoll made a last attempt to get his message through. 'Look,' he said. 'I don't give a shit whether you believe me or not, or who's right, or who's wrong. For once in your life, pull your head in. Just do what I've said.'

'So Feng can sneak out to the tower and back while my guys are busy dumping cars in some stupid creek? If you have any more good ideas like that one, do me a favour, will you? Keep them to yourself and get off my fucking phone.'

By hanging up to drive home his point, Gorman had created a new problem, Driscoll realized. Suddenly, Melinkov's call to Collier had become more critical – so critical that it had been a mistake to think the Russian could handle it by himself.

Hoping the MP would still be on the line, Driscoll hurried back to the kitchen, said a hasty thank you to the woman, then went straight out to the car.

Melinkov wasn't on the phone to anyone. He was leaning over the front of the Renault, smoking a cigarette and consulting a map he'd spread out on the bonnet.

'What did Collier say?'

'My call to his mobile is redirected to his office, but from there I receive a recorded message from a Sheila Stanton to say she is not presently at her desk and that Mr Collier is at an important meeting from which he cannot be disturbed. You have better luck with Gorman?'

'No.' The hollow in Driscoll's stomach had been replaced by a knot, and what he'd thought was apprehension had given way to something rather more unpleasant. 'He wouldn't listen.'

'I see.' Melinkov continued looking at the map. 'Then we can rely on no one but ourselves.'

'For Christ's sake.' Driscoll ripped the map off the bonnet. 'It's damn near one o'clock, and we're a three hour drive away from Grain. We might as well be on another bloody planet.'

'You are wrong. I did not expect Gorman to listen, so while you are talking to him, I think of another solution. If you will please get in the car and return the map to me, I will direct you to where it is we must go.'

'Where? What do you mean?'

'Less than three miles away lies the South Sussex Flying School. From the airstrip there, you will find us a nice aircraft in which you can fly us to the estuary and the creek.'

'Steal a plane?'

'When we have such little time, the longer we do nothing, the more of it we waste.'

In any other circumstances the suggestion would have been ridiculous. But if there had ever been a need for an off the wall idea, this was it, Driscoll thought; a plan so crazy that it took no account of what they were going to do if they got as far as the estuary, but maybe, irrespective of the risk and of how much luck they'd need to pull it off, the only plan that stood the remotest chance of working.

CHAPTER 21

Melinkov's navigational skills were being tested. By using his cell phone and endeavouring to read the map at the same time, he'd nearly instructed Driscoll to turn the wrong way on to the A27, and now he was having to look for signposts too, he wasn't doing any of it very well.

It had been Driscoll's idea to call Sir Oliver Fox, a last effort to contact someone who had the authority to either stop the torpedo from leaving its launching cradle or, if it was going to be too late for that, to prevent it from reaching the deeper water of the estuary.

'For Christ's sake,' Driscoll said. 'The number's in the memory. If you can't find it, give the phone to me.'

'The number is already ringing.' The Russian braced himself for another of Driscoll's overtaking manoeuvres.

At high speed on the open road, the Renault was a liability, capable of passing other vehicles only if Driscoll was brave enough to intimidate oncoming drivers, and only then if he kept his foot planted firmly on the floor. It was also overheating and smelling powerfully of hot oil.

To give the engine a chance to catch its breath, and now Melinkov was speaking on the phone, he eased back on the throttle and waited for some good news.

There wasn't any. The call was over as soon as it had begun.

'Sir Oliver is not at Energex,' Melinkov said. 'According to his secretary he too is at a meeting. I think it will be the same one Collier attends.'

Driscoll was past caring where either of them were. That they were making themselves unavailable within an hour of Beijing's deadline was a sick exercise in self-preservation, he realized, a reminder of how to play the game by men who'd written the rules. Faced with the possibility of the public refusing to believe that an horrific loss of life from a gigantic explosion in the Thames could ever be an accident or an act of God, Collier and Fox were conducting business as usual – their defence should the Martello Tower prove not to be the source of danger Gorman had promised them it was, and a means of insulating themselves from the repercussions that would follow.

'There.' Melinkov pointed ahead to a pair of open gates and a large white sign that stood at the entrance to The South Sussex Flying School.

Inside the gates, a road with speed bumps led to a group of what looked like old World War II buildings surrounding an area of broken-up tarmac that had grass growing through the cracks.

The buildings, though, were in good repair and freshly-painted, as was a nearby clubhouse or office of more recent vintage and a glider winch that Driscoll could see at the far end of the grass airstrip.

Of more interest were the aircraft; a Beechcraft Baron and an Ikarus C42 fixed-wing microlight that was parked on the tarmac between a line up of well-used Cessna 172s and a brand new Glasair Sportsman.

'One of these will be satisfactory?' Melinkov asked.

'Depends if any of them are fuelled up.' Driscoll was tense, knowing they'd have little opportunity to check, and worried about Melinkov being heavy handed once they had. 'We'll try for a Cessna.'

'To start such an aircraft, first we must obtain an ignition key?'

'Yeah.' Driscoll brought the Renault to a halt alongside the office building. 'I'll see if I can get one.'

'No, no.' Melinkov was already halfway out of the car. 'It is best I do this.'

'You don't have to whack anyone.'

'I shall do whatever is necessary.' The Russian had started to head off when Driscoll called him back and pointed to a Piper Super Cub that was coming in to land.

'Ah.' Melinkov nodded. 'I see. By this means we can save ourselves much trouble, can we not?'

'As long as it's got something in the tank.' Driscoll watched the Piper touch down at the end of the strip and waited for the pilot to commence his taxi back to the clubhouse.

'He brings his plane to us.' Melinkov said. 'We shall go and say hello to him so you may inspect his fuel gauge. Then, providing you are satisfied, we can be on our way.'

199

To do what, Driscoll wondered? In a plane as utilitarian as a Super Cub, what were the chances of them reaching the wreck before two o'clock? The engine cowling showed that the Piper was one of the later models but it was still a tail-dragger, and even with the most powerful version of the Lycoming engine it would still have a cruising speed of not much more than 80 knots, or maybe 100 or 110 miles an hour if they were lucky with a tail wind.

In one respect, luck was already on their side. The Piper's rear seat was unoccupied, and the pilot had either mistaken them for other school trainees or had simply decided to be friendly.

Cutting back on the throttle he brought the plane to a standstill near the Renault, then clipped up the window and lowered his door. 'You scheduled for a solo?' he asked.

Indicating that he couldn't hear above the noise of the propeller, Driscoll sauntered over to the cockpit and smiled while the young man took off his headset.

'You waiting?' The pilot repeated his question.

'Yep.' One look at the fuel gauge had told Driscoll what he needed to know. He nodded at Melinkov who'd come to stand beside him, then stepped back to let the Russian take over.

To save a few seconds, Melinkov used both hands, slamming one in to the pilot's stomach to release the buckle of his harness, and the other to haul him bodily from the cockpit by the collar of his jacket.

In spite of being winded and taken by surprise, the young man was commendably quick. But he wasn't quick enough. Before he could connect with his fist, Melinkov had broken two of his fingers and kicked him hard between the legs.

It was another demonstration of how uncompromising the Russian could be, but Driscoll was too preoccupied to concern himself with anything except the need to get the Piper airborne before somebody somewhere sounded the alarm.

While Melinkov dragged the pilot clear of the undercarriage and left the young man to nurse his injured fingers and his testicles, Driscoll installed himself in the cockpit, carrying out a hasty pre-flight check, hoping he'd be able to talk the Russian out of accompanying him now that Melinkov would be of no more use.

The alarm was not long coming. A man had emerged from the office and three more were running from one of the other buildings.

'You stay here,' Driscoll shouted. 'Explain what's going on, and if they don't believe you, try Sheila Stanton again. Tell her she's got less than half an hour to get hold of Collier.'

'I think not. I prefer to take my chances in this little plane with you.' Melinkov clambered in to the seat behind. 'But unless you hurry, we shall both be staying here.'

He was right. The men were no more than fifty yards away, and now they'd seen the pilot on the ground, they'd started yelling and running with more urgency.

In case one of them had the bright idea of blocking the airstrip with a car, Driscoll opened the throttle wide, guiding the accelerating Piper away from the buildings until he could swing out across a bumpy stretch of unmown grass.

His short cut was only partially successful. The plane was sluggish, still moving at a comparatively low speed when he turned on to the smoother surface of the strip.

But apart from a solitary seagull 200 yards in the distance, nothing was in the way, and as far as he could determine, no other aircraft were coming in to land.

His takeoff was uneventful. Within a few yards, the tail came up as the plane gathered speed and began to bounce. Fifteen seconds later, long before they reached the seagull, Driscoll felt the controls go light, and the Piper was in the air, climbing at a rate of nearly a thousand feet a minute into a watery blue sky.

To avoid losing airspeed by banking too quickly, Driscoll put the Piper in to a long gentle turn to the north before he settled down to set a course that he hoped would lead him to the intersection of the Medway and the Thames.

Behind him in the cockpit, Melinkov was shouting something and pointing at his watch.

Whatever message the Russian was trying to convey, Driscoll didn't want to hear it. He didn't need to be reminded of how short of time they were, and if Melinkov had more advice to offer, he didn't want to hear that either.

Retrieving the pilot's headset from the floor, he started looking for the jack point on the instrument panel, discovering that in his rush to get in he'd stood on the plug and crushed it flat.

The back up system was similarly useless. A built-in microphone and a speaker in the roof panel were either inoperable or the engine noise was drowning out any transmissions that were being radioed to the stolen aircraft.

It didn't matter, Driscoll decided. Whether or not Air Traffic Control already had the Piper on their screens, with so few people knowing about the danger to the *Richard Montgomery*, it would be a while before anyone linked a shipwreck in the Thames with the theft of a light aircraft from a Worthing flying school.

Preferring to concentrate on more immediate concerns, at an altitude of 2000 feet he let the Piper flatten out, leaving the mixture on full rich in the hope of extracting a few more vital knots of airspeed while he tried to refine his plan of attack.

The plan was simple. It was simple because it had to be, and because it was the only one he'd been able to think of – a high risk gamble that required him to identify a creek he'd never seen before and to then somehow or other ditch the Piper in the mouth of it.

Simple it might be, but Driscoll knew the plan had major weaknesses. As well as relying on his ability to stall an unfamiliar aircraft at the right moment without tipping the Piper on its nose and drowning him and his passenger before they could get out, it also assumed they were going to arrive there before the expiry of the deadline.

Their current lack of progress was not the Piper's fault. With the airspeed indicator reading 86 knots, and with a marked absence of the tail wind he'd been hoping for, the plane was already at the top end of its performance range, and in the last few minutes, having concluded that it was flying as fast as it could be reasonably expected to fly, he'd stopped fiddling with the controls.

Spread out below him now was what he thought was the town of Tonbridge, a rough halfway point that it had taken them over a quarter of an hour to reach – a measure of how much longer it would be before they reached the marshes and the creek.

So what was he worried about, he wondered? With clear skies and an estimated arrival time of 1.49, providing the creek was easy to locate, he'd still have eleven minutes in hand – more than long enough to carry out a couple of experimental stalls at suitably safe altitude before he was forced to make his final run.

The thought should have been reassuring. But it wasn't. The knot in his stomach was still there, and even though being back in the cockpit of an aircraft was helping to reassure him, just as he knew he couldn't afford to ditch in the wrong place, so he knew that if he delayed his run too long, they'd risk not being able to get out before the torpedo blew the whole damn plane to bits.

For the next ten minutes he concentrated on navigation, keeping an eye open for fighter jets or helicopters that he half expected to appear from nowhere and not bothering to correct his course until he got his first glimpse of the water.

He was too far to the west, and now he had his bearings he wished he'd started to reduce his altitude much earlier.

Easing the stick forwards he began a steep descent, lining up the Piper's nose with the mouth of the Medway and waiting until he was over the coastal saltings of the Isle of Grain before he checked his airspeed and commenced his search for the creek.

Away to his right, the outline of the Martello Tower was unmistakable and as grim as ever. Viewed from the air its disconnection from the present was complete – a mythical fortress that could have just arisen dripping from the mud bank which until today had been its home.

For Driscoll it was a landmark, a point of reference if the creek was going to be difficult to find.

It wasn't. Of the three waterways cutting through the marshes, only one had a warehouse and a jetty standing at the end of it.

Melinkov had identified it too. Leaning forwards to attract Driscoll's attention he waved a hand and pointed.

It was an unwanted distraction. What the Russian hadn't seen was a trail of discoloured water leading away from the base of the jetty to the centre of the creek.

Because it had been faint and indistinct, Driscoll banked the Piper and reduced his altitude to 200 feet before returning for a closer look.

He hadn't imagined it, but instead of fading out as he'd first thought, there were signs of it elsewhere – not just near the jetty but throughout the entire length of the creek, a hundred yard-long line of lighter coloured water that eventually led out into the estuary itself.

Driscoll had been slow to understand the significance of the trail, but now he did, he knew exactly what it was.

It wasn't a trail. It was a wake – evidence of a fundamental and unforgivable miscalculation.

By failing to realize that the torpedo would need to be launched well ahead of two o'clock if it was to complete its journey from the jetty to the wreck on schedule, he'd made the worst mistake he could have made.

He felt sick, incapable for the minute of piloting the Piper that was heading out across the waters of the estuary and losing height as rapidly as it was losing speed.

Alerted by Melinkov pounding on his shoulder, he opened the throttle and eased back on the stick, maintaining his bearing while he tried to decide what the hell he was going to do.

Now that the eleven minutes he'd allowed for ditching the aircraft had become eleven minutes to the time of impact, he found himself trying to imagine what a two mile-high eruption of mud and water was going to look like and wondering how far away he'd need to be if a blast of such improbable proportions was not to convert the Piper into pieces of confetti.

Beneath his starboard wing the Martello Tower had again swum in to sight, a reminder of the nets that had once been strung across the river – defences from another time that had they still been in place would have protected the *Richard Montgomery* from the warhead that was bearing down on it.

If Driscoll had not been looking at the tower he would never have seen more streaks in the water, the same kind of streaks he'd first noticed in the creek.

They were intermittent – long dashes leading east across the estuary in the deep water channel that skirted the base of the tower, a witness of the torpedo's progress that would be visible only from the air, and then only from directly above or maybe at a shallow angle from behind.

Before he could check, the Piper had crossed the wake and he lost sight of it until he banked again.

He was a hundred yards from the line of streaks when the reason for them became more obvious.

To compensate for the current, the torpedo was fishtailing slightly as its guidance system made the necessary adjustments to its course. But it was porpoising too, occasionally coming so close to the surface that for a brief moment or two before it dived again he had a clear view of its outline.

The body of the torpedo was white and blunt-nosed, about eight feet long with cruciform tail fins at the rear, just ahead of which were mounted twin Minn Kota propulsion units.

It was remarkably slow moving, rising every twenty seconds or so, but travelling at not much more than five or six knots.

Its slowness alone was adding to its menace, and now Driscoll could detect more of the streaks or dashes, as well as them showing where the torpedo had come from, they showed where it was headed – a mile-long arrow pointing directly at the rusting masts of a wreck that very soon was going to turn the quiet waters of the Thames estuary into a hell of boiling flame and tidal waves.

If stealing a plane and thinking he could crash land it in a creek had been crazy, in Driscoll's mind now was an idea bordering on lunacy – a plan so desperate that believing he had the skill to bring it off was about as realistic as believing he had the resolve to try.

The thought of trying was making his stomach worse, and the chill that had been creeping over him was starting to affect his co-ordination.

Was it possible to fly a Super Cub with its tail wheel dragging in the water, he wondered? And if it was, what if his timing was off, and instead of nudging the rear of the torpedo with his wheel, he made contact with the warhead?

Nothing would happen, he told himself. Nothing. A warhead designed to detonate on impact would be too risky in case of a miss. It would have a magnetic sensor, he decided, or maybe one triggered by an on-board GPS unit as he'd first imagined.

Not that it was going to make much bloody difference, he thought, not when there was such a disparity in speed between the aircraft and the torpedo. Even with the Piper close to stalling, it would still be travelling ten times faster than its target – so much faster that any approach from behind would be almost as dangerous as tackling the damn thing head on.

In the end his decision was made easy.

Fifty or sixty yards to the north of the wake he could see an area of shallower water, a long stretch of it that had formed at the edge of the mud-bank on which the remains of the *Richard Montgomery* lay. Too far away to interfere with the torpedo, the shallows were close enough if the thing could be knocked sufficiently off course to bury itself in the mud before its guidance system was able to regain control and correct the error.

Committed to the only tactic he thought might work, and too scared to consider what was going to happen if it didn't, at an altitude of thirty feet, Driscoll waited for a glimpse of the torpedo's tail fin. Then, gritting his teeth, he commenced his run at right angles to the wake, counting down the seconds while he reduced height until he had the Piper's wheels skimming a few inches above the water.

His guess of when the torpedo would next break the surface was nearly as good as his estimate of where it would.

The tail fin had appeared immediately ahead of him at a distance of not more than eighty feet, leaving a line of bubbles to provide him with the only reference point he was going to have.

Altimeter firmly stuck on zero, flying by instinct and ready to sense the first tug on his tail wheel, Driscoll tightened his grip on the stick and prepared himself.

Whether the manoeuvre would have been successful he would never know.

At the same instant muzzle flashes stabbed out at him from the upper level of the Martello Tower, a hail of bullets tore away his tail plane and most of his starboard wing.

For a light aircraft travelling at such low speed, the consequences were more severe than he expected.

The Piper slammed in to the water on its side, smashing its fragile fuselage to pieces before the wreckage cartwheeled in a cloud of spray.

The water was cold, but the taste of it was not unpleasant. More surprising was the quantity of water. A torrent of it was gushing through the broken windshield, filling the cockpit in a matter of seconds and pinning him back against his seat.

Except that it wasn't just the water, he realized. It was the remains of the Piper's instrument panel that was crushed against his chest – a twisted mess of aluminium that was making it impossible for him to find the buckle to release his belt.

For a while he continued fighting to free himself, refusing to abandon the struggle until he breathed in his first lungful of liquid mud and only giving up because by then he knew with absolute certainty that he was going to die.

CHAPTER 22

The three-day-old newspaper was still lying on the bedside table where the staff nurse had left it. Driscoll had been meaning to throw it away, but because the report on page five continued to be his sole source of information, he kept imagining that if he read between the lines often enough he might get a hint of what the hell had really happened.

The report was a sloppy piece of journalism, written by someone who'd been too busy coming up with a cute sub-title to question officially released misinformation that had been designed to explain away those events the public had witnessed, and which therefore were impossible to cover up. Predictably, the end result was a write-up that was as sketchy as it was misleading.

For want of anything better to do until Collier arrived, Driscoll lay back on his pillow and read through the wretched thing for what he promised himself would be the very last time:

AIRBORNE JOYRIDERS MEET MUDDY END

Efforts are being made to recover the wreckage of a light aircraft that was shot down over the Thames estuary yesterday afternoon. According to the Air Traffic Control Centre in Southend, the plane, a 1994 Piper Super Cub, was stolen by two men from the South Sussex Flying School near Worthing and tracked by radar to the Isle of Grain in Kent, after which on several occasions it strayed dangerously close to the international no-fly zone surrounding the wreck of the USS *Richard Montgomery*.

The Ministry of Defence are making no apology for the manner in which the aircraft's flight was terminated, pointing out that in the interests of public safety, and because of the pilot's refusal to acknowledge repeated radio warnings to stand off and keep clear, it became necessary to use all reasonable force to bring down the aircraft as expediently as possible.

It is understood that the aircraft lies submerged in shallow water at the edge of a substantial mud-bank which made the rescue of the pilot and his passenger an unusually difficult and particularly messy job for the Coast Guard and the paramedics who attended the scene.

Although the pilot has been hospitalized, neither of the men are reported to be seriously injured. Police are expected to release their names later in the week at which time appropriate charges will be laid.

So superficial and so carefully worded had been the officially released version of the story that Driscoll could be sure of only two things – that by some stroke of good fortune Melinkov had managed to survive as well, and that either the torpedo had never reached the *Richard Montgomery*, or if it had, somehow or other it had failed to detonate.

Whether or not the Piper's crash had anything to do with it, he had no idea. Nor did he have any idea how he'd escaped from the sinking aircraft. When the real reason for the crash had been so effectively disguised, almost from the minute he'd woken up in hospital and started asking questions, he'd felt as though he'd been living in an information vacuum.

That none of his questions had been answered was an understatement. Melinkov's cell phone was as dead today as it had been yesterday and the day before, neither Sir Oliver nor his secretary were returning calls, and according to the Energex receptionist, as of Tuesday, Mr Gorman had ceased to be an employee of the company.

Frustrated by a near total information blackout and feeling more than well enough to take matters into his own hands, by yesterday evening, Driscoll had been close to discharging himself, changing his mind only after he'd received a telephone call from Collier.

The call had taken up the best part of twenty minutes, an artificially friendly enquiry to find out how well he was recovering, followed by an assurance that it wasn't just the British government who were indebted to him, but a number of other people who were equally anxious to express their gratitude – unnamed, influential people who recognized very clearly who they had to thank for preventing what could have been a peace-time disaster on a truly unprecedented scale.

At the time, in between trying to get answers, Driscoll had barely been able to control his cynicism, accusing Collier of being evasive until the MP had announced his intention of coming to see if he'd be sufficiently fit to attend a meeting at the Chinese Embassy in London later on this morning.

Since then, Driscoll had grown progressively more suspicious, unwilling to believe that anything much had changed, and concerned that he could again fall victim to some new manipulative twist combining Rebecca Wilson's death and his supposed drug trafficking with the theft of an aircraft from a flying school in Sussex.

It would depend on how grateful Collier was going to be, he decided, or maybe on the government's level of paranoia and how determined they were to prevent the truth from leaking out.

As tired of speculating as he was of lying on a damn hospital bed, he went to have his shower, taking longer than he intended to because the steam took the edge off the rawness in his throat and made it easier to forget what it felt like to have a mouthful of laryngoscopes and bronchoscopes.

His breathing was less laboured too, he realized, and this morning he wasn't coughing up quite so much of the Thames as he had been.

He returned to his room to find the staff nurse waiting for him. Although she was a stern-faced woman with the bedside manner of a dock worker and hands to match, she'd adopted him almost from the time he'd been admitted and had been looking after him and fighting with him ever since.

'Here.' She tossed a large brown paper parcel on to the bed.

'What is it?'

'Shoes, socks, underwear, two shirts, a suit and a nice silk tie. I looked in case it was a shipment of marijuana or cocaine.'

'Shame you've been disappointed.' He grinned at her while he unwrapped the paper. 'Do you know who sent it?'

'One of your girlfriends.' She pointed to a card that had fallen out.

It was a with compliment slip that had the name Sheila Stanton printed on it – an indication not of Collier's thoughtfulness, Driscoll decided, but more likely of how formal today's meeting was going to be.

He held up the tie. 'What do you think?'

The nurse shook her head. 'Wearing that isn't going to make you feel any better,' she said. 'And it certainly isn't going to make you look any better.'

'Does that mean I have to shave myself again this morning?'

'Unless you can persuade Miss Stanton to do it for you, whoever she is.' The nurse looked at him. 'Are you sure you'll be all right?'

'Yep.' He was more than sure, already assembling his questions in his mind, as anxious for Collier to arrive as he was to be out of here.

Thirty minutes later, sitting next to the MP in the rear seat of a chauffeur-driven Daimler, Driscoll had the answer to the first of his questions. 'Melinkov must have been quick,' he said. 'I was jammed in the cockpit pretty damn well.'

Collier nodded. 'He said if he hadn't used a knife to cut your harness you'd have gone down in the plane without a doubt. As I understand it, the water wasn't deep, but, of course, if you're trapped you can drown in a couple of feet. If you don't already know, you have more than that to thank Melinkov for. According to the paramedics, if he hadn't got the worst of the mud and water out of you before the pair of you were picked up, you'd either be dead by now, or looking at a life-long bronchial problem.' Collier glanced across the car. 'As things are, I'm pleased to see you don't look too much the worse for wear.'

'Was it Melinkov who told you about the torpedo?'

'He didn't need to. It was found lodged in the undercarriage of the plane.'

'Still armed?' Driscoll was beginning to appreciate that he'd been even luckier than he thought he'd been.

'I don't know.'

'Where's Melinkov now?'

'I'm sorry.' Collier looked apologetic. 'I don't know that either.'

'And there's been no sign of Feng?'

'No, but after today I don't believe we'll have to worry about him anymore.'

'Why not? The *Richard Montgomery*'s still there. It didn't blow this time, but that won't stop Beijing having another go, will it?'

'I'm confident they won't try again. That's one of the reasons I thought you might care to come with me this morning. In the circumstances, inviting you seemed the very least I could do.' Collier opened his case and took out a sheet of paper. 'Which brings me to this. I'd like you to read it before we get to the embassy. It's a copy of the last email we received from Feng. My secretary forwarded it on from Santorini.'

'What was she doing there?' Driscoll could guess. 'Did you send her to find out where Natalie Washburn had gone?'

'And to avoid us having a break in our communication channel. Before you ask, all I can tell you is that we were able to trace Miss Washburn's movements only as far as Hong Kong. For the moment, could I suggest it would be more profitable for you to concentrate on the wording of the email?'

Driscoll couldn't see why. Except for the implied threat to the *Richard Montgomery* and the mention of a specified deadline, the wording was much the same as it had been in the other emails he'd seen.

Collier cleared his throat. 'I hardly like to bring this up,' he said, 'but it's best we get it out of the way. Without going into details, I can say there's no longer any suggestion of you being involved in the Rebecca Wilson affair. Thanks to Energex, her husband has received a large payout from a hastily arranged life insurance policy he didn't know his wife had taken out, and if necessary we might be able to implicate Feng in the death of his wife – an unfortunate case of a Chinese narcotics dealer mistaking Mrs Wilson for Miss Washburn perhaps.'

'After a drug deal had gone wrong?' Driscoll couldn't keep the cynicism out of his voice.

'We'll see.'

'So Gorman's the only casualty, and Energex are coming out of this smelling of roses.'

'I wouldn't say that. Providing Beijing accepts the compensation they've been offered – and after our meeting today, I think they may be glad to – the company's directors will be contributing the lion's share of the payment.'

'Big hooray,' Driscoll said.

Collier ignored the remark. 'Gorman's incompetence is another matter,' he said. 'I appreciate what you and Melinkov think of him, but it wasn't entirely his fault that you ended up in hospital. Even if he'd known the army had taken the precaution of stationing a heavy machine-gun in the Martello Tower, after a kamikaze performance like yours, you were always going to get yourself shot down.'

'And Gorman was always going to get himself fired?'

'Probably.' Collier appeared to be thinking of something else. 'It's funny, isn't it?' he said. 'The first way mankind found to handle conflict was by using sticks and stones, bows and arrows, guns and bombs. Then after we'd discovered we're all part of a global economy, instead of going to war, we adopted the second way – a more civilized initiative that allows governments to control other countries by withholding aid and imposing trade sanctions.' He paused. 'Now we've got this.'

'What?'

'The third way – war of a kind we've never seen before – a completely new means of settling our differences that relies on the triggering of what are supposed to look like unpreventable accidents or acts of God. It's a rather disturbing development.'

For politicians, the concept wouldn't be disturbing, Driscoll thought, it would be irresistible. 'No voter backlash,' he said, 'because the public never know what's going on, and no military build-up because all you need are people like Melinkov and Feng to handle the nasty stuff.'

'Well, yes – although it's a little harsh to suggest it's only governments and the armed forces who benefit.'

With most of his questions answered, Driscoll wasn't inclined to prolong the discussion, preferring to keep his opinions to himself while he tried to figure out where, if anywhere, he fitted in to the new scheme of things.

Having reached no conclusion by the time the car pulled up outside the front entrance of the Portland Place embassy, he switched his attention to matters of more immediate importance and made an effort to look as though he understood what they were doing here.

The Chinese aide who greeted them in the foyer introduced himself as Mr Liu, apologizing for the absence of the ambassador before escorting them to an austere first floor room that had a large, unflattering portrait of President Hu Jintao decorating one wall, and an abstract painting of what Driscoll thought could be the Shanghai skyline hanging on another.

'Please to be seated.' The aide placed a small tape recorder on the table and pointed to it. 'You have no objection?'

'No, not at all.' Collier was so relaxed he could have been home talking to his wife. 'It's good of you to see us at short notice,' he said. 'Since I'm not representing the sole interests of my own government today, but also those of the US Administration and the Russian Duma, rather than summoning the ambassador to a formal meeting in Whitehall, I thought it more appropriate for Mr Driscoll and I to come here.'

'I see. Your visit is in connection with what, precisely?'

'Cementing the good relationship between our countries by co-operating with each other.' Collier smiled. 'Allow me to explain. First of all, we know the People's Republic is suffering from an increasing number of industrial accidents. Three years ago, you had the tragic blowout of your Gao Qiao gas well in Chongqing in which more than two hundred people died and nine thousand were injured. Then, last November, there was the unfortunate explosion in your PetroChina benzene factory in Jilin province. As I understand it, the result of that was a discharge of something like a hundred and fifty tons of mercury in to the Songhua river, and a chemical slick that's contaminated the water supply of millions of people.'

The aide was looking uneasy. 'You mention these events for what purpose?' he asked.

'Well,' Collier smiled again, 'in an increasingly dangerous world where harmonious international relations have become essential, countries must help each other and work together if tragedies of a similar kind are to be avoided in the future.'

The statement had been taken word for word from the first paragraph in Feng's last email, Driscoll realized – the reason why Collier had wanted him to read it, and why, if Liu had recognized it too, he was being careful to pretend he hadn't.

'I am not sure I understand,' Liu said. 'How is it you propose that we work together?'

'Through technology.' Collier leaned back in his chair. 'I'm not suggesting China is in any way lagging behind the rest of the world, but I think you'll be finding it more and more difficult to recruit the highly skilled foreign workers your industries need if your safety record continues to deteriorate, and of course, when so many of your major rivers run through other countries as well as your own, it's in no one's interest to see them poisoned by accidents that are easily preventable if you have the right technology.'

'Which Russia, Britain and the United States are willing to provide?'

'Indeed. The expense to the People's Republic won't be insignificant, but I've been asked to make it clear that Moscow, London and Washington are happy to subsidize the equipment cost and cost of installation. Just as an example, without the latest protection technology, any one of your major oil refineries could suffer serious damage from a fire or an explosion should they be accidentally hit by lightning during the next big electrical storm.'

'I see. Your offer of such technology is most generous.' Besides looking uneasy, the aide was swallowing.

'It's regrettable how dangerous the world has become, isn't it?' Collier said. 'When we have Islamic extremists planting bombs everywhere, and you have Uighur terrorists operating right across Xinjiang, until we learn to co-operate, it's always going to be hard to know whether an accident is really an accident or an act of terrorism that's been designed to look like an accident.'

Driscoll had long ago decided not to join the discussion, respecting Collier's superior diplomatic skills and impressed by the way the MP had promised retaliation in kind should the Chinese be rash enough to persist with their so-called reparation programme.

It was pretty damn clever, Driscoll thought, a blunt threat masquerading as an offer of help that was going to create a standoff and stop Beijing from trying their hand again in the future – a message conveyed so smoothly there could be no suggestion of it being a threat at all.

The embassy aide knew exactly what it was. Judging by his expression, he also knew he'd been outflanked. He stood up and bowed. 'The ambassador will be most pleased to receive this information,' he said. 'By the week's end I think you should expect to hear something from him. In the meantime, on behalf of the Chinese People's Republic I thank you for this kind consideration.'

Now the meeting was at an end, Driscoll felt as though he'd been watching actors performing in a stage play, an exchange between men so accustomed to representing the views of their governments, it was impossible to tell whether they had any of their own.

He waited until he was accompanying Collier back to the car before asking whose bright idea that had been.

'I wish I could take the credit for it.' The MP continued walking. 'Unfortunately, I'm afraid I can't. It came from your friend.'

'Look,' Driscoll said, 'just because Melinkov dragged me out of the plane it doesn't mean he's my friend.'

'Not him. Miss Washburn.'

'What?' Driscoll stopped him. 'What are you talking about?'

'Three days before the 27th, she telephoned me from Shanghai with a most interesting proposal. We had a long and very profitable conversation.'

'Jesus.' Driscoll was confused, not sure he was hearing this correctly. 'Are you telling me it was her idea to play the Chinese at their own game?'

'Indeed it was. Apparently, shortly after you left for Chelyabinsk, she decided the pair of you had become so mixed up in a situation you stood little chance of getting out of, that she needed to do something about it. If I remember rightly, she used the word manipulated.'

Driscoll was too bewildered to care what word she'd used, unable to believe he could have ever distrusted her so thoroughly and worried that he was either jumping to conclusions or misinterpreting what he'd just been told.

Collier rested his case on the roof of the car. 'As you and I both know,' he said, 'Miss Washburn is a resourceful young woman. She's probably more astute than you and I put together. She managed to make contact with one of the Uighur separatist leaders she'd met while she was researching the Chinese oil industry and suggested that if, during the next big thunderstorm, he could arrange for a small accidental explosion to occur at the Huai River oil refinery, he and his men could well find themselves in possession of a large number of brand new Kalashnikov assault rifles. The concept's admirably simple, and it allows us to prove we have the capability of doing what we've said we can. It will also cost very little.'

Driscoll had stopped listening. After living with his doubts for so long, only two things mattered now. 'So she never was working for Beijing,' he said.

'No, of course she wasn't. I've already explained. She was just doing everything she could to look after you and get you out of the mess she thought you were in.'

'I have to see her,' Driscoll said quietly. 'Where is she?'

'I have no idea. But she did say that, if you happened to ask, to tell you she was certain you'd know where to find her.'

CHAPTER 23

The taxi had slowed down, but the driver was looking for the villa on the wrong side of the street.

'It's OK.' Driscoll could see it. 'This is fine. You can drop me here.' He paid the fare and stepped out into the afternoon sunshine, feeling the air warm on his face, breathing in the smell of the ocean and the scent of flowers he could remember from the last time he'd been here.

Away to his right, the Aegean was the same painted sea it had been before, the sky was as blue as it had been on the day he'd left and, in the front garden, the lower branches of the two olive trees were still entwined in the same peculiar embrace.

Wanting to drink it all in, for nearly a minute he stayed out in the street, no longer sure it was such a good idea to be arriving unannounced, and with no real idea of what he was going to say to her, let alone what he would do if she wasn't here.

Even after he'd climbed the white stone steps and rung the doorbell he remained uncertain, wondering how best to break the ice and rather wishing he'd taken the precaution of telephoning first.

Someone was home. But it wasn't Natalie who opened the door: it was Melinkov, grinning like an idiot while he pumped Driscoll's hand and pulled him inside.

'You are surprised?' The Russian couldn't stop grinning. 'You do not expect to find me here?'

Driscoll was more put out than surprised, unable to get a proper look at Natalie until Melinkov realized he was in the way.

She was standing barefoot in the hall, hands by her side, apparently too unsure of herself to come forward.

Although Melinkov had started retreating discreetly to the terrace, still she seemed to be in no hurry to say hello, making only a half-

216

hearted attempt to look as though she was pleased to see him.

'Hi there,' Driscoll said.

She shuffled her feet. 'I wasn't sure you'd come.'

It would have been easier to believe her if she hadn't been wearing the halter top and the yellow skirt he'd bought her from the little shop in Fira – a clear way of reminding him of how things had been before, he decided. 'If you didn't know I'd come, why tell Collier you'd be here?'

'I didn't tell him that.' She wiped away some tears. 'Well, not exactly.'

'For Christ's sake.' Driscoll shut the door behind him. 'Just come here, will you?'

She took a step, hesitated, then ran straight to him.

To protect his bruises he caught her in mid-air, wrapping his arms round her and swinging her off her feet before he pushed her against the wall and kissed her on the mouth, allowing the taste of her tears to bring back a kaleidoscope of half-remembered images.

There were dozens of them – one of her in the Shanghai restaurant mixed up with his attempt to keep her alive in the kitchen of his brother's house, another of their car crash in her Fiesta, and blurred memories of the meetings with Collier and Feng that had brought them here to Santorini before everything had started to go wrong. And now he had another one for his collection – what should have been the best of them all had Melinkov not been here to take the edge off it.

She'd guessed what he was thinking. 'Melinkov isn't staying,' she said softly. 'He's on his way to somewhere else. He just called in to tell me I don't have to worry about Feng any more.'

'Did he say why?'

'I didn't ask. But he explained what you've been doing. I know what happened to the train in Russia, I know all about the SAFOD project at Parkfield, and I know what you did last week in England. Melinkov says he doesn't know anyone who would've tried to fly a plane like that.'

'Did he tell you if it wasn't for him I'd be at the bottom of the Thames?'

She shook her head. 'He said you'd bought yourself a ticket to Johannesburg, though. Is that where you're going?'

'Depends.'

'On what?'

'You.'

'Oh.' She started to smile but caught herself in time.

'Do that again,' Driscoll said.

'No.' She put a hand over her mouth.

This was what he'd remembered about her most – not just her eyes, her figure and the flawless honey colour of her skin, but the broken smile she was trying to stop him seeing.

'You're embarrassing me.' She tried to wriggle away. 'If you mean what you say, we don't have to go anywhere. We can stay here for as long as we want. Collier's going off to visit his daughter in Tennessee, but he said if there was somewhere I'd like to go, all I have to do is contact Sheila Stanton and she'll arrange to have everything paid for me.'

'Lucky you.'

'Mm. Are you going to keep holding me off the ground like this?'

'Unless you can think of something better for us to do while Melinkov's around.'

'He's ordered a taxi for three o'clock. If you want to talk to him before he leaves, I can bring coffee out on to the terrace.'

'OK.' Driscoll put her down. 'If he asks how long we're going to be here, say we don't know yet.'

Melinkov hardly looked in the mood for asking questions. He was lounging in a canvas chair smoking one of his cigarettes and staring out to sea.

'Thanks for what you did,' Driscoll said. 'Collier told me.'

'It was nothing. Like the people of Sheerness and the Isle of Grain, we both are fortunate, I think. You suffer from no bad effects?'

'Bruises and a bit of a cough. How about you?'

'A small sprain of my left knee, but I am otherwise OK. I am most pleased to see you. I was not certain you would be here.'

'Are you on your way home?'

'No, no.' Melinkov shook his head. 'I have already been back to Russia. I make a special trip there to tell my daughter that Mr Yukos is paying for the surgery she needs to make her well again. For her it is the best news she could have, and for me also, of course.'

'That's really great.' Driscoll was pleased for him. 'So where are you off to now?'

'Energex have been instructed to send someone to North Korea. The Kim Jong regime is refusing to listen to the United Nations, and because the government does not care if their international aid is cut

218

off and their people starve, a new way will be used to stop them from developing nuclear weapons and testing their long-range missiles.'

'The third way?'

'Ah.' Melinkov grinned. 'Collier has explained this to you. I visit Korea for a short while only – just long enough to learn what unfortunate accidents can be made to happen there.'

Driscoll wished he could be surprised. But he wasn't. What Collier termed the third way was too good a tool for politicians to ignore, he thought, a zero risk technique that the Chinese had given to the rest of the world without appreciating what the inevitable consequence would be.

'I bring something for you.' Melinkov reached into his satchel and took out a small roll of paper. 'My daughter Catherine has drawn this for you. I have explained that you do not wish me to be your friend, but when I tell her what it is you do in England, she thinks it will be nice for you to have this.'

It was a pencil sketch of an aircraft flying over water at low altitude, a remarkably well-drawn picture that no nine-year-old should have been able to produce.

Driscoll was at a loss to know what to say, unable to reconcile the image of an innocent and gifted daughter with the one he had of her father, and wondering if he should have made a greater effort to thank Melinkov for rescuing him.

He was still feeling guilty when Natalie brought out the coffee. Whether she'd overcome her dislike of the Russian or was just doing a good job of concealing it, Driscoll wasn't sure.

What she couldn't conceal was her happiness.

She had a permanent smile on her face, and now she'd come outside and had the sun in her hair, she was looking so impossibly desirable that even Melinkov was having trouble keeping his eyes off her.

Pulling up a chair she sat down facing the Russian and crossed her legs. 'Are you going to tell us why I don't have to worry about Feng?' she asked.

'It is very simple.' Melinkov inspected his coffee cup. 'He is dead.'

This time Driscoll's surprise was genuine. 'What happened to him?'

'It is not important.'

'We can ask Collier. Or did Collier have something to do with it?'

'He would not answer your questions. After losing his first wife to cancer, certainly life has not been kind to him, but just because he

learns that Feng has burned his son to death at the Hotan airstrip, it
does not mean a politician of his standing would act unwisely.'

'So he didn't arrange to have Feng killed?'

'There will be no suggestion of it. I hear only that after you and I are
taken off the mud-bank, two of the men Energex had stationed on the
Isle of Grain are returned to London where they are told to keep a
watch on the Chinese Embassy.'

'Told by someone who needed to know whether Feng was still in the
country?'

Melinkov shrugged. 'Who can tell? Whatever the truth may be, all
we can be sure of is that two days later a Chinese property investor
from Hong Kong who goes by the name of Jun is found dead after the
embassy BMW he drives is filled with a fentanyl nerve gas from a cylinder someone has hidden in the boot.'

Guessing where the cylinder had come from was one thing, Driscoll
decided, but it was probably best not to know who'd asked Melinkov to
put it there.

Natalie wasn't going to press the point either. She'd moved her chair
and had been resting a foot on Driscoll's ankle while she finished her
coffee and listened to Melinkov's account of what had happened. Now,
though, she wanted to change the subject.

She picked up the pencil sketch and studied it for a moment. 'Did
your plane really look like this?' she asked.

Melinkov shook his head. 'In such a small cockpit it is necessary for
the passenger to ride behind, but my daughter is a little girl who wishes
to draw her father sitting beside the pilot.'

Had the circumstances been different, Driscoll wouldn't have
minded spending an afternoon in the sun indulging in small talk and
catching up on news. As it was, his sense of frustration was making it
hard for him to concentrate and he was relieved when a ring of the bell
announced the arrival of the taxi.

Natalie said her goodbye to Melinkov out on the terrace, leaving
Driscoll to accompany him to the front door.

'You're not going to like it in North Korea,' Driscoll said. 'There are
better places.'

'You and Miss Washburn are in one of them, I think. It is my wish
for you to both enjoy your stay here.'

'We will. You look after yourself.'

'Of course.' Melinkov shook hands, then hurried down the steps, glancing back briefly to shout '*Udachee ee da pomozhet tebe Gospod*' before he got in the car and slammed the door.

Hoping Natalie might be able to provide a translation, Driscoll went to see if she could.

She wasn't on the terrace. The coffee cups had been cleared away, but she wasn't in the kitchen either.

She was in the bedroom, lying on the bed with her hands behind her head and her eyes closed. 'Has he gone?' she asked.

'Yeah, he's gone. Do you know what *Udachee ee da pomozhet tebe Gospod* means?'

'Something like good luck and may God be with you.' She turned away from him on to her side. 'Do you have any more silly questions like that you want to ask me?'

'No.'

'Then it's all right if I go to sleep now, is it?'

'Sure. If you don't want to talk, I'll find something else to do.' Kicking off his shoes he lay down behind her on the bed, then, after waiting for her to relax, carefully lifted her skirt and slipped his hand between her thighs, half-expecting her to resist, but realizing she wasn't going to when she moved to make herself more comfortable.

Reluctant to spoil things by rushing, for a while he contented himself by kissing the nape of her neck, taking his time to slide his other hand under her halter so he could brush his fingertips against her nipples.

She liked him doing it, responding by removing her top and quickly pressing her breasts back in to his cupped hand to heighten her enjoyment until her nipples became more swollen and she was ready to open her legs for him.

As though she'd wanted him to know how long she'd been waiting for this, and how much she'd been hoping it would happen this afternoon, she was wearing nothing beneath her skirt, trembling slightly when he first touched her, but soon surrendering to the pleasure of his caresses when he became more enterprising and began to tease her.

Almost too aroused to know what she was doing, she was wonderfully wet, inviting him to explore her by curling up tighter on her side, and encouraging him by gradually raising her knees before she was suddenly overtaken by her own demands and no longer able to control herself.

Before he could stop her she rolled on to her back and sat up, fumbling in her haste to help him strip off his clothes, then wide-eyed in anticipation, gathered her skirt round her waist and reached out to hold him in both hands.

By now, Driscoll too was lost, intoxicated by the smell of her hair and her perfume, so conscious of the silky tautness of her skin that he could think of nothing but the urgent need to take her and possess her.

Pushing her back on her pillow, he made her look at him.

'Please,' she whispered. 'I don't want to wait.'

He didn't want to either, allowing her to guide him inside her until she was fully penetrated before he stopped kissing her in order to catch his breath.

But she'd already closed her eyes and begun to move beneath him, arching her back and spreading her legs wider, no more capable of lingering than he was, and so eager to seek her release that, for Driscoll, the act of making love to her had assumed the qualities of a dream – an hallucination, or some imagined fantasy because he'd died in the plane crash after all.

But there was nothing imaginary about the way she'd begun to shudder, and a second later, the climax they shared was as real and as sensuous as anything he'd ever wanted to experience – a burst of such intense pleasure that only she could have given him, and their reward for all the hurt and all the wasted weeks they'd spent apart.

Now it was over, he was unwilling to break the spell, trying as hard as he could not to cough, but in the end losing the battle and waking her up.

'Hi.' She smiled at him. 'Is that you?'

'I'll let you know after I've got some fresh air in me. You stay here. I won't be long.'

'Why do I have to stay here?'

'Because you're too sleepy to do anything else, and because from now on I have to know exactly where you are, or where you're going to be.'

'Oh.' She smiled again. 'So you know where to find me whenever you want to?'

'Right.' He pulled the sheet up over her, kissed her on the forehead, then went to the bathroom, wrapped a towel round him and walked out slowly on to the terrace.

The shadows were lengthening and the air was a little cooler, but Santorini was still drowsing in the sunshine, and in this part of the world at least, things seemed very much as he wanted them to be and how they should be.

But how long would it last, he wondered? As government after government joined the other players in the new game, how many months or years would it take for everything to change?

He was glad when he heard her call out to him, and pleased that instead of her staying where he knew he'd be able to find her, she was coming to find him – a reminder that, after today, someone else would have to save the world because, thanks to her, he had more important and far better things to do.

AUTHOR'S NOTE

Although the scenarios in this book are fictitious, nearly all other elements of the story are based on fact.

The People's Republic of China continues to explore for oil in the Tarim Basin and elsewhere in the world, and radioactive waste from Russia's nuclear reactors continues to be processed at the Mayak Chemical Combine Plant in Chelyabinsk.

Meanwhile, for the moment at least, in California the San Andreas Fault Observatory at Depth is providing data that will help scientists predict when the Big One is most likely to occur.

In Britain, the situation is similarly fragile. Number One, The Thames is still for sale at the bargain price of £700,000, and remains an alarmingly convenient address from which to attack a target that over the last sixty years has been allowed to become so dangerous it can no longer be made safe.

CDP